# HONG ON THE RANGE

Also available in the Millennium science-fiction/fantasy series

# HONG ON THE RANGE

## William F Wu

**HUTCHINSON**
London  Sydney  Auckland  Johannesburg

Millennium Books and the Millennium symbol are trademarks of
Byron Preiss Visual Publications, Inc.

First published in 1990 by Hutchinson Children's Books
an imprint of Random Century Group Ltd
20 Vauxhall Bridge Road, London SW1V 2SA

Random Century Australia Pty Ltd
20 Alfred Street, Sydney, NSW 2016

Random Century New Zealand Ltd
PO Box 40-086, Glenfield, Auckland 10, New Zealand

Random Century South Africa (Pty) Ltd
PO Box 337, Bergvlei, 2012, South Africa

Book edited by David M. Harris

Typeset by Deltatype Ltd, Ellesmere Port
Printed and bound in Great Britain by
Mackays of Chatham PLC, Chatham, Kent

British Library Cataloguing in Publication Data
Wu, William F., 1951–
Hong on the range
I. Title
813.54 (J)
ISBN 0-09-174479-2

This novel is dedicated
to some of *my* travelling companions:

Rob Chilson
Michael D Toman
Lynette Meserole
and
Tom Meserole,

whose annual William F Wu Going Away Parties
finally got me out of town;

and to the memory of
Dorothy M Johnson,
this homage
to all her fine work.

Illustration by Phil Hale, Darrel Anderson and Richard
Berry

# Acknowledgments

Special thanks in writing this novel are due to David M Harris, Byron Preiss, Brian M Thomsen, and Ellen Datlow.

Support, suggestions, and other contributions also came from Rob Chilson, Diana Gallagher Wu, Chelsea, and Wicket the doggie; thanks to all.

# One

I had been trudging across the prairie under the hot sun for days, ever since Independence, when I saw the buzzards circling overhead in the distance. They were wheeling high, not expecting to feed very soon. With a tired hitch at the straps of my pack and bedroll, I changed direction just enough to find whatever had drawn them.

First I could only see that something large was displacing the tall buffalo grass ahead. Then I reached the spot and found a steerite lying down with his steel legs neatly folded underneath him. They gleamed silver in the sun and his hinged metal tail swished back and forth, its brush swatting the flies that buzzed around the natural hide of his meaty, biological middle. As I pulled my battered hat off by the brim and squinted at the steerite, he turned his steel bovine head towards me, short horns and all.

'Hi, there,' I said.

'Hello,' he answered pleasantly. He had been programmed with excellent enunciation and a trace of a Boston accent. 'Good day to you. Where are you bound?'

I untied my red bandana and wiped off my forehead with it. 'I'm going to Femur to look for a job. Pardon my asking, but . . . have you lost your herd? What are you doing here?'

'I am merely waiting. Have I lost my herd? More accurately, my herd has been rustled.'

'Rustled?'

'I dutifully escaped. None of my comrades suc-
ceeded in this endeavour. Since our trail crew ran off,
I have no trail boss to whom I must report. Nor am I
honour bound to join the herd after it has been
rustled.'

I nodded towards the mark stamped onto the
shining metal base of his tail, where it extended from
his natural hindquarters. 'Waiting for what? You
still have your serial number.'

'Oh, yes. I am fully programmed and ready to
report to any authority who can restore me to my
legal owner.'

'Who's that?'

'I don't know. We get basic programming for
herding, pasturing, and speech, but little precise
data. Of course, we can accumulate information as
we go, but no one ever told me the owner's name or
where to locate him.'

'I guess the trail crew was supposed to get you
there?'

'Indeed they were, those cowardly louts.' He
lowered his head modestly. 'I am led to believe that
my mechanical parts are quite expensive. Not to
mention my beef.'

'And you're just waiting? How long are you going
to wait before you do something?'

'Until I think of something to do. My owner's
insurance has an expiration date embedded in my
programming. When his time to file a claim on my
theft is up, then my progamming changes and I
become a maverick without ownership restrictions.'

'Would you mind visiting the city of Femur?
Perhaps someone there can check your serial
number and return you.' I didn't add how much I
would like the ride.

'I would appreciate being taken there. Would you be so kind?'

'Of course,' I said, putting my hat back on. I retied my bandana and eased the straps of my pack off. The bedroll was tied to it. 'Would you mind carrying me?'

'Be my guest. Shall I rise now or wait for you to mount first?'

'Uh – go ahead and get up.'

He rose with that awkward half-jump that cattle seem to have. I then put both hands on his back, half jumped myself, and clambered on. The straps on my pack could just be stretched to hang from both of his short horns, leaving the pack resting neatly on the back of his neck, bedroll and all.

'In which direction shall we locate the town of Femur?' he asked politely.

I leaned forward, hanging on to one of his horns, and pointed with one arm down low where he could see it. 'Straight thataway. It's a long cluster of wooden buildings on the stage route right in the middle of rolling prairie, or so I'm told. The largest town in the area.'

'We shall see if the information is correct.' He swung into a walk.

I jerked backward from the start and grabbed onto my pack. The pull on his horns didn't seem to bother him, so I held the pack as a kind of handle, like the straps were reins. His middle was broad and well fed, making my straddle more awkward than I would have liked, and his gait was completely unfamiliar. My moccasined feet dangled out to each side. Still, any ride beat walking, even on a steerite.

'By what name may I address you?' he asked over his shoulder.

'I'm Louie Hong.'

11

'My serial number is ST 4006.'

'Pleased to meet you.'

'And I, you.'

After walking for my entire trip so far, riding was even more of a luxury than I had expected. We fairly seemed to eat up the ground; in fact, periodically, my mount did pause to munch on the ground cover. When one such break had been concluded and we were on our way again, I offered a little conversation.

'You seem to be in good condition,' I observed. 'Those buzzards would have had a long wait. You weren't even out looking for water when I found you.'

'I wasn't thirsty,' he said mildly.

'How long have you been on your own?'

'Two days and a fraction more.'

'Which direction were you headed in? Your herd, I mean.'

'Northwest, approximately. I surmise we were destined for the high plains to the distant north, but I may have been incorrect. Perhaps we were meant to feed the railroad crews to the west.'

'I haven't seen the railroad in these parts,' I said. 'I hear the stage that passes through Femur stops at a railroad depot.'

He nodded courteously, but had no further comment.

'Serial numbers are hard to remember,' I said. 'Would you mind having a name?'

'Not at all. As a matter of fact, I always wished to be called Chuck. I think it an elegant play on words, considering the ultimate destination of certain portions of my middle. What do you think?'

I laughed. 'Glad to meet you, Chuck.'

'And I, you. Do you sing, sir?'

'Uh – sing?'

'Yes. Occasionally the cowboys would entertain the herd with archaic cowboys songs, I believe sometimes evolved to reflect modern times. They seemed to consider it a duty based on folk beliefs.'

'You want me to sing to you?'

'Please do not feel pressed if you find the activity onerous. After all, they only did it in the evening after supping. And you are not a cowboy.' He plodded on a few steps and then added, 'I always found it comforting, personally.'

'I . . . don't know.'

'Allow me to demonstrate. Let me see.' He cleared his throat and started singing.

> *' "Oh, roast me not on the lone prairie—"*
> *These words came low and mournfully*
> *From the stainless lips of a young steerite*
> *As he malfunctioned at the fall of night.'*

He waited modestly for a moment, still ambling along, and then asked, 'What do you think?'

I hesitated, rocking back and forth on his bony spine. 'Very moving,' I said finally. 'I'm not familiar with, uh, this version.' I raised my head to adjust my bandana around my neck and saw something on the horizon. 'Hey, I think I see it.'

Chuck lifted his head and turned it slightly to the side to eye the uneven cluster of shapes in the distance. 'A modest settlement, at best. Nevertheless, we shall arrive shortly.'

We had been crossing trackless prairie, but Femur was, as rumoured, a long string of wooden buildings lining a strip of road. It was smaller than I had hoped. The narrow road ran across our path, meandering slightly to avoid small rises in the terrain. I could see the dry ruts cut into the bare earth of the road by wagon and stage wheels.

'Do you know where to go in town?' Chuck asked me.

'No, I don't. Maybe if we go around one end and walk down the middle of the street, we can read the signs.'

'Quite so.' He changed his direction slightly, aiming for the left end of the little town.

When we got to the road, he made a right turn around a small pigsty by the side of the livery stable and started down the middle of the street. On both sides, rough boardwalks fronted two-storey wooden buildings erected side against side. They all had distinctive false fronts on the top storey. Nobody was on the street.

Ahead of us, somebody came stumbling fast out of a pair of swinging doors, propelled by a boot just barely visible between the doors. A moment later, another guy strode out, obviously in stern pursuit. Chuck halted so fast that I fell forward over his horns.

'Oh, my,' said Chuck.

I pushed my hat up so I could see.

Both guys were standing in the street ahead of us. The first guy out was a bulky fellow, shaped something like Chuck, scowling in the sunlight as he clenched and unclenched his fists. He kept them high as he circled his opponent warily on Model C-5 Abilene Accordion ankles.

The other guy was a bit shorter and of medium build. He had straight, shoulder-length brown hair neatly brushed back, and a fancy black frock coat with tails whipping slightly in the breeze. His black ribbon tie was also fluttering over his white shirt and silver vest. If he had any special parts, I couldn't see them, but he wore his gun low and strapped down to his silver trousers.

14

'Fisticuffs?' Chuck asked. 'Pugilism?'

'Looks that way,' I said. 'At least.'

'I request that you please dismount. I intend to depart the immediate vicinity until the belligerence has ended.'

'Okay.' I pulled my pack free of his horns and hopped off. 'Thanks for the ride.'

'You are of course welcome.' Chuck trotted away with his ears flattened against his head, his legs scissoring quickly beneath the boxcar body.

The guy in the fancy clothes stood still, composed, turning just enough to keep the other fellow in front of him.

'It don't make you clean!' The big guy was yelling. 'You can't deny it. We all know who you are.' He sniffed loudly.

The gunfighter said nothing.

The cowboy suddenly quit sidling around and reached for his gun. The gunfighter's hand went real quick to the handle of his, and the cowboy jumped back. In fact, he jumped so hard that he triggered his model C-5 Abilene Accordion ankles. The mainsprings went off together, propelling him backward through the air a few feet, where he hit the hitching post just over the small of his back, flipped around it with his legs a spinning blur, and thumped facedown on the boardwalk.

You've got to watch those sensitive reflexes.

Loud guffaws from inside the swinging doors echoed up and down the dusty street before the guys inside turned away. It was the kind of town that would mostly have folks come in from ranches after sundown or on Saturday night. Nobody else seemed to be around.

The gunfighter sauntered up the street, not dallying and not hightailing, either.

Clutching my pack, I headed cautiously for the saloon, keeping an eye on the cowboy across the street. He was just starting to recover from his close nasal examination of the wood grain. When he rolled over on his side and looked at me, I stopped.

'What do you want, scrawny?' he demanded.

'Nothing.'

He turned his head and tried to spit into the street, but his mouth was dry. Instead, he wound up making a weird face for nothing.

Apparently his Abilene Accordions were okay. He got up and leaned against the hitching post to dust himself off. I was already forgotten.

That was normal enough for Louie Hong, control-natural. It was also why finding a job was tough.

That was why I had headed west to Femur.

I stopped outside the saloon doors and squinted into the dark interior. It was the only place with a sign of life. The crowd inside turned out to be only five guys sitting around one big table looking bored. I was glad to see the crud on the floor, though.

I pulled open one of the swinging doors as slowly as I could, hoping to slide inside on my moccasins without making any noise. As soon as the door opened, more sunlight hit the assorted sawdust, dead bugs, and dried mud on the floor. All five guys looked up immediately in case further excitement was forthcoming.

They still watched me as I walked over to the bar and laid my pack on the table.

The barkeep was a burly guy with thinning curly brown hair. He had shining silver Pan-Brite Steel Wool sideburns on fleshy, sun-reddened cheeks. As I stood there, he dried his hands on his spotless white apron and then shoved my pack onto the floor beside me.

'This bar is for drinks, sonny,' he said. 'Name it.'

'I am an honest young fellow looking for employment,' I said politely. 'I will do anything.'

'Sorry, sonny.' He turned away.

'I could sweep up in here,' I called after him. 'Swamp out the floor after you close.'

'I do that,' he growled over his shoulder.

'You said anything.'

I looked to see who had spoken. It was one of the guys at the table. I picked up my pack. 'That's right.'

He was sitting in the centre of the group, lounging back in a chair tilted up on its two rear legs. He was a tall, heavy guy in a battered, wide-brimmed brown leather hat and a long sheepskin vest. His shirt was a deep red with gold buttons and his bandana was bright yellow, except for the dust it had collected. He was clean shaven and rather decent looking, over all.

He frowned suddenly. 'You ain't a natural, are you? A control-natural?'

Everyone around him bristled slightly.

'Yeah.' I started for the door.

'Hey, where ya goin', cowboy? I just might have a couple of newbits for you.'

I hesitated, looking back. They were all grinning real big. 'For what?'

'You're too choosy, fob,' said the guy on his right.

I started to look at him, but the first guy let his chair fall to the floor with a bang and stood up. The others followed his lead.

'Run down to the livery and pick up seven horsites. Tell 'im they're Duke's horsites and give 'im this.' He flipped a coin towards me.

It spun fast in a rainbow arc, sending yellow flashes across the room to sparkle on the wooden walls. I caught it and looked it over. It was a solid gold double bison, the kind with the charging buffalo on one side and the dead one with its feet in the air on the other.

When I looked up in surprise, he winked at me.

'We're goin' over to get our pay at the bank. You meet us there double-quick, I'll let you keep the change.'

'Yessir!' That could be quite a bonus, depending on how long they'd been in town. From the looks of them, they hadn't been off the road long at all. I hightailed down the street, my pack slamming against my back, remembering the livery stable I had passed riding Chuck.

I skidded to a halt in front of the stable, throwing up little clouds of dust with my moccasins. Nobody was in sight. Just before I started inside, I heard a faint whimpering sound from around the back of the stable and a quiet voice. It sounded like Chuck.

The horsites could wait another minute. I made a long detour around the pigsty to get behind the stable. Back here, I could see down the rear view of all the buildings on this side of the street.

At first I didn't see him, and when I did, I almost didn't recognize him. He was lying in the shadow of the stable against the rough wood grain, a tangled pile of stainless steel head, skeleton, electronics, and tail. All the meat and hide was gone. A large pool of syntheblood blackened the ground under him.

'Those ham-fisted clods,' he wailed. 'Those mitten-fingered slobs!'

'What happened?' I edged closer, staring at him. Whoever had done the job had been quick and sloppy. I had never seen the innards of a steerite before.

'I've been slaughtered by experts! I've been butchered by the best! Those thieves couldn't cut steaks by a blueprint! They couldn't trim fat with a scalpel! I'm just so *embarrassed* . . .' He began to cry.

'Well – I'll be right back, okay? I got to do something. You just hang on right there.' I ran back around the pigsty again and into the front of the stable.

'Hey! Anybody home?' I demanded.

'Quit yelling, quit yelling.' A short, ragged guy in a grey beard came stumping out of one of the stalls holding a shovel, walking with a stiff-legged, side-to-side motion. His beard stuck out in all directions like he'd been struck on the head by lightning and never got over it. The walk was more telling, though. Underneath the baggy blue pants, he had a pair of Prairie Village Grippers. They were an early model of specialized thighs marketed towards professional wranglers. Nobody had ever been able to walk right in them.

'Duke wants his seven horsites,' I said firmly, backed by the authority of the coin in my pocket.

'Those stalls there,' he said, tilting the handle of the shovel as a pointer. 'Forty-seven newbits.'

I tossed him the double bison as casually as I could. He snapped it out of the air, gave it a glance, and stuffed it into his trouser pocket. I watched carefully as he counted out the change, which was considerable.

I split the change between my pants pocket and my pack. Then I gathered up the horsites, which of course were designed much like Chuck except that they didn't have his intelligence or his ability to speak. Unlike steerites, horsites normally had a rider or driver to guide them individually.

As I led the horsites up the street, I saw more signs of life than before. At the far end, some people were piling into a stagecoach. I read the signs over all the storefronts until I found 'First Ferric Bank of

19

Femur', which didn't look any different from the other storefronts that I could see.

The horsites didn't want to stand still. I kept getting tangled up in the seven sets of reins as they shuffled around and turned sideways and nudged each other. I was just ducking under some of the reins and trying to shift some of them from one hand to another when a bunch of guys ran out of the bank yelling and hollering and firing guns in the air.

The horsites all started and shied as the guys started jumping into the saddles, yanking the reins out of my hands. I dodged out of the way and found the stagecoach barrelling down on me, its team spooked by all the shooting and shouting. When I stopped and whirled around, I found the last of the horsites I'd been holding pulled away riderless and more guys bursting out of the bank, yelling and hollering and shooting at *me*.

I spun around again and leaped high for the stage as it rolled past. My hands slid and scraped helplessly on the smooth surface for a moment before I got hold of one of the straps holding the boot shut. I hung on hard, bouncing against the back of the stage, with both feet kicking wildly for a footing as we raced out of town.

# Two

Duke and his gang were riding out the same end of town as the stage. The only difference was that as soon as they had cleared the last building, they cut around it and lit out north over the open prairie. The stage, of course, stayed on the road winding westward.

I had finally managed to get both feet braced on something firm; I couldn't tell what and didn't care. Behind me, a spontaneously formed posse was just mounting up and thundering out of town. In the heat of action, they all turned at the end of town and went after the gang. So far, I had been forgotten.

The stage was still bouncing along at high speed, maybe just for good measure. I was still afraid of being shaken off, especially as my hold on the strap began to tire. So I leaned my head around the corner of the stage to see if there was any chance of working my way inside.

One of the passengers saw me and started in surprise. He was a young guy with sandy hair, maybe my age, but tall and thin.

'Say! There's someone out there,' he shouted.

Another guy immediately stuck his head out the window, along with a gun levelled at me. It was the gunfighter I had seen in the street, only he was bareheaded now and his long hair trailed in the wind. His eyes were deep-set and shadowed, his face lined and dried by the sun. After an intense, momentary stare, he withdrew again.

I was relieved, but still hanging on precariously. The first guy, though, opened the door. It swung back toward me and I looped one arm through the open window. When I shifted my weight to it completely, the young passenger took my outstretched hand and pulled me in close. He helped me inside, and a moment later I fell into a seat beside him with the gunfighter across from me.

One more passenger was inside. She was a slender young woman sitting primly on the opposite seat of the stage but as far from the gunfighter as she could get. Her straight blonde hair was tied back under a small lavender hat that matched her snug, full-length dress. White lace lined the top of the tight collar around her neck. When she saw me looking at her, she turned her gaze out her window.

I remembered to take off my hat and hold it.

The gunfighter's hat was in his lap. He was studying me, but his gaze was casual, as though I had already been dismissed. I looked away.

Out the window, I could see the posse just disappearing over a gentle rise in the distance. I wouldn't mind if they never remembered me. In the meantime, Femur could do without my services as a labourer.

'Late for the stage, huh?' the young fellow next to me called over the rattle of the bounding stage and the hoofbeats of the horsites pulling it. He smiled pleasantly. 'Harris Nye.' He held out his hand.

I looked at it for a moment, not sure what to do with it. Then I remembered and shook hands with him. 'Louie Hong.'

'Did they get your luggage loaded?'

'Uh – this is it.' Belatedly, I remembered my pack, which I was leaning back on against the seat. I pulled it off and held it on my lap.

'Ah. You travel light, I see.' Harris nodded approvingly. He spoke to the gunfighter. 'Good planning, don't you think? Personally, I have a lot of extra specials with me, so I need lots of luggage. I'm Harris Nye.'

The gunfighter nodded lightly before Harris could offer his hand.

By this time the stage was slowing down. Four horsites weren't going to pull this much weight very far at top speed, after all. Soon it had settled into a normal, swaying walk.

'Bit of excitement back there, huh?' Harris said happily, looking around at everyone. 'I'd heard life was different west of the Mississippi. Oh, by the way . . . I'm from east of the Mississippi.'

The gunfighter smiled faintly and looked out the window again. The woman looked at him like he was a piece of scenery.

'Does anyone know who they were? I wonder if I've read about them,' Harris said.

'Duke Goslin,' said the gunfighter, without turning his head.

'Really?' Harris sat up straight, wide-eyed. 'I've heard of them. Carver Dalton and Tether Chen are in his gang, right?'

The gunfighter nodded, still gazing out the window.

'Wowee. Think of that.'

Now that the gunfighter wasn't watching me, I kept sneaking glances at him. He was older than I had thought at first, and was probably someone else Harris had read about. I couldn't see any hint of specials on him, but I didn't doubt he had some.

For that matter, they were invisible on the woman, too. Of course, sitting like we were, none of us revealed any special parts – or lack of them – by our movements. I couldn't see any on Harris, either.

So Harris was an overeager young adventurer thinking he was going to have fun across the Mississippi, with bags full of special parts. The kind one could carry in luggage could be easily interchanged on expensive modular mounts that he would have implanted in various places. I had seen his sort passing through Missouri from time to time while I was growing up.

'Well.' Harris settled into his seat, still grinning cheerfully. 'This is quite a trip for me. Joining the great resettlement migration and all.'

'I didn't see you purchase a fare,' said the woman suddenly. She looked squarely at me with deep blue eyes – Finegrinder & Denton's Barbilou Bluebells, I was pretty sure, now discontinued.

'This is Miz Eulalie Prang.' Harris swung his head back and forth between us several times.

I looked back at her without saying anything.

'I once read,' said Harris, 'that sometimes a driver will let somebody ride on top for free.'

'Sometimes,' I said. I leaned forward and put on my pack. Then I stuck my hat on again. Riding up top would be better than having a paid passenger demand that I be abandoned on the prairie.

I stood on the bench, leaning forward because of the ceiling, and opened the door. The stage was moving leisurely now, so manoeuvring wasn't so dangerous. I reached up and grabbed the rail that ran around the outside of the roof and swung out.

Somebody shut the door behind me, probably Harris.

I pulled up far enough to see the backs of the two drivers. They might have let me ride along if I had asked, but I wasn't so sure they would like my joining them without that particular courtesy. Two big suitcases and a huge trunk were strapped onto

24

the roof. Hoping to use all that luggage to hide in, I pulled all the way up as slowly as I could, lest my weight unbalance the stage too much.

I had just gotten one foot up over the railing when the shotgun rider noticed the tilt. He looked over his shoulder at me, scowled, and then started climbing onto the roof. My foot was stuck on the railing so I couldn't lower it, and I was suddenly in no rush to get all the way up there.

He was a tall, slender guy like Harris, but much older and not given to smiling in all directions. That was all I saw before he took my shirt front in one hand, my belt buckle in the other, and lifted me up into the air. The blue sky swirled around in a circle and then I thumped onto the ground hard, cushioned a mite by my pack.

I lay there with my wind knocked out, watching the back of the stage go on without me. Harris stuck his head out the window to look but didn't say anything I could hear. I closed my eyes, struggling to get my breath back.

By the time the creaking of the stage had faded away, I was able to roll over onto one shoulder and watch the swaying vehicle shrink in the distance. The sun was low in the sky over it.

Well, I was no worse off than I had been before I reached Femur, except that now I was severely banged up, had nowhere to go, had a shutgun rider mad at me, and was wanted for bank robbery.

And my hat had fallen off.

I crawled over and got it, then stood up to dust myself off. The sun was still hot, and this humid air wasn't going to cool off much. I looked around.

The tall grasses of the rolling prairie waved endlessly in all directions. At least I had a road to follow now. Since Femur no longer beckoned, except with a rope, I started west.

I was too tired to walk very fast. Harris had plenty of energy, and I supposed that one's taste for adventure was higher if one had the money to ride during the day and sleep under a roof at night. Not being a control-natural, of course, made the big difference.

Walking made me think of Chuck, then, for the first time since I had left him. I had promised to come back, and I felt bad about not returning. That was life in the west, though. Everyone was transient these days, this side of the big river. You made friends one minute and then never saw them again.

I heard the hoofbeats and saw the dust ahead in the road before I could see the rider. As long as no one came up behind me from Femur, I was probably safe. I watched him come on.

His mount was an unusually large white stallion horsite that cantered casually down the road. He himself wore shiny black boots, grey trousers, a long-sleeved matching grey shirt with fringe, and a white hat. From here, his face was a weird blur.

When he got closer, I could see that he was wearing a clown mask. The face was white with lots of red and orange and yellow, with blue trim. It was smiling goofily.

He pulled up in front of me. 'Hi, there, fellow traveller. Are you in need of assistance?'

'Sort of,' I said. 'I could use a home, a job, and a girlfriend. Failing those, a fistful of double bisons would do. But I would settle for a ride west, or even a roof under which to spend the night.'

He pushed his hat back on his head. Behind the mask, his hair was black. 'You have reached a sorry pass, indeed. Do you know who I am?'

'No.'

He drew himself up straight. 'I . . . am the Long Ranger.'

'Oh.'

'And this is my fiery horse, Goldie.'

I took another glance at the big white mount. 'Goldie?'

He tilted his hat forward and leaned down at me. 'Don't you believe me?'

'The real one lived in olden times. Everybody knows that.'

'Yeah, well, never mind that part. I'm the new one. *Understand*?'

'Okay, okay. I mean, who cares?'

'Here. This'll prove it.' He reached down to hand me something.

I took it. It was a red jelly bean. I ate it.

'Now, then. Exactly what, young fellow, has brought you to this unfortunate state of affairs?'

'Well . . . being a control-natural didn't help any.'

'*Oh*. In that case, forget the whole thing. Gimme back my . . . aw, you chewed it up already.' The Long Ranger shook his head and spurred Goldie. They took off down the road past me.

He would have found out sooner or later, anyway.

I plodded on. Around one bend, I spied a clump of low trees away from the road. It suggested some shelter and maybe some water for the canteen in my pack. I left the road for it just in time, since the horizon had turned red by the time I reached it.

The trees were cottonwoods, rather short and stumpy, but taller in the sunken creekbed than they had looked from the road. The creek was nearly dry and offered nothing to drink. Since my spontaneous departure from Femur had left me without time to buy food, I had nothing to do but take my blanket out of my pack, use the pack as a pillow, and go to sleep in the waning light.

A weird hissing sound woke me up in the darkness. It sounded like sniffing. That could mean anything from a fox to a coyote to something larger than that and even hungrier than I was. I felt around in the dark until I located a small rock. Then I sat up suddenly, threw it, and yelled, 'Yah!'

Two guns clicked into cocked positions. Now that I was sitting up, I could see two silhouettes by a small yellowish fire. It had been hidden by a couple of tree trunks before.

One of them sniffed loudly.

'Come out of there, slow and easy,' said the other.

I did. My habit of sleeping in my moccasins paid off again. When one lived the way I did, being ready to run was useful.

'Hey, it's our little buddy from the bar,' said the one who had spoken before. He lowered his gun. 'Come on over to the fire.'

I got my first look at him by the firelight. He had a wide forehead under a reddish brown hat, big wide round eyes, and a face that narrowed sharply to a pointed chin. As he holstered his gun with his right hand, I caught sight of his left. Instead of a hand, he had a series of shiny blades on a Swissarmie Brand Swivel.

'Dalton's the name,' he said, with a nod. 'This here's Smellin' Llewellyn.'

The other guy sniffed a few more times and holstered his own gun. They both sat down by the fire and I did likewise, not wanting to snub their invitation. They had meat on a little frying pan, just starting to sizzle.

'Say,' said Smellin'. 'This is the guy? I didn't get a

good look outside the bank. He's the same one who rode the steerite I told you about.'

I recognized him, too. He was the cowboy with the Model C-5 Abilene Accordion ankles I had seen almost thrown down on the gunfighter in the street. His friend was Carver Dalton. I had a vague memory of seeing him in the bar next to Duke.

'If you hadn't run off after that steerite,' said Carver, 'Duke wouldn't have had to hire him to do your job.'

So that last riderless horse I had been holding had been Smellin' Llewellyn's. I looked at the sizzling steaks on the frying pan with a new prejudice.

'I got enough meat for the whole gang, didn't I?' Smellin' demanded. He sniffed again. 'I found you all again, didn't I? And I shared it once we all got together again, didn't I? So's we could split up after that?'

'Yeah, all right.' Carver jerked his thumb toward the fire and looked at me. 'If that was your steerite, you're entitled to dinner. You did a right job for us with those horsites.'

'Thank you,' I said, still staring in shock at the portions of Chuck frying away in front of me. Eating him didn't quite seem right, somehow, but neither did starving.

Carver reached into a cloth sack of some kind and threw another hunk of Chuck onto the frying pan.

I looked over Smellin' Llewellyn. His nose was a bit large, unusually straight, and exactly proportioned. It looked a lot like a Hayashi-Chang Da Bizi, but I couldn't be sure. That might account for his odd nasal habits.

He saw me looking at him and sniffed again. 'Hay fever,' he said briefly. 'That was your steerite, wasn't it?'

29

'We were just friends,' I said, sniffing the steaks a little myself. They were getting more tempting every minute.

'I had to split the meat with the stable hand who helped me. Didn't have time to dally. But I didn't know you was hooking up with Duke and the boys. No hard feelings?'

'No.' I shrugged. Chuck was still functioning, after all; he was just a lot skinnier.

'We figure we're safe for the night,' said Carver. 'The whole gang split up for the time being.'

I nodded, relieved. After all, I was safer with a couple of notorious outlaws on my side than I was alone.

'Well . . . eat up,' said Carver, throwing a steak onto a metal plate and handing it to me.

'Thanks.' I pulled out my Cubby Scout knife and ate up.

Sleeping out under the stars was a lot more romantic the first couple of times I had done it, back when I was a little kid. It would have been more comfortable this time with a fire for company, but Carver and Smellin' had kicked it apart when they had finished cooking and heating coffee, leaving only coals that could stay alight till morning. Also, sleeping out under the stars would have been more reassuring with company than alone, except for the company.

I had never heard of Smellin' Llewellyn, but Carver Dalton was known for cutting up more than steaks. In fact, Smellin' was the one who had done that. I felt real safe from outsiders like posses and the Long Ranger and the shotgun rider.

In fact, I felt so safe that I lay awake most of the night listening to Smellin' sniff and snort in his sleep.

We were too far from any farm to hear roosters. At

the first light of false dawn, Carver got up and tossed sticks on the coals, then poked the fire together again. The smoke woke up Smellin', and I got up because I had nothing better to do. Breakfast was the same as dinner, only I didn't want as much.

'I've been thinking,' said Carver. 'We can't just leave you afoot. Can we, Smellin'?'

Smellin' sniffed and shook his head. 'I guess we owe him. What say we get him a ways from Femur, anyhow?'

'That's what I figure.' Carver nodded. 'Then we can tell him where to meet us later and between times—' He turned to me. 'You'll be on your own.'

I nodded, looking back and forth between them. As far as they were concerned, I was in the gang. Between them and the posse, this was no time to argue.

Smellin' kicked the fire apart and we were on our way by the time the sun threw slanting yellow rays across the eastern prairie. Carver mounted the normal way. Smellin' took one little hop to land hard on his Model C-5 Abilene Accordion ankles. The force of his weight triggered them, and he sprang off the ground right into the saddle. Then he grinned and leaned down to help me up.

I rode with my arms around Smellin's waist as we bounced along. They seemed to know where they were going. I still didn't want to pester them with questions.

They ignored the road. We set out overland, westward and slightly to the north. Since they didn't make conversation, I didn't, either. The chance of saying the wrong thing seemed too high.

Life was just moving right along. Yesterday morning, I had been Louie Hong, footloose wanderer seeking honest work. Now I was Louie Hong, footloose wanderer and wanted desperado.

# Three

When the light picked up, we hurried into a canter. Every so often, we came across a small farm nestled into the prairie, but Carver and Smellin' were not too scrupulous about riding through ploughed fields. Before long, I could see a thin line of smoke rising from a couple of low buildings in the distance.

The stagecoach was out front, the team still unhitched. Apparently the road wound among the rises and dips in the rolling country, following some olden-time route. If you knew where you were going and rode overland on a horsite, you could make up a lot of distance in a short time.

Cantering through the corn sprouts helped considerably, of course.

Just as we got close to the stage stop, we broke into a full gallop, I guess to make a dramatic entrance. At the front door, they both reined up sharply with a practised ease and swung their legs back over the horsites' rear ends to dismount. Trouble was, I was still sitting behind Smellin', who knocked me clean off the horsite with his leg.

I landed on my back with a thump, looking up at the cool morning sky. This perspective was becoming all too familiar.

'I guess that's twice I owe you,' said Smellin', taking my arm and hauling me up. 'I forgot. I don't normally take passengers.'

'Careful,' said Carver, inclining his head towards the door.

Smellin' followed Carver, leaving me to catch my balance alone. I followed them crookedly, then had to stop in the doorway behind them when they paused.

The stage passengers were sitting around the room finishing breakfast. It looked like hot cereal of some kind – not too appetizing, but at least it wasn't more of Chuck. All of them looked up at us.

The gunfighter was sitting motionless on the hearth with the bowl of porridge on a plate in his lap. He and Smellin' were staring at each other. I edged away from Smellin' slightly.

'Got more breakfast, Louella?' Carver asked pleasantly, moving inside.

'Sure, Carver.' A large woman standing off to the left stirred a big pot over a small cookfire in the corner. 'Come on in.'

The casual conversation broke the tension. Smellin' followed Carver with another wary glance at the gunfighter. Everyone relaxed a little. A minute later we were all standing around the wall eating some sort of tasteless mush. The seats were all taken.

Harris Nye was looking us over with a silly grin. He had mush on the front of his shirt. The blonde in lavender, Eulalie something, was eating in small, precise bites, not looking up. Her little feet were laced up in black hightop shoes with points. Then I turned and saw the two stagehands standing by the cookstove.

The tall, rangy shotgun rider was glaring at me over his bowl of slop. I was sure that only the presence of Carver Dalton and Smellin' Llewellyn stopped him from chucking me out the door. Next to him, a shorter guy with a Chilbob Retractable

Horsewhip wrist was just dropping an empty bowl in a tub of dishwater.

I straightened around again, pretending to ignore them. My knees were shaking, though, and cereal fell off my spoon onto my foot.

'So, Louie,' Carver said just a little too loudly. 'I hear you intend to take a trip.'

'Well, uh . . .'

Smellin' jabbed me in the ribs, hard, with his elbow. My bowl of mush slid off my plate and turned over on the floor.

'That's right,' I said belatedly, picking up my empty bowl.

Louella came bustling over with a dripping, dirty mop and began by slopping it over my moccasins.

'Driver.' Carver turned to the guy with the horsewhip wrist. 'How much fare is required to take a passenger from this stop to the railroad depot?'

'The name's Creel.'

'Now, you just hold on a minute.' The shotgun rider pointed at me with a long, skinny arm and finger. 'That there feller is a stowaway. I throwed him off the stage yesterday. We don't gotta take him.'

'Easy, Snake.' Creel nodded to Carver. 'Fare's higher for a stowaway.'

'I said, how much?' Carver shifted his weight and studied Creel.

'Oh . . . I figure two double bisons.'

'What?' Carver straightened. 'You're shorted. That's enough for a fair horsite. That railroad depot isn't very far.'

'So take him yourself,' said Creel calmly. 'If you don't, it's a far walk. Posses usually ride.'

Carver grinned, then, and so did Smellin'.

I sneaked a look around the room. Harris was

staring wide-eyed at everybody. Eulalie was watching Carver carefully. Even the gunfighter was smiling faintly.

'I can spare one,' said Carver. He flipped a spinning coin to Creel, who snatched it out of the air.

'Me, too,' said Smellin'. 'More where they came from.' He tossed one to Snake, who bobbled it a few times and then dropped it on the floor before bending down to get it.

'And for that price, he gets to the depot. Period. No mistakes, no accidents. Right?' Carver snapped out one of the larger blades on his Swissarmie Brand Swivel hand and started cleaning the fingernails on his other hand with it.

'He'll get there,' said Creel, watching Carver's blade carefully. 'After that, he's on his own.'

'And just in case anybody's wondering,' said Smellin', 'we're only carrying a few of those on us, for luck, say. Most of 'em are on their way elsewhere.' He looked particularly at the gunfighter, who had already returned to his bowl of cereal.

The gunfighter stopped moving and gazed into his bowl for a long moment. Then he looked up slowly with just his eyes. 'Are you addressing me?'

Harris was looking back and forth between them with his mouth open.

Smellin' shrugged slightly and looked away. Then he went to take his dishes to the tub of water.

The gunfighter turned his attention back to his cereal.

Carver winked at me and grinned as he went to do the same.

Louella had picked up my dishes. Now I felt out of place, standing there alone. I went over to sit by Harris on the hearth.

'I saw your spill yesterday,' he said quietly. 'You must be pretty tough, huh?'

In the far corner, Carver and Smellin' were chuckling with Creel and Snake. I didn't want to stay with the outlaws, and I didn't want them to leave me behind, either.

'Are you new in the gang?' Harris asked. 'I haven't read about you, I don't think.'

'I'm not exactly in it,' I muttered as low as I could. I had a suspicion that my new colleagues would not take kindly to my real feelings on this subject.

'What's that? Couldn't hear you.'

'I'm not exactly in the gang,' I whispered hoarsely, eyeing the outlaws across the room.

'What?' Harris said loudly, frowning in puzzlement. 'You say you're *not* in the—'

'Just joined up,' I declared heartily, aware that every head in the room except the gunfighter's had turned at the sound of his voice. 'Just signed on, I did. Oh, yeah.' I smiled real hard, till my teeth hurt from clenching them together.

'I see.' Harris slapped his knee. 'Well, don't worry, Louie. I bet within a few weeks, you'll be in every magazine east of the Big River. Your picture will be on every cover, your name on every—'

'Okay, okay,' I said testily, glancing at the outlaws in the corner. Carver was grinning big.

Harris's eyes widened in horror at my tone. 'I'm real sorry, Louie. I didn't mean to make you mad. Oh, no. Not me. Nosirree, not me, I wouldn't do that.' He put both hands up, palms forward, pushing air away from me.

The gunfighter finished eating and took his bowl back to the cookstove.

Harris kept his eyes on him all the way.

'Any more, Doc?' Louella asked him.

36

'No, thanks,' he answered. He came back to the fire and sat down on the hearth again.

'Are you a physician, sir?' Harris asked. He had watched him walk all the way back, too.

Doc gave him a very long, steady stare.

I was just starting to sweat when he gave a hint of a smile.

'I used to be,' he said quietly. He shifted on the hearth and gazed into the fire with that same ghost of amusement.

Carver and Smellin' walked to the door and Carver caught my eye. He jerked his head toward the door for me to follow.

I did, glad to get away from Harris even though I had gone to him in the first place to get away from them. Outside, they motioned me over to the horsites, away from the building.

'Don't suppose you know where to go,' Carver suggested, leaning one elbow on a horse rail.

'Where to go?'

'We're all meeting out west to split the take,' said Smellin'. 'Between here and there, you're on your own, like we said. But you'll be safe once you make it out our way. And Carver and me, we figure Duke brought you in.'

'I'll be shorted if I know why,' said Carver. 'We don't speak for Duke, you understand. But anyhow – you got anywhere else to go?'

That was more blunt than I wanted to hear.

'Could be,' I said, squinting up into the morning sun at him.

'Okay by us. Just thought you might want to meet up.' Carver shrugged and started to turn away.

'I didn't say I wouldn't,' I added quickly.

'So you didn't.' Smellin' grinned at Carver.

'So where is this place?'

'It's a hideout clear over yonder in the Sierra Nevadas.' Carver nodded confidentially.

'The *what*?' I stared at both of them. 'That's all the way across the country.'

'Suit yourself.'

'No posse ever formed would follow you that far,' said Smellin' easily.

'Is that the only reason?' I demanded.

'It's near a mining town called Washout.' Carver glanced over his shoulder at the house. 'You get that far and ask around some. You'll find it.'

'Is that the only reason you're going so far?' I asked again.

'Fact is,' said Smellin', 'that Femur posse won't follow you past the railroad depot. Make sense?'

I was about to ask them again when the door opened and they both stiffened.

Snake and Creel came out grinning at them, though, and went to hitch the horsite team to the stagecoach.

Carver nodded to me and touched the wide brim of his hat. 'See you out there, eh?'

'Imagine that,' Smellin' said as they walked away. 'Us talking to a control-natural, of all things.'

'Well, *I* didn't hire him on.'

They both laughed as they saddled up. Several minutes later, they cantered westward across another sprouting cornfield. I stood there watching them go.

The Sierra Nevadas were a long way off. Still, getting on the train to dodge the posse made sense. Carver and Smellin' were probably too well known to risk a train depot themselves. When the stage was ready to go, I was on it, again sitting next to Harris across from the other two.

Creel cracked his whip over the team and the stage pulled out at a creaking walk. Doc and Eulalie both settled into comfortable positions and gazed out their respective windows. The rolling waves of prairie grasses began to pass by.

'Perhaps this would be a good time to take stock of my trip so far,' Harris said cheerfully. He drew in a deep breath. 'What fresh morning air. The magazines are right.'

No one said anything.

'I said the magazines are right.'

Doc and Eulalie gazed harder out their windows.

'The magazines say life itself is different west of the Mississippi. They're right, I say.'

'I think you told me that yesterday,' I said as politely as I could.

'It's true today, too. You know, ever since I crossed the river and passed under the Arch, every place I have seen is steeped in history.'

'Everywhere is steeped in history.' I shrugged. 'People just know more about some places than others.'

He looked at me in surprise. 'Really?'

I gazed out the window. This could be a much longer trip than I had expected.

'Of course, this part of the West is heavily settled, according to my guidebook.' He relaxed against his seat. 'Only yesterday did I realize that the towns are growing smaller and farther apart.'

No one spoke.

'It was the first area open to resettlement.'

I shrugged again, watching the prairie grasses wave at me.

'The farms, too,' he added. 'I don't see any fields out there now at all, do you? Open prairie stretches in every direction.'

I nodded wearily. Travel by stagecoach can wear people out surprisingly fast.

Pretty soon Harris fished around in a small leather valise and pulled out a worn little digest of some kind. I couldn't see the title and didn't want to ask. He started reading.

Glad to have the silence, I leaned against the side of the stage and closed my eyes. In some ways, this was even more uncomfortable than the ground I had spent the night on, but I was suddenly very sleepy. I drifted off before long.

Hoofbeats in the distance woke me up. I was sweaty from the heat. Across from me, Doc was also just stirring in response to the sound.

Harris was alert and eager for the next adventure.

The stage didn't stop. Soon the guy in the clown mask came galloping past us and then slowed to hail Creel and Snake.

'Say! Was that who I think it was?' Harris asked excitedly.

Doc was leaning slightly to look out the window.

'Who do you think it was? I couldn't see,' said Eulalie, from the other side.

'He wore an elegant grey suit,' said Harris. 'And a mask with the face of a clown. Who else could it be but the legendary masked rider of the plains?' said Harris.

'Who?' Eulalie wrinkled her nose.

He elbowed me. 'Am I right?'

'He calls himself the Long Ranger, if that's what you mean.' I rubbed my rib cage where he had jabbed me.

'Ha! I knew it.' He slapped his thigh. 'I knew it.'

'Good morning, Creel,' said the Long Ranger. 'You too, Snake.'

The stage was still moving. The Long Ranger was riding at a walk alongside the driver's seat.

'Get lost,' Snake growled.

'Morning, Long Ranger,' said Creel.

I couldn't see any of them, but Creel's voice had a hint of laughter. If I had leaned out the window, I would have seen the Long Ranger plain enough, but I didn't want to attract notice. All of us inside the stage were listening.

'Did you gentlemen know that the bank in Femur was robbed yesterday?' the Long Ranger asked.

Doc looked straight at me.

Creel cleared his throat. 'Well, now, as it happens, we chanced to leave town to a lot of whooping and hollering and gunshots.'

'Aha. So you know more of this matter than you are telling.'

'I didn't say that,' said Creel.

'Why didn't you tell me about this last evening when I greeted you on the road?'

'Ya didn't ask,' said Snake, in more of a growl than before. 'Move on, willya?'

'I am asking you now. What did you observe during the holdup?'

'You got me,' said Creel. 'I thought they were just helping us out of town. A big send-off to get us on our way.'

The Long Ranger hesitated. 'Do they do that often?'

'Never,' Creel said amiably.

I could almost hear him grin. Across from me, Doc relaxed and gazed out at the passing prairie again. Apparently those two double bisons really were worth something.

'You guys aren't very nice,' whined the Long Ranger. 'What did I ever do to you?'

'We didn't rob that bank,' said Creel. 'We can't help you.'

'All right.' The Long Ranger sighed. 'Here. I have a jelly bean for each of you.'

41

I couldn't resist. Twisting around, I leaned out the window to look.

'Git away from me with that thing!' Snake yelled. 'Back off, you!'

'Easy, Snake.' Creel was laughing.

'If you don't like red, you can have a different colour. How about silver?'

'A silver jelly bean?' Creel asked, still laughing.

'I said back off! Creel, git us outta here!'

'I'll take it!' Harris shouted, leaning over me to stick his head out the window.

At that moment, however, Creel unleashed his whiplash wrist and cracked it over the team. The stage jerked with the sudden speedup and took off, throwing Harris onto the little floor space between the two benches. Doc and Eulalie looked down at him with benign indifference.

'Farewell,' called the Long Ranger, making his horsite rear up.

I was pretty sure he was waving with his hat, but I wasn't going to look.

Even as we thundered along, creaking and bouncing, Harris managed to climb back into his seat. Once there, he just hung on without talking.

Nobody complained.

After a while, the stage slowed down again. We settled into the familiar rhythmic, swaying pace, but now I was wide awake. As I watched the endless miles of grasslands go by, I realized that Harris was right.

I should say, his magazines were right. Missouri had been one of the first areas of heavy resettlement. As we left its western border behind, signs of civilization were becoming scarcer every hour.

# Four

The depot wasn't much. The railroad ran across the prairie with a minimum of grading, and the depot was just a small rectangular wooden building with benches outside on a little boardwalk platform. A big overhead wooden water tank for the locomotive stood next to it. The place was silent and motionless except for the prairie wind across the tall grass.

I itched to get out when the stage creaked to a halt, but I waited for the others. Control-naturals got used to waiting. Eulalie climbed carefully out of the stagecoach first, fussing with her long dress. Harris glanced nervously at Doc, who responded with a slight nod and debarked next. Once Harris had stretched his long legs to the ground and made room, I finally jumped out.

The others went to retrieve their luggage. Snake got up on the top and started bouncing baggage on the ground. Creel opened the boot.

Harris had two very large brown alligator suitcases. They were heavy, judging by the thumps they made on the sod when they hit and the slouching, staggered gait he used to carry them, with his valise tucked under one arm. From the boot, Doc took a small black suitcase in one hand and a matching smaller bag in the other. Eulalie owned the solid wooden trunk, which Snake and Creel rolled off the top with a thud that shook the ground and kicked up a cloud of dust. They had to carry it to the platform for her.

Since I didn't have any luggage, I hurried ahead, around the end of the depot. One person was sitting on one of the benches that lined the boardwalk platform.

She was hard to see clearly, slumped on a bench with a battered, wide-brimmed, brown leather hat like Duke's hiding her face. Her hair was dark brown and braided into two long strands that looped down and then up under her hat again. A shapeless, weatherbeaten leather bag sat between her feet. It might have been a pack like mine. Her clothes were plain and worn.

If she had any special parts, they were not evident.

The ticket window was closed. I banged on it a few times and glanced down the road the way we had come. By now, someone in the posse just might have remembered the guy who had jumped on the stagecoach right after the robbery.

Nobody opened the ticket window.

I sat down at the far end of the same bench, tapping my feet nervously. A posse could move much faster than any stagecoach.

In front of us, the railroad sat on its ties, with little yellow flowers and tufts of grass growing around it here and there. Beyond it, prairie grass stretched northward to the horizon.

'Hello,' I said after a moment.

'Shut up,' she said, without turning to look at me.

I complied.

Doc brought his luggage to the bench next to me and sat down. Snake and Creel dropped Eulalie's trunk with a thump on the end of the platform, and nodded to her politely. Creel caught my eye and winked as they walked away. A moment later, I could hear the stage pulling out on the other side of the building.

Eulalie sat down at the opposite end of Doc's bench. Harris carefully set his luggage down near her trunk. Then he sat down in the middle of my bench, between the laconic stranger and me, and stretched out his long legs.

'Hi,' he said to her brightly.

'Shut up,' she said again.

'Pardon me.' He looked hurt. 'I meant no offence. Is etiquette different here? I was not aware of behaving improperly. Perhaps I am woefully ignorant of the prevailing social values. If I did give offence, it was my mistake, and—'

She let out a terrific scream and clamped her hands over her ears. Then she started singing softly to herself, apparently to drown out any stray sounds that might leak in.

Harris looked at me in surprise. 'What did I do?'

I almost screamed myself. Instead, I managed to shrug. Then I put a finger to my lips for silence.

Harris nodded gravely and leaned back on the bench, studying her.

I glanced over at Doc and Eulalie. They had been watching, but they turned away in unison when I looked in their direction. Doc straightened his string tie and brushed dust off his black coat. Eulalie tugged slightly at the tight collar around her neck and patted her face with a lace hanky.

I still couldn't see any signs of specials on Eulalie either, except for her Finegrinder & Denton's Barbilou Bluebells.

'I believe I will stretch my legs and examine the track,' said Harris.

When he had wandered off, I was just able to hear the song the stranger was singing under her breath as she stared at the planks in the platform under her feet:

45

*'Do you remember Sweet Betsy from Pike?*
*Who crossed the wide prairies and just out of spite*
*Never told no one what she was about*
*Knew what she was doing and never did doubt.'*

That wasn't the version I remembered, but it fit the old tune. Then I heard the wooden door over the ticket window slide up. Doc and Eulalie got in line and Harris started back from the tracks, where he had been balancing himself on one of the rails with his arms out to each side like it was a high wire.

I jumped to get in line and glanced down the road again. It was still clear.

My singing companion quit singing and sneaked a peek up at me.

'Ticket window's open,' I said.

'Leave me alone,' she snapped, but she got in line behind me.

Eulalie was first. As she got her ticket, I fished around and located all the newbits I had left from fetching the horsites for the gang. They totalled fifty-three. I had no idea how much a ticket would cost or how far this would get me.

Eulalie moved away and Doc stepped up to the window. 'To the end of the line, wherever it is.'

'Thirty-three newbits to the railhead,' said the voice in the window. 'Wherever it happens to be when you get there.'

'Fair enough.' Doc nodded and paid up.

I stepped up to the window after him. The ticket master was just a robot head sitting on the counter. It didn't even have a body. The head was in the shape of some brown bear or weasel or something with very large, humanlike blue eyes. It was wearing a roundish dark blue helmet with some kind of bright yellow wing design painted on the front.

'To the end of the line,' I said jauntily, sliding thirty-three newbits across the counter.

A trapdoor opened under the money, spilling the fair inside somewhere. A ticket appeared in the creature's mouth. When I took it, his eyes blinked green at me.

'Where is the railhead, by the way?'

'It moves every day, bub. By the time you get there, somewhere in the Rockies, I'd say. That's where it is now, and you'll move faster than it will. Next!'

I took one step away and then leaned back. 'What kind of animal are you, anyway?'

'I'm a wolverine, you moron.'

'In *Kansas*?'

'Next!' he shouted around me at the young woman.

I was too antsy to sit anymore. Instead, I walked out to the tracks where Harris had been. From there, one could look both directions and see the rails run exactly straight for miles until they came together near the horizons. On the eastern side, I could see a train, tiny in the distance, coming this way, with a wisp of smoke trailing above it.

Suddenly I gasped slightly, squinting in the distance. A small dust cloud had appeared along the road. Of course, it might not be the posse. It could be any large group of riders moving fast and just happening to follow my route.

Doc and Eulalie were sitting down in their previous spots, but Harris was now in my seat. The nameless young woman was back in her seat.

'Train's coming,' I said to the group at large, bouncing up and down anxiously on my feet.

Nobody answered.

I glanced back nervously at the dust cloud. It was closer.

'As I understand it,' Harris was saying to the young woman, 'depots like this often turn into bustling towns. If I had the money and no other plans, I would invest in this prairie land right now.'

She sat with her arms folded, staring at her feet.

'I'm willing to wager that real estate around this depot will be worth quite a bit.' Harris nodded confidently. 'Oh, yes. This will be quite a little town before long. Femur will wither on the vine unless it gets a railroad spur.'

She snatched up her bag and began pacing down the boardwalk away from everybody. It wasn't very long, and she turned around to pace back. I looked at the train again and bounced up and down harder.

The train was much larger, and I could feel the ground rumbling slightly. Sunlight glinted silver off the top of the locomotive. The smokestack was puffing black clouds.

'Isn't that stupid train here yet?'

I jumped in surprise. She had followed me out to the tracks. Harris was now perusing his guidebook back on the bench.

'It's pretty close,' I said, backing away from the tracks. Over the road, the dust cloud was bigger than ever.

I had never ridden on a train before. When it finally arrived, it was smaller than I had expected, the roofs of the cars only about four metres from the ground. It slowed with a squeaking of brakes and a slight hiss of steam. The engine was silver with red trim and had the shape of ancient locomotives, I guess since it burned wood to make steam, but its top surface was mirrored with solar panelling. Behind the wood car, it was pulling a passenger car, two cattle cars, and a caboose.

A conductor came out the door at the front end of

the passenger car, moving down the two steps attached to the car even before the train stopped. He held on to a railing with one hand and steadied his black cap with the other. The train stopped so that the engine was under the big water tank.

'All aboard,' said the conductor, without putting any effort into being heard.

The young women shoved past me and climbed on. I followed her, aware of the others gathering behind me. The conductor moved aside to make room on the steps.

The car was crowded. The seats were in pairs along each side with an aisle down the middle. Only one pair was empty when I first looked down the length of the car, but the young woman ahead of me threw herself into that window seat.

I could have sat next to a couple of strangers but I was curious about her. Half expecting her to shout at me or even change seats, I moved down the aisle and sat next to her. Nothing happened.

When Harris came down the aisle and smiled at her, I figured out why. She seemed to consider me preferable company, however slightly. The others all had to find aisle seats apart from each other.

Harris found one right behind me.

As the train pulled out, I watched the little depot slide away, looking across my seatmate. The dust cloud arrived at the depot in a great rumble of hoofbeats that I could hear even over the rumble of the train. I leaned away from the window, lest someone in the posse see me.

I sat stiffly until I was sure that the train was not going to slow down again. Just as I let out a long breath of relief, I heard one set of galloping hooves come right up alongside the back of the train. When I saw a riderless horsite cantering away from the train, I knew that one member of the posse had managed to jump on board.

I wasn't sure what to do. Certainly nobody in Femur knew who I was, though the bartender and the hosteller had seen me clearly enough. Maybe I could fool the guy by acting casual.

My seatmate was also gazing out the window.

The train was a lot faster than the stage, and a lot smoother, too. I took a breath and said, 'Not bad, eh?' Then I shut up.

She shrugged.

Since she hadn't told me to shut up, I figured I'd try again.

'What's your name?'

She hugged the leather bag on her lap.

After a moment, I thought maybe she hadn't heard me.

'Betsy,' she muttered finally, looking at the back of the seat in front of her.

'Oh – like the song?'

She smiled for the first time. 'Yeah.'

'My name's Louie.'

'My name's Harris,' said Harris, leaning over the back of my seat and shoving his hand at her.

She reached up without turning to look at him and shook the tips of his fingers politely.

'Say, how about this train? Great, isn't it?' He patted me on the shoulder. 'Great, huh?'

'Yeah,' I said, glancing at her.

She was looking out the window with intent fascination.

'These trains are quite intriguing,' said Harris. 'I was just reading about them on the platform back there. Did you know they have an integrated mix of solar power and steam? Huh?'

'Yeah,' I said quietly. Whoever had jumped on

the train from the posse must have grabbed onto the caboose. That meant he would have to get to the passenger car by running along the top of the cattle cars. That was what was taking him so long.

Betsy studied the prairie harder.

'That was the best substitute they could make when the old fossil fuels ran out,' said Harris. 'The solar power means they don't have to burn up the wood as fast as they would otherwise. We could be going as fast as forty miles an hour, huh?'

I too was gazing hard at the unchanging scenery, sweating heavily, waiting for a stranger to throw open the door at the back of the car.

He nudged me. 'Huh? What do you think? Forty miles an hour?'

'Maybe,' I said. 'Say, it might be in your guide-book.'

'Good idea!' He sat back, finally, to consult it.

Betsy caught my eye and grinned a little.

I couldn't stand the suspense. Finally I heard the sound – the rear door opened and footsteps came inside. It slammed shut again. I didn't dare show my interest by turning to look.

I closed my eyes, breathing hard, waiting for footsteps to march up the aisle towards me. None came. After a while, I realized that either he had found a seat or else he was still back there watching everybody. I decided not to move.

The train rolled across some untold miles of prairie that was flattening out into high plains. The solar battery brought the train up to about half its total speed and then the steam power added the rest. Added to the rhythm of the train as it swayed slightly along the tracks was the barely audible serenade from Betsy under her breath, as she sang to herself. I could not catch any more words over the noise of the

51

train, but I clearly heard only that one tune, over and over.

Carver Dalton and Smellin' Llewellyn had said the Femur posse wouldn't follow me past the depot. They had almost been right.

I had been sitting with my eyes closed, but not quite asleep, when Betsy suddenly broke off her singing with a gasp. Her weight shifted in the seat as she moved, and I turned to look. A big herd of dark brown shapes was coming into view through the window.

I leaned forward a little to look.

'Buffalo!' Harris breathed in my ear. He was leaning over the back of my seat again, looking out our window. 'Huh, Louie? That's right, isn't it? Huh?'

'Looks that way,' I said, neglecting to mention that I had never seen any before, either.

Betsy's eyes were wide with wonder.

'American bison,' said Harris. 'I read about them. The wild herds were totally wiped out at one time.'

As the train moved forward, the herd came fully into view. It was some distance from the tracks and unconcerned with the train. A few of them looked up before returning to their grazing.

'Small domestic herds survived the wild ones,' Harris added. 'When the land west of the Mississippi was depopulated, they broke free and thrived.'

'They're pretty,' said Betsy quietly.

'Pretty?' Harris giggled. 'I think they're funny looking.'

I couldn't count them before they would be out of sight but the herd was big. For all I knew, they might not have natural enemies anymore. Predators had fared even worse on the plains in distant years past than the bison.

Other passengers were watching them, too. In a few more minutes, they had been left behind and everyone settled back in their seats. I sneaked another look at Betsy, wondering if she was a control-natural like me.

We would have to become better acquainted before I could ask a question that personal.

'You like animals?' I asked her.

'Shut up,' she said without rancour.

I did.

I had been dozing when the conductor came to the front of the car.

'Next stop, Compost Hill,' he said. 'Water stop for the train, too. Thirty minutes if you want to stretch your legs.' Then he walked down the aisle with a facility that ignored the swaying of the car.

'Tickets,' he said to Betsy and me.

As we handed them over, I glanced down at his feet. They were Filadelphia Ferrous Felines, with black-furred cat toes and steel claws for gripping. The wooden floor of the aisle was scarred with his countless trips up and down the length of the car. He punched our tickets with a solid brass punch-thumb I had never seen before and handed them back. Then he moved on to Harris, behind us.

The train slowed and came to a stop at a depot and water tank that were nearly the same as the last one, except that they were on top of a long, gentle rise in the ground and the ticket master in the window was a chicken head here instead of a wolverine. The whole place smelled funny.

All the passengers stood up, so getting out of the train took a while. Betsy followed me out. I could hear Harris talking cheerfully to someone behind us.

If I was under suspicion, this might be the time for

my pursuer to make his play. All I could do was look nonchalant. As the passengers spilled out, I strolled briskly down the length of the train to put some distance behind me.

Some of them were actually getting off here. Others walked up and down the platform aimlessly while more wandered around the corners of the depot to see if anything else was here. A few went to look at the robot chicken head.

I wove through them all, heading for the caboose because it was somewhere to go. Some of the other passengers stopped to peer through the slats in the cattle cars.

The orange caboose looked like the ones in pictures I had seen. It appeared to be empty and I didn't dare snoop too closely. Being wanted for bank robbery was enough trouble.

The passengers at the cattle cars seemed to feel the same way about them. They were drifting away as I reluctantly drifted back, nervously glancing around to see if anyone was watching me. I stopped, then, hearing a faint but familiar voice. It was singing.

' "Oh, roast me not on the lone prairie"—
These words came low and mournfully . . .'

I moved up close to look between a couple of slats in the second cattle car. 'Chuck? Is that you?'

The singing stopped. I heard some quiet mutterings and the sound of heavy hooves shuffling about.

'Louie?' Betsy said behind me. 'What are you doing?'

'Uh—' I turned and glanced around. 'Keep your voice down, okay?'

A pair of steerite eyes appeared between the slats in the car. 'Who's out there?' Chuck whined fearfully. 'Friend or foe?'

'Chuck, it's me, Louie,' I leaned down a little so he could see me. 'What are you doing in there?'

'You said you were coming back for me,' he complained. 'I trusted you.'

'Didn't you hear the shooting?' I whispered. 'I got caught up in a bank robbery.'

'A promise is a promise.'

'It was an accident. I meant to come back for you.'

'So you say.'

'Come on, Chuck. I almost got shot.'

He sniffed haughtily.

'I'm a wanted outlaw now. Part of the gang that pulled the job.'

His eyes widened slightly.

'So how did you get here?' I waved at the cattle car.

'Here?' Chuck sighed. 'Back in Femur, I got enough solar power in my cells to crawl from the back wall of the stable out to the prairie grass. I'm still very gaunt, but I grazed enough so I can stand now, thanks to my superior metabolism. I wasn't very strong, though. Then somebody threw me onto the back of a wagon and sold me, I think. So here I am.'

'That's an illegal sale,' I said. 'You were stolen property. It doesn't count.'

'That's terrible,' Betsy declared.

I turned in surprise.

'Well, it is.' She stiffened in embarrassment. 'Can we rescue him?'

'I don't know,' I said slowly. 'Look, Chuck, I'm riding on this train. I'll see if I can think of something. Have you heard how far they're taking the herd?'

'No, but we all surmise that we are going west to feed the railroad crew.' He hesitated. 'The steerites in this car are all nice fellows, but they belong here. As you are aware, I do not.'

'I'll try to think of something,' I told him. 'Meanwhile, we better get away from here so we don't arouse suspicion.'

I started back for the passenger car. Betsy followed. I thought I could hear Chuck sniffling in the cattle car as we left.

# Five

I was quiet until the train was under way again. When the sound of the engine and the rumbling of the cars could cover my voice, I leaned towards Betsy.

'I don't know what to do,' I said. 'He's a steerite.'

'*I* know he's a steerite. You think I'm so dumb I don't know a steerite when I see one?' she demanded.

I sat back a little in surprise. 'No, no. I mean, I have to be careful. It's not like letting a person out.'

She eyed me suspiciously from a sidelong angle.

'If someone sees me letting him out, they'll have me arrested for rustling.'

'Well, didn't you say you were a bank robber? If you're already a wanted man, what difference does it make?'

'Keep your voice down!' I hissed. 'It's a mistake! I didn't rob any bank.'

'You told Chuck you were a member of the gang.' She hesitated, studying me. 'Frankly, you don't look much like a bank robber to me.'

'Thanks,' I said. Then I wondered if that was a compliment.

'So are you or aren't you?'

'Well . . . I'm a member of the gang but I didn't know anything was wrong. I was just hired to hold their horses.'

'A likely story. So what are you going to do to rescue your friend?'

'I don't know. I have to think of something.'

'Well, I should hope so.'

After that, she went back to singing to herself. I leaned back in my seat and watched more prairie go by. When the sun began to go down, I got hungry and found myself thinking of Chuck in altogether embarrassing ways.

Betsy and the other passengers all had provisions with them. Behind me, Harris was explaining the contents of his guidebook to some other passenger. I contented myself with loosening my moccasins and going to sleep.

The train made little stops occasionally all night that I was sleepily aware of. I did not fully awaken until the sharp sunlight came slanting through the windows. When I looked out, we were passing huge piles of rubble and the broken hollow shells of old buildings.

'Aha,' Harris said sleepily. Then he stopped to clear his throat. 'That would be the remains of Denver, no doubt.' His voice was gravelly with sleep.

I stretched and looked out. The destruction was very old. Prairie grasses waved all around and in the remains of the city. The sod was high against the sides of the walls that were still standing. Birds fluttered away here and there, disturbed by the passing of the train.

The train slowed down again somewhere in the middle of all the rubble. The conductor stuck his head in the front of the car, yawned, and said, 'Denver. Thirty-minute stop.'

When I got up, I saw that the passengers had thinned out considerably during the night. Apparently most of them had been travelling to the small stops we had made across the plains. I followed Doc out of the car.

A small town was growing here amidst the old rubble. The train depot here looked just like the others I had seen, a simple rectangle made of unfinished planks. Inside, it was just an empty room with a single restroom in one corner and a jerky dispenser in another.

The dispenser was a cast-iron pillar as tall as I was in the shape of an ear of corn. The green and yellow paint on it was faded and scraped. A human-shaped mouth in dull red opened near the top. I dropped a large number of newbits into the mouth. A moment later, strips of jerky rolled out of it. I grabbed them in handfuls. All but one piece went into my pack.

'Corn-fed beef, a product of the high plains,' intoned the robot mouth from a voice deep inside the dispenser.

'Thanks,' I said. The jerky was even tougher than usual, but I went into the restroom chewing on a stick of it. I had no way of guessing how old it was. Certainly nobody was growing corn here now.

Maybe somebody just stuck new jerky into the machine every so often. More likely, old jerky.

When I walked outside again, I saw that more of the passengers were getting off here. Meanwhile, Harris was standing by himself, looking off into the distance. Doc was brushing dust off his black coat with his black hat as he headed towards the depot, glancing about at everyone in his alert but unhurried way, and Eulalie was walking in a little circle to one side, blinking her Finegrinder & Denton's Barbilou Bluebells around at the new day. Betsy was peering into Chuck's cattle car.

I was afraid to show too much interest in Chuck. After a bit, Betsy wandered back to the little group and stood near Eulalie. Then I joined them.

When I turned, I saw what Harris was staring at.

Tall mountains rose up nearly on top of us and stretched north and south as far as I could see. I had been too sleepy and distracted when I had gotten off the train to look up.

I had never seen anything like them.

'Any idea who he is?' Betsy asked quietly.

'Huh?' I looked at her.

'That quiet man.' She was asking Eulalie. 'He looks familiar. Are you acquainted with him?'

'Certainly not,' Eulalie snapped. 'He has been a gentleman to me, however,' she added mildly.

'Perhaps I can be of help,' said Harris. 'I've been thinking about his nickname, "Doc".'

'Something else in your guidebook?' Betsy sneered.

'This was in a magazine article I read when I was still east of the Mississippi. It told of a paediatrician who became a gunfighter when he moved west of the river.' Harris looked toward the depot. 'I wonder. Can this be the notorious Doc Alberts?'

'I saw a poster of Doc Alberts once,' said Betsy. 'I don't remember the picture very well.'

I looked around to see what else I had missed. Towards the front of the train, the crew member called a fireshovel was loading lumber into the wood car as the water tank poured water into the locomotive. A solitary man came out of the depot.

'Oh,' said Harris, with interest. 'That's the fellow who got on the train late. Galloped up to the caboose on horsite, I'm told, and leaped on. That's the kind of adventure you don't see back east. Yessir.'

I began to sweat again.

He was a very stout, solid-looking man standing in a knee-length brown tweed coat and a low, broad-brimmed tan hat. The robot pig head in the ticket window oinked cheerfully as he passed. Harris openly stared at him.

'Well?' Eulalie sniffed. 'I suppose you think this fellow is Alexander the Cheese-Grate.'

'No,' said Harris quietly, still staring. 'I believe that is the famous bounty hunter, Prism Chisholm.'

A tickling chill ran up my spine. I stifled a gasp and looked closely at the stranger's eyes. They were hard to see in the shadow under his hat brim. Prism Chisholm reputedly had complex eyes with a variety of unusual abilities.

The Femur posse would have quit when they reached the railroad depot. A bounty hunter wouldn't stop at all. He just might have been in town at the right time. If the bank had offered a reward for the robbers, he could have ridden out after the posse on his own.

He might also have had time to get my description before he left.

I thought quickly. Word couldn't have preceded the train here to Denver. Telegraph lines hadn't gone up across the prairie, and wireless hadn't worked since old times on account of the solar irregularities, as they were called. So at least he was the only one I had to worry about.

So far.

We all stood quietly watching the stranger walk towards us. He nodded briefly to the group and got on the train. For just a moment, his eyes had glinted strangely under his hat, reflecting multiple facets.

'That's him,' Harris whispered, turning to watch through the windows as he walked down the aisle in the train car.

'Another ruffian.' Eulalie sighed. She gathered up her lavender skirts and climbed back on, too.

'I wonder if the quiet gentleman really is Doc Alberts,' said Harris. 'So many famous individuals in one place – not excluding yourself, Louie. But

61

don't worry – I'll never say a word about you or Doc to Prism Chisholm! Not me, no sir!'

'Uh – thanks,' I said, with a glance at Betsy. I caught her looking at me just before she turned away.

'Perhaps Doc could help me with my specials,' Harris mused, mounting the train car in his turn. 'Since I bought them just before leaving, I haven't really had time to practise with them. I would like to develop some facility with them before their use is really necessary.'

I stood back to let Betsy on the train car ahead of me. She punched me in the arm. Holding the sore spot, I went on up after Harris.

The car was now empty except for our party from the stagecoach and Prism Chisholm, who sat in the last row of seats against a window. The rest of us took our previous seats anyway. The view was the same everywhere. Doc followed us on board, and the train started into the mountains.

I still hadn't thought of a way to free Chuck and now I was more worried about my own problems. Even if I did free him, I had no idea what he would do in the middle of the Rocky Mountains by himself. If he wanted to get out of the mountains, riding on the train was probably the best way to do that.

'I am heartened by the growth of towns out west here,' Harris was saying across the aisle to Eulalie from behind me. 'By reading about the terrible biological ravaging in years past of the land west of the big river, as they call it, I found out that nothing human could live here for a long time.'

'I know,' she said primly from her seat a few rows away.

'Intrepid explorers ventured this way during that time.' His voice was earnest. 'But when the current era of constant sunspots and flames commenced, even wireless contact with them could not be maintained, and most of them never returned east to tell of their adventures.'

'I know that, too,' she said sharply.

So did I. As Harris droned on, I turned my attention to Betsy, who was singing to herself again and watching the startling scenery as the train slowed down going up a long, steep slope. Maybe I could still throw Prism Chisholm off the scent by acting like a regular traveller.

'So,' I said cheerfully. 'Where are you headed?'

She kept on singing for a couple of lines. 'None of your business,' she said between verses, still tapping her foot in time. She picked up the next verse without missing a beat.

I still couldn't make out the words but the tune was the same as before.

Maybe she wasn't a control-natural after all. Maybe she had a recording in her throat that she liked to replay and lip-sync. I couldn't tell.

The engine was now chugging hard. No wonder they had loaded up on lumber again. At least they could find more firewood on the forested slopes, as opposed to the open plains, if they needed it. The crew had to put on a lot more steam to make the trip through the mountains since sunlight was often blocked from the solar panels on the train by clouds and neighbouring peaks.

The ride up and down the slopes was uneven, proceeding at slow chugs uphill and then headlong races downhill before we coasted as far up the next slope as the momentum would carry us. We always slowed before taking curves. I could see the tracks had followed mountain passes whenever possible. Great peaks rose up on each side constantly before giving way to more of the same.

For the time being, I couldn't do anything about Prism Chisholm. I was dozing when Betsy spoke to me.

'Do you hear something?' she asked.

'Huh?' I was still half asleep.

'On the roof.' She pointed up.

I blinked and looked up at the wooden beams in the ceiling. At first I only heard the laboured chugging of the train. Then I thought I heard footsteps.

I turned around. Harris was asleep in the seat behind me. So was Eulalie, across the aisle from him, but Doc was leaning back in his seat watching the ceiling, too. I looked farther back.

Prism Chisholm was staring at me, his eyes glittering off their many facets.

I swivelled around and slid down in my seat, sweating heavily.

Betsy looked me over but said nothing.

With a heavy thump, a second set of footsteps joined the first. They were walking slowly across the roof of the car from somewhere in the middle towards the front. The train was puffing up a steep grade slowly enough for some agile individuals to hop aboard.

The footsteps reached the front of the car and were followed by scraping sounds as the visitors climbed down a ladder. Then the door was flung open and two men in long, plain yellow dusters staggered unsteadily inside to catch their balance. The coupling between this car and the wood car ahead creaked loudly until one of them slammed the door shut.

'No need to worry, folks,' said a short, slender guy with heavy glasses. A wire ran from behind his back somewhere up to one of the earpieces on his glasses. 'We won't be troubling you.'

The other man was considerably taller but stooped so that his head was only a little higher than his friend's. His duster hung loosely on him, flapping around his arms and body. His movements were all strange, as though he were poised to jump at any moment. He walked slightly bent at the knees and waist and held his elbows angled back. In order to hold his head level to the ground, his neck actually had to be tilted back a little bit.

'Wesley,' he said sternly, resting a hand on the smaller man's shoulder. It left a greasy handprint on his duster. 'Folks, what he means is, we won't be troubling you if you don't trouble *us*.' He held up a gun in his other hand.

I was trying to slide unobtrusively lower in my seat, behind the one in front of me. The crack between the seats allowed me to look forward. I could turn and see everyone else.

'Ah, yes,' said Wesley. 'That is what I meant. I shall make the correction in my brain. Thanks, Alkali.'

Alkali nodded and looked over the group in the car. Combined with a long, pointed nose, his posture gave him a ratlike appearance.

Wesley started down the aisle.

'Hold it,' said Alkali, grabbing his arm. Alkali's hat slipped down towards his eyes and he pushed it up again. It was ugly, a sweat-stained reddish affair with an unusually wide brim.

I had a vague recollection of that hat from Femur during our escape. One of the bank robbers had worn it. I had seen both of these guys before, standing around Duke in that Femur saloon. Neither one of them had spoken.

'Wesley,' said Alkali. 'Look who's here.'

I flinched and followed his wary gaze. Now they

were both looking at Doc. He was looking back, not moving.

I slid down to the floor, farther out of sight.

Suddenly Alkali shot out one long skinny arm and pointed a crooked finger at Doc. 'You. We got no quarrel with you.'

Doc looked at him for a long moment. Then, without otherwise moving, his eyes moved slightly to Wesley. They stayed on him.

'Me, neither,' said Wesley, shrugging and looking away.

Alkali's gaze fell upon Harris and he aimed his crooked finger at him. 'Doc. Is he a friend of yours?'

Doc didn't even look over at him. Instead, he smiled faintly and folded his arms.

'You a control-natural?' Alkali demanded, aiming his pointed face at Harris.

'Me?' Harris tried to laugh. 'Not me, no, sir. No sirree. Not ol' me. Nope.'

'Let's see your specials, dude.'

Wesley laughed. Light glared off his glasses, giving him a momentarily eyeless look.

'They're in my luggage,' Harris said meekly. 'I got rid of my old ones.'

'So they all say.' Alkali grinned and shook his head.

'We're losing time,' said Wesley. 'I estimate we have two minutes and fourteen seconds left before we cross the crest of this mountain and begin the western slope.' He shrugged again. 'I hate to be the one to say it.'

'Oh – yeah,' said Alkali with a sigh. 'Let's go.'

In the last row, Prism Chisholm had pulled his hat brim low enough to cover his eyes. He was too professional to risk a shoot-out under a disadvantage.

The train was still straining up a long slope. Wesley and Alkali moved down the aisle, keeping their balance by holding the tops of seats. Alkali walked with a strange springy step that seemed to bounce through all his joints in arhythmic waves.

I ducked my head as they passed. Their footsteps reached the back of the car. Then they opened the rear door and started a lot of banging and creaking and thumping.

The door swung shut on its own. I sat up and leaned over the arm of the chair to look. They were gone.

Betsy snickered and made chicken noises at me.

Suddenly the entire car shuddered and jerked forward. A loud screeching sound started right behind us but quickly faded as the train, or what was left of it, crested the rise and shot down the far slope fast, picking up speed, throwing us all forward in our seats. Alkali and Wesley had unhooked the cattle cars and caboose.

The screeching was caused by their working the hand brakes on the detached cars. By timing the uncoupling just right, they would have been able to stop those cars on the short stretch of track at the top of the slope where gravity would not work against them too hard.

Meanwhile, we had already left them far behind as we rolled on down the mountainside.

The steam whistle broke into a loud scream mingling with the screech of our own brakes as the trees outside the window blurred to a green smear. The clicking of the rails under the wheels of the train sounded like chattering teeth, or else my chattering teeth sounded like rails clicking. I gripped the sides of my seat hard, hoping we would start up another slope to slow our momentum before we came to a curve. Next to me, Betsy was staring out the window wide-eyed.

Finally the train's downward plunge began to level off. We had reached the bottom of the slope. The brakes whined on until finally we came to a sudden, jerking halt. The train made little squeaking and hissing noises even after it had stopped.

So did I. Anxious to get onto solid ground, I pushed myself up and hurried on quivering knees to the end of the car, leaning on the tops of seat backs with my hands as though the train were still moving. At the door, I paused to look down for the steps.

At least two people slammed into me from behind and I watched the ground rise up to thump into my chest, knocking out what little breath I had left.

Betsy, Harris, and Eulalie all stumbled over me in their rush to get out of the car, too.

I rolled over and looked up. Far above me, craggy, snowtopped mountain peaks angled against the blue sky. The air here was cool and dry.

Prism Chisholm descended the steps from the car with dignity and stepped over me, his many-faceted eyes glowing several shades of green.

I heard people jump from the locomotive. Their footsteps ran behind my head, out of sight. The crew was going to look at the freed coupling behind the passenger car.

After a while I managed to stand up and brush myself off. The slopes around us were heavily forested in pine and all kinds of leafy hardwoods. Brown gravel crunched under my feet as I moved away from the train.

'You've been rustled,' Prism Chisholm said quietly to the crew. His eyes were now colourless again, but sparkled in the sunlight.

The fireshovel turned to look. He was a tall, broad

man with Nittany Block VI shoulders and Flumper Corporation PoppedEye forearms, one ending in a large steel clamp to grab logs and one ending in a shovel to move coals. Smoke and soot covered him.

'Wesley Coon and Alkali Springs jumped on the roof of the passenger car and disconnected the last three cars,' said Prism Chisholm. 'My infrared eyesight tracked them along the roof from the moment they hopped on. According to my microscopic study of the dust on their dusters, they recently crossed the Kansas plains, which was no surprise to me anyway. My reading of their skin temperature suggests considerable stress over the last few days out of Femur. By now, they've rustled the steerites out of the cattle cars and started them through the forest.'

The fireshovel followed all this without much interest.

The conductor came up alongside the fireshovel. 'Not much point in going back, then,' he said. 'We can pick up the cars on the return in another day or two. Tell the engineer.'

The fireshovel nodded and started away.

'All aboard,' muttered the conductor with a sigh.

# Six

The first to board again, Prism Chisholm returned to his old seat at the back of the car.

Eulalie gathered the skirts of her long lavender dress together and sat down next to Doc, who hadn't left his seat. He was lightly brushing dust off his matching silver vest and pants. Harris sat down behind him.

Betsy hesitated, looking at the empty seat by Harris, then turned to sit in the window seat in front of Doc. I sat next to her on the aisle again. If Doc noticed how everyone clustered around him, he gave no sign of it.

As the train started forward, Harris let out a deep breath. 'Wesley Coon and Alkali Springs,' he said quietly with a nervous glance over his shoulder at Prism Chisholm. 'And they actually spoke to me!'

'More ruffians,' sniffed Eulalie, fanning herself with her lace hanky.

'Two more famous members of Duke Goslin's gang,' said Harris, giving me a glance this time.

I looked away.

Betsy studied me for a moment again before looking out the window and starting to sing to herself once more.

I figured that Wesley and Alkali were simply pursuing their normal activities on their way to Washout. After all, it was a long trip to the gang's rendezvous. I just had to find a place to settle down as soon as I could and let all the gang members leave me far behind as they travelled on westward.

Maybe Prism Chisholm had been tracking Wesley and Alkali. He could have been following Doc. Perhaps he was travelling just to see the sights out west.

I didn't believe any of that.

'Chuck,' I remembered aloud suddenly. 'They've got him.'

'Well, of course,' said Betsy sharply. 'You can't do much for him now, can you? Some friend you are.'

I sighed and closed my eyes. Chuck was on his own again. For that matter, I had to watch out for myself. Prism Chisholm certainly knew Wesley Coon and Alkali Springs. Maybe he was planning to follow me to find the rendezvous point.

My eyes shot open again. Following *me*? Without thinking, I whirled around to look.

Prism Chisholm was gazing straight at me with those sparkling unfocused eyes.

I spun around again and slid down in my seat, wondering what his eyes could read about me.

The train made better time, of course, chugging forward without the added weight of the steerites and their cars. We threaded through the highest of the mountains and gradually started downward again. The far slopes were less forested than the mountain regions we had already travelled. Occasionally in the distance I could see what looked like the sparse forest and barren rock and sand of high desert.

As time passed, I sneaked more looks out the window past Betsy, still waiting low in my seat. The grading beneath the railroad was newer here, the gravel roadbed recently sculpted. Marks in the earth showed where materials had been laid. Fresh fields of stumps had been left where the railroad crew had cut lumber for ties.

Finally the train slowed to a crawl as we entered the camp of the railroad building crew. Tents lined the sides of the railroad and workers milled about in the narrow spaces among them. I had thought they would be toiling away beyond the railhead.

I glanced up. The sun was already behind a mountain to the west. Darkness fell quickly up here.

Maybe I could find work here.

The train creaked slowly to a stop. Outside, people were talking and yelling raucously. The tents of the railroad camp were crowded together in the space between the railroad itself and the steep slopes on each side.

The conductor stuck his head in the door at the front of the car. 'End of the line. You can pick up a stagecoach here to points west.'

I grabbed my pack and my hat and hurried off the train. The locomotive had stopped right behind the freight train that moved the workers and their supplies. People bustled all around me.

I walked quickly, without a clear destination, hoping to lose myself in the tents and the crowd before Prism Chisholm got off the train. The stained and dirty tents were laid out in uneven rows, making makeshift alleys between them. After I had turned a couple of corners, only the smokestacks of the locomotives on the trains were still visible. Prism Chisholm was still out of sight.

I turned to the nearest person. She was a heavyset woman in a faded blue flower-print dress sitting on a stool in front of a tent. As I watched, she carefully dripped oil from a small can into an exposed hinge in the back of one knee.

''Scuse me. Where can I find the crew chief?'

She scowled at me. 'What do you want with him?'

'I'm looking for work.'

'*What?*' She reared back and heaved the oil can at my head.

I ducked. The oil can missed the back of my head, knocking my hat forward a little, and I ran.

After I had skipped through the crowd and turned a few more corners, I glanced back. She too was out of sight. I straightened my hat and looked around.

I found myself gazing closely at someone's belt buckle.

Very slowly, I reared back and looked up. Far above me, the man's face was a full-whiskered dark profile against the setting sun, topped with a cowboy hat that came to a sharp point in the front. Nearly blinded by the sunlight, I lowered my gaze all the way down to his legs. One ended in a large steel-wheeled foot. The other had an ordinary foot but a powerful Abilene Industrial-Strength Accordian ankle.

'Something you want, fella?' he demanded.

'Uh—' I didn't want this guy mad at me too. 'Do you know, uh, where the stagecoach is? I just got off the train.'

'It was here,' he said. 'But it's gone. Left long before that train showed up.'

'It did?' I backed up a little, so I could see him without injuring my neck.

'Yeah.' He had a reddish face hidden inside a gold and grey beard. 'Fact is, those drivers didn't much like the air around here, with talk of the strike and all.' He grinned and punched a fist into his other palm.

'Strike?'

'Say, just who are you anyway?' He eyed me carefully. 'Just travelling through, you say?'

'I . . . think so.'

'You think so? What's that supposed to mean?'

'Yes. That is, unless there's something to do here—'

'You mean scab?' he shouted, lifting me up by the shirtfront.

'No! Not me, no, never,' I said quickly, though it was muffled by the cloth he had pulled up over my mouth. My feet were dangling somewhere off the ground, kicking back and forth.

'That's better,' he said, still holding me up in front of his face. 'Maybe you don't know what's going on. You see, we've all stopped work. Tonight around the campfire, we're going to have a meeting and decide what to do next.'

'Can 'ou mut me wown?' I asked, with a corner of my collar in my mouth.

'Huh? Oh, yeah. Sorry. I'm Jed Kenney, rail messenger.' He let go.

I thudded onto the ground on my back. His face was once again a distant silhouette against the bright sun. 'I'm Louie Hong. Uh – I think I'll mosey on back to the train.' I scooted away, got up, and trotted off.

I found Harris, Eulalie, and Betsy standing together where they had got off the train. They were watching the workers hustle past in all directions. Doc was nearby, leaning over a water barrel in his hat and shirtsleeves, sprinkling water on his black coat and dabbing at it with a cloth. His gunbelt was readily visible now that his coat was off.

Our train was now slowly chugging around a small, temporary loop of track, about to head back east again.

I didn't see Prism Chisholm.

'We're told that the stagecoach has left without

us,' said Harris. 'Quite authentic, wouldn't you say? The uncertainty of life on the frontier, the casual attitude toward—'

'It was scared off by the strike,' I said.

'Strike?' Harris blinked. He looked around at the railroad workers. 'You mean these people are *anarchists*?'

'An entire camp full of ruffians,' said Eulalie. 'And we're stuck here.' She edged towards Betsy. 'Honey, you and I should get acquainted. We ladies must stick together under trying circumstances.'

Betsy wrapped her arms around her pack and hugged it, stepping away sideways.

The sun was already down, though the sky directly above the pass was still bright with waning day. People were moving up the track, towards the railhead in front of the freight train, carrying wood of all kinds: raw logs, leafy branches, folding chairs, footstools, cut lumber.

Doc shrugged his coat back on and started in the same direction as the general migration of workers.

Harris and Eulalie both followed him. Since I had nothing better to do, I joined them. I could hear Betsy singing softly to herself as she fell in line behind me.

The pile of wood sat on the graded roadbed squarely in front of the freight train and the last tracks that had been laid. It was already maybe forty feet high, and more wood was thrown onto it as I approached. Small yellow flames were just beginning to crackle along the bottom. Scores of workers formed a great ring around the growing fire, all of them in the shadow of the mountain to our west.

Ahead of us, Doc leaned against a small tree that had been left standing. The rest of us stopped nearby, not wanting to crowd him.

'Louie,' said Harris. 'I bow to your superior experience. What do you suggest we do in the absence of the stagecoach?'

'Stay here, I guess.' I had no intention of going back to Femur, at any rate. Someone walked up to Eulalie, distracting me.

'Excuse me, ma'am,' said a large man in leather chaps and a fringed buckskin coat. He touched the brim of his felt hat and sniffed. 'You obviously don't belong to the railroad crew. May I ask if you arrived on the train from Denver?'

'That is correct.' Eulalie eyed him carefully.

'I'm to meet a man here named Prism Chisholm. Have any of you folks seen him?' He had a long, fleshy face and a prominent nose that reminded me of Smellin' Llewellyn's.

Harris and Betsy both looked at me.

'He was on the train with us,' I said slowly. 'Haven't seen him since.'

'Me neither,' said Betsy.

He touched his hat brim again, sniffed again, and trudged off into the crowd.

Harris watched him go.

'Another friend of yours?' Betsy demanded.

'No.' Harris shook his head. 'That is the finest living tracker on the frontier. I am convinced now that Prism Chisholm is in fact on someone's trail.' He looked at me.

'The finest living tracker on the frontier?' I asked, with a voice that was suddenly dry. 'So who is he?'

'Sniffin' Griffin,' he said. 'The man who has had an ongoing feud for years with a member of Duke's gang named Smellin' Llewellyn.'

'Are you serious?' Betsy started laughing.

'Rumour has it,' he added gravely, 'that one of them bought a supposedly unique special proboscis and olfactory sensor and the other stole its secret.'

'Perhaps that would be justification for a vendetta among these types,' said Eulalie.

Shouting and cheering had risen up around us. Someone had stood up in front of the fire and was haranguing the crowd.

'. . . or we'll never get a decent wage!' he cried. The black silhouette in front of the rising golden flames raised two huge arms that ended in gigantic blocks. He was a driver, a man who could pound in railroad spikes in one massive blow or drive piles into the earth with a couple of them.

'Look what we've given!' A woman chimed in, rolling forward clumsily on caterpillar tread feet. 'And what do we get in return? Nothing!'

'Nothing!' The driver shouted again, raising his blocks. 'Nothing!'

The crowd began to chant in time with his gestures: 'No-thing! No-thing!'

I backed up a little, alarmed at the atmosphere, scanning the crowd. It was an angry ring around the bonfire. Everyone was chanting and jumping with raised fists, or clamps, or mallets . . . tongs . . . hooks. . . .

Firelight glittered off a pair of multifaceted eyes toward the back of the circle, not far from us.

I ducked away from the fire. Just a few yards away, by the first row of tents, I was alone in the darkness. Now was the time to find out what I could. I skipped around a couple of tents and sidled up to the crowd again, crouching in the shadows, near Prism Chisholm and Sniffin' Griffin.

'Since I was going to meet you here anyway,' Prism Chisholm was saying, 'I decided to take the job.' He had to talk loud to be heard over the crowd.

'I got to hand it to you,' said Sniffin' Griffin,

sniffing. 'Here I thought we were going to be stuck with security jobs on the railroad and you got us a real bounty job instead.'

'You'll like it even better when you hear who pulled the job,' said Prism Chisholm. He smiled slightly, his face just barely outlined by the flickering firelight. Flames shone in his sparkling eyes.

'You mean . . .' Sniffin' Griffin tilted his hat back and twitched his nose a couple of times.

'Duke Goslin and his gang.'

'And a certain ol' buddy of mine. Well, well.' Sniffin' Griffin turned and started to pace thoughtfully. 'I do like that. I do indeed. I'll enjoy sniffing him out – hey, is somebody back there?' He peered in my direction.

Suddenly panicked, I scampered behind another tent. Then I ran, turning corners every chance I got. After a while, I realized there was no sign of them behind me. Breathing hard, I slowed down but kept walking, still zigzagging aimlessly.

They hadn't chased me. That just meant Sniffin' Griffin hadn't gotten a good sniff and Prism Chisholm hadn't bothered to take a good look. With those eyes of his, he might have picked me out in the dark by my body heat or something.

Looking out for more surprises, I wandered through the alleys among the tents, sweating freely and trying to figure out what to do.

My fear had been right; Prism Chisholm and now his partner were following me to find the money. I had to lose them somehow. Even if I could get a job here at the railhead, they would question me before they moved on. I had to find some way to keep going.

I heard a hissing sound off to one side, but paid no attention to it. Someone might have left a coffee pot over a cookfire. I kept walking.

Something hissed again.

I walked a little faster.

'Hey!' a voice whispered after another minute.

I whirled around, ready to run.

'Louie? Over here.'

The voice wasn't behind me. It was again from one side, out of the darkness beyond the last row of tents.

'Louie, it's me – Chuck.'

'Chuck?' I whispered back, approaching him. 'I can't see you.'

He stepped forward a little and a flicker of light from the big bonfire shone off his stainless-steel head. It looked gigantic now on his scrawny body. He was hardly more than a hide-covered skeleton.

'I escaped,' he said proudly.

# Seven

The chanting and shouting around the bonfire had grown louder. I crept up close to Chuck, staring at him.

'What happened?'

He gave what might have been a shrug of his skinny shoulders. 'When those two rustlers started driving us over the mountain, I slipped away into the trees to one side. They didn't even see me. Besides, they didn't know how many of us there were.'

'Since none of you cost them any money, I guess they didn't care if they lost one along the way.'

'Well, it *was* dangerous.' He pouted. 'I was on my own again. I do seem to have a certain facility for escape when I deem it necessary.'

'I didn't mean it wasn't dangerous—'

'Of course not,' he sniffed.

'So how did you get here?'

'I kept the railroad in sight and followed it. I saw you in camp down here before sundown.' He lowered his head and pawed idly at the ground. 'Um, do you suppose . . . that is, I'm not sure where to go now. I was wondering . . .'

'Maybe we could help each other,' I said slowly. 'Only stay out of sight, will you? If someone else doesn't rustle you, they'll butcher you again. This whole camp is full of hungry workers.'

Chuck glanced around nervously.

So did I.

'In what manner shall we proceed?' he whispered.

'I'm not sure. I could tell everyone you belong to me, but this is a pretty wild place. They might not care.'

'How terribly uncivilized.' He shook his head from side to side in disapproval.

'Can you get along on your own for a while? Maybe I can figure out what to do.'

'I suppose,' said Chuck. 'Grass is scarce here but not totally absent. Also, I expect to find some of the unfamiliar native flora of this altitude edible as well. I will remain in the vicinity and await your advice.'

'Okay. I hope I think of some.'

Chuck withdrew into the shadows and started up the slope away from the camp.

I hurried back down the tented alleys towards the bonfire. Betsy seemed to like Chuck. Maybe she could think of something.

The roaring of the crowd had grown louder than ever as everyone had marched the short distance from the high flames of the bonfire to the freight train. As I came up behind the mob looking for Betsy, I saw that all the cars had been uncoupled. Some of them had already been turned over on their sides; now the locomotive itself had been surrounded on three sides by the biggest and strongest of the railroad workers. The entire mob was chanting, 'Heave! Heave! Heave!'

The locomotive was rocking farther over on each chant, then rocking back slightly before the next shove. Finally, with one more great shout from the crowd, the locomotive tipped over and fell with a crash onto its side. Cheers rose up everywhere.

I caught a glimpse of Doc in the firelight. He and the other passengers from the train were jostled in the middle of the mob. No one was paying attention to them; they must have been caught up when the workers had suddenly decided to assault the freight train. Now they were trying to work their way out but the crowd was too tightly packed.

'Here he comes!' someone shouted. A tall, four-armed silhouette, standing on the side of the over-turned locomotive, pointed down the track to the east with two outstretched arms.

A rail messenger was speeding toward us – Jed Kenney, the guy who had dangled me over the ground in order to have a face-to-face palaver. His wheel foot was carefully balanced on one of the rails and the Abilene Industrial-Strength Accordion ankle over his other foot powered him as he kicked off the ground alongside the track. As he approached the overturned train cars, he raised up on his wheel and braked to a stop, throwing up a small shower of yellow sparks.

'They're almost here!' Jed shouted to the crowd. 'They came overland from a mining camp. They're almost at the main tent right now!'

Angry shouts rose up from the mob.

'Who's here?' I yelled at someone nearby. 'What's he talking about?'

'The strike breakers,' he answered grimly as he pushed forward into the crowd. 'Out-of-work miners from some town gone bust. Yancy Havoc's pets!'

Their shouts had become incoherent, but suddenly the crowd broke down the side of the tracks in a body, passing the overturned freight cars. I got a glimpse of Harris towering head and shoulders over Betsy, Eulalie, and Doc, all of them carried along by the mob. Beams of light shot forward here and there as workers with lamps inset in their foreheads switched them on.

From where I stood, I could see the front of the

mob mounting the raised roadbed behind the freight train. Two more rail messengers joined Jed; they could move the fastest. Then a grader rolled up after them on caterpillar-tread feet, swinging his one big shovel-bladed hand for balance and raising his regular hand clenched. He was followed by a great hammer-fisted driver, maybe the one I had seen earlier. After him, the mob followed in a jumble of shapes that merged into one dark mass marching down the railroad they had laid.

I trotted after them, afraid of losing my fellow train passengers. They weren't exactly friends of mine, but unless they found out I was a control-natural, they were close enough. I followed the mob at a short distance so I wouldn't get caught up or trampled if they all changed direction suddenly.

Just over the rise, a big luxurious tent up on a bluff overlooked the tracks. As the mob marched down the roadbed, a light came on inside the big tent. A man's silhouette walked to the front and threw back the flap. Shouts and jeers rose up from the mob as they saw him.

The workers who had lights shined their beams on him from wherever they were in the crowd. He was of medium height, slightly heavy, wearing a low black hat and frock coat. A red string tie blew over his shoulder in the wind. His vest and trousers were also black, but the gunbelt he wore was lavishly tooled brown leather.

When he swept back the side of his coat to free his gun, I saw the fast, quirky motion of a Triple-Jointed Gatlinburg gun arm. So did the mob. They quieted, watching him warily.

'Yancy Havoc,' someone shouted. 'Come down here and talk face to face!'

It was Jed Kenney, still standing in the front rank.

The man in the spotlight of fifteen or twenty headbeams sneered as he looked down over the mob. Then he stopped and peered forward, squinting. 'Doc,' he called. 'Is that you, Doc?'

Slowly, the workers in the mob moved away from his line of sight, parting in the middle until Doc and Yancy were staring at each other along a long dark sloping corridor of strangely twisted and misshapen bodies. Their similar clothes made them look like partners. As the silence between stretched awkwardly, though, they looked more like enemies sizing each other up. They had locked eyes from under their broad-brimmed black hats, their string ties fluttering and their long coattails swaying.

'Evening, Yancy,' Doc called back.

'Evening, Doc.' Yancy grinned. 'You looking for me?'

'No. Just passing through until the stage left early without me. If you have another one, I'll keep going.'

'I don't have any,' Yancy called back. 'That's an independent line. They'll come back when they feel like it.'

'Evening, Yancy.'

'Evening, Doc.'

Doc turned around and looked pointedly at the people blocking his way back toward the camp.

None of the workers had noticed Doc until Yancy had spotted him. They didn't quite know what to make of him or this conversation. Slowly, they parted in front of Doc and allowed him to walk out of the crowd. Behind him, Eulalie and Betsy and Harris hurried through the space after him.

The mood of the crowd had broken. They looked back at Yancy, uncertain now. I turned away to join up with my fellow passengers again.

'Look!' someone in the mob shouted.

I spun around

A crooked line of white headlamps was coming over the crest of the next rise down the track. The brilliant circles threw beams of light that jiggled and danced across the dark sky in rhythm with the footsteps of those wearing them. On the bluff overlooking both crowds, Yancy threw back his head and laughed.

'The strikebreakers!' Jed Kenney shouted. 'Get 'em!'

The railroad workers surged forward with a roar of fierce cries, their anger awakened by the sight of the other mob. The strikebreakers thundered yells back at them and came charging down the slope. The beams of headlamps staggered crazily from both mobs as they ran together.

Jed Kenney skated forward along one rail, raising a big stick. A short, heavyset miner ran forward and slammed into him, holding him around the middle with trunklike arms that ended in steel picks. A railroad driver barrelled forward with his massive arms high and clashed with a mining driver among the strikebreakers with the same kind of arms. They strove against each other, neither one capable of gripping the other with their fingerless hammerhead hands. Then the two sides closed completely.

Screams and cries rose up from the battle jammed into the narrow pass over the railroad, punctuated by the clang and clank of steel against steel and the thump of fists against flesh. If the railroad workers prevailed over the strikebreakers from the mines, I didn't know what would happen. However, if the strikers broke ranks they would flee back toward me, into the camp.

I didn't want to get caught in a rout. With a worried glance over my shoulder, I jogged after Doc and the other passengers. Doc was picking up his luggage where he had left it beside the tracks. That left Harris's suitcases still there next to Eulalie's big trunk. Betsy had kept her bag with her, as I had my pack.

On the edge of camp, I spotted Harris standing on the tracks looking intently at the distant battle raging behind me.

'Fascinating,' Harris said to himself.

I skidded to a stop and looked back. The mobs fought on in the distance, a rumbling, crashing silhouette lit up by their own headlamps, with jagged edges constantly shifting and flowing. Screams and shouts came to us on the night wind.

'I wouldn't stay here,' I said, trotting past him.

'Really? You wouldn't?' He sounded surprised.

I caught up to Betsy and Eulalie and looked back again. Harris was following reluctantly.

'We ladies must find quarters for the night,' Eulalie was saying as she hustled after Betsy. 'We must be especially careful among these socially questionable specimens.'

Betsy hummed loudly to herself and hurried after Doc.

'Can you help me carry my trunk?' Eulalie asked, prancing behind.

Doc was standing with his luggage at his feet, in the bright glow of the bonfire that still roared high into the darkness. He had his hands raised palm-forward to warm them. As I watched, he glanced up at us and then past us to the battle down the track.

The clashing mobs still struggled, but the railroad workers had been forced back. The headlamps and the beams that were shot by both sides in all directions were no longer in lines but in a great jumble, with the vast majority of them worn by the miners. The battle was coming closer to the camp, step by grudging step.

Doc had taken one of the safest spots in the pass, next to the fire. Betsy took a spot near him. Eulalie huddled behind her.

Harris had picked up his suitcases but was dawdling, walking backward so he could watch the fight.

Suddenly renewed shouts and cries rose up from the battling workers. I looked up just in time to see some of the railroad workers break and stampede this way. Whirling, I ran towards the fire but saw Doc walking away from it towards the slope, carrying his luggage. As usual, Betsy and Eulalie were right behind him.

That was good enough for me. Instead of going to the fire or following them, I ran straight towards the part of the slope closest to me. Faint firelight washed over it, showing me the steep brush-covered mountainside where it rose behind the farthest row of tents.

Before I got there, shouting and footsteps closed in around me. Someone heavy knocked me over and I rolled on the gravel. When I stopped moving, two dark shapes were wrestling on the ground beside me.

One had an injured leg and was trying to crawl forward by pulling himself along with his big steel clamp hands. The other was a skinny, rangy woman with hydropump biceps that held the injured man's arms tight against his body. The guy on the bottom was grunting and straining to move; the woman had her teeth sunk into his shoulder.

I had no idea which side either one of them was on.

More people stumbled around us among the tents, shouting and running and dragging others to the ground. They flashed in and out of the firelight, throwing shadows on the sides of the tents. All of them seemed huge and strong and angry.

I managed to stand up next to a tent, but my way was blocked by the fistfights and wrestling on all sides.

Hoofbeats sounded to one side. Chuck had trotted down the slope and was threading his way through the fighters. His stainless-steel head reflected the golden flames of the fire. As skinny as he was, he was still heavier than most people, even here.

'I suggest you climb on my back,' he called over the din, stopping in front of me. Someone stumbled backward into him and bounced off, causing Chuck merely to glance back in annoyance.

'You sure you can hold me?' I looked doubtfully at his narrow back.

'A silly question,' said Chuck. 'It is to laugh. Hurry up, will you?'

'Okay.' I grabbed onto his horns to brace myself and threw one leg over him. His spine and rib cage provided a much narrower seat than before. 'Let's go.'

He took several steps, paused to let a couple of people roll past us on the gravel as they grappled with each other, and then trotted up the aisle between the tents. When he reached the slope of the mountain, he started to climb it in little jumps. I hung on hard to his horns and around his middle with my legs.

The slope was so steep that I was nearly upright as I clung to him. After a sustained but very jerky ride, he stopped.

'I am winded,' he huffed. 'Please descend.'

'Thanks for the rescue, Chuck,' I said, getting off. 'That was very brave.'

He lowered his head modestly. 'I have

experienced some hard lessons since first we entered Femur.'

I looked out over the narrow pass. We were about twelve metres up the slope, certainly high enough not to worry about exhausted combatants accidentally trampling me. Both mobs had arrived in force and the battle of dark shadows and sweeping headlamps was scattered throughout the camp. Tents crumpled to the ground as their poles were knocked aside in the crush.

On the far side of the camp, up the slope, I could just see Prism Chisholm and Sniffin' Griffin moving out of the way of the surging battle.

On the same slope, but overlooking the bonfire in the opposite direction, the other passengers stood safely watching, too. Eulalie's trunk remained down by the tracks. The others had their belongings with them.

As I watched, Doc straightened his hat and his tie and walked away. He was probably looking for some privacy to 'shoot rabbits'.

'This is terrible,' said Chuck, watching the brawls beneath us. 'Why are these fellows hurting each other? Why don't they be nice?'

'Just be glad you don't have to work for a wage, Chuck,' I said, watching two huge barrel-shaped men strain against each other and grapple for a hold. One had a Lumberjack Nine Axeblade hand; the other had trapped it in a massive steel pincer.

'You don't, either,' said Chuck.

'Yeah, but I'm looking for work.'

'But you just said . . .'

'Not now, okay?' I wasn't too sure what I meant, either.

'But if you don't want to work for a wage, why—'

'Chuck, let's go join the other passengers.' When I looked, though, they were gone.

'As you wish.'

'Come on, Chuck.'

'Where?' He peered around in the dim light.

'I'm not sure.'

'Okay.' Chuck followed me anyway.

I had to find my way along the slope in the flickering firelight among rocks, bushes, and trees until I got past the battle that was now scattered throughout the tents. Betsy was just disappearing behind the tall, blazing fire down below, apparently the last in line of their group. I picked my way down the slope, to angle behind the bonfire to the west after her.

When even Betsy was out of sight, I tried to hurry and tripped over a rock. The resulting stumble carried me at a run down the rest of the mountain-side before I could catch my balance again.

Chuck cantered up alongside me. 'Why are we running?'

'Uh – so they don't leave us behind.' I kept trotting around the fire and he accompanied me.

In just a few moments, we mounted the graded roadbed. We were past the railhead now where no tracks had been laid yet. I was straining to look into the darkness ahead.

The firelight barely limned Betsy's hat and her looping braids as she trudged after the others lost in the night beyond her.

'Where are we going?' Chuck asked me again.

'I'm still not sure,' I said. 'But I think Doc just decided not to hang around the railroad camp any longer. Since the stagecoach isn't here. . . .'

'Oh, no. Do you mean to say that he is just going to *walk* the rest of the way?'

'It looks that way, don't you think?'

'But . . . across the desert? How far is he going?'

'You got me.'

'It could be thousands of kilometres!'

'Could be.' I shrugged.

'And the others are going with him?' He shook his head. 'I can hardly believe it.'

'I doubt they've thought it through. Maybe they think he's just going to find a place to spend the night. For that matter, maybe he is.'

Chuck considered this as we hurried along. 'What are your plans?'

'Well . . . I figure I left the Femur posse behind, but a man named Prism Chisholm worries me. He and a partner named Sniffin' Griffin are following me to find the loot from the bank robbery.'

Chuck studied me sidelong with one eye. 'No fooling? You robbed a bank?'

I sighed and shook my head.

# Eight

We made good time on the graded roadbed, but we didn't catch up to anyone. Since they weren't likely to leave the road, I wasn't worried about losing their trail, but I was too tired to gain on them much. From the way Chuck was panting and wheezing, he was in no condition to carry me.

Soon the bonfire was no more than a small yellow light in the distance behind us. A splattering of stars overhead and a curved sliver of moon offered very little light here. At least the night was so clear that I didn't really need any shelter.

Finally I came to a reluctant stop on the gravel. Chuck stopped next to me, huffing.

'I'm worn out. What do you say we stop for the night?' I asked.

'I say, agreed. But why haven't they stopped?'

'I guess Doc will walk as long as he feels like it. If the others are scared to be left behind, they'll push themselves to keep up.' I pointed to a couple of boulders up on the slope. 'Just in case someone comes this way tonight, or even in the morning, let's go up there.'

He nodded assent, still panting, and we climbed up the slope. I found a comfortable spot over the boulders and curled up. He lay down with his back to me, close enough for us to keep each other warm in the chilly mountain air. As I drifted off to sleep, I could hear him munching on grass that he had found growing nearby.

I woke up at dawn with a start and looked around.

'Morning,' Chuck said pleasantly. He yawned and then chomped on another sprig of grass.

'I'm thirsty,' I said.

'This is indeed a dry climate. Mountains should provide plenty of water, however, and I will undoubtedly smell it as we go.'

I got up and stretched, looking back down the roadbed toward the camp. 'Prism Chisholm didn't see us leave last night or he'd be here already, but he's probably looking around the camp for me now.'

'Quite so.' Chuck half-jumped to his feet. 'I grazed off and on during the night. With that sustenance and the added solar energy that daylight will provide, I am able to offer you a ride, at least while I am refreshed.'

'Huh?' It took me a minute to unravel that. '*Oh.* Thanks.' I clambered aboard and he carefully meandered down the slope back to the roadbed, leaving the morning shadow of the eastern mountain for a strip of sunlight. There he resumed our westward trek.

I pulled out another strip of jerky and jerked off a piece with my teeth. I probably could have patched my moccasins with it if necessary. 'Is this how this crud got its name?'

'Huh?'

'Never mind.' I twisted around to look back toward the camp. 'No sign of anyone yet.'

We were going down a gradual slope, rounding a curve.

'The end of the road is in sight,' said Chuck.

'What?' I whirled around, panicked. 'What do you mean?'

'I *mean*,' he said petulantly, 'that the end of the road is in sight.'

About sixteen metres ahead, the graded roadbed came to a halt. This was as far as the railroad crew had advanced before going on strike.

Chuck ambled to the end of the grading and stopped. Then he reached down over the last of the bare gravel to pull up something else to eat. 'Well?' he said with his mouth full.

'Well what?'

'Exactly where do we go from here?'

The slope had widened from a mountain pass to a broad, rather sandy descent. Trees were scattered throughout it, blocking our view of the other passengers ahead, wherever they were. Ridges stretched into the distance on each side but were lower than the mountains we had been travelling through. I couldn't see any footprints in the grass and underbrush.

I was sure Prism Chisholm could have. Maybe he would yet.

Chuck had raised his head to sniff the breeze.

'We'll just have to keep going, I guess,' I said.

'I smell water to the left, not very far away. Let's go drink up.'

'Good idea.'

He stepped off the roadbed and started for the line of trees to one side. It looked narrow, as though it followed a streambed. I had to slide off him when we got to the trees to avoid getting skimmed off by low-hanging branches. As he followed his nose through the underbrush, I clung to his tail and ducked under branches and stumbled over roots. Before long, we came to a clear, narrow brook running silently over rounded brown-and-whitish rocks.

I lay down to splash water on my face, then cupped my hands for drinking. Downstream next to me, Chuck waded his front legs into the stream and lowered his head to drink.

Then he paused.

'Do you hear that?' he asked.

'Huh?' I looked up, with water dripping off my face.

It was another verse to the tune of 'Sweet Betsy from Pike.'

*'Beyond the great bison, beyond the high range,*
*And into the desert where all was so strange,*
*She travelled so far and she travelled so well,*
*And what she was doing, nobody could tell.'*

I looked upstream after Betsy's voice but didn't see her. Chuck stepped all the way into the water and started wading that way. I scrambled up and jumped in after him, gasping as the icy water swirled into my moccasins.

*'Singing too-ra-li, too-ra-li, too-ra-li-ay . . .'*

I grabbed Chuck's tail again and slogged after him. Around the next stand of trees and bushes, Betsy was just strapping her pack shut. She jumped up at the sound of our splashing, ready to run.

'Betsy, it's me, Louie,' I called.

'Shut up,' she said casually, looking at Chuck. 'Say, is this your friend?'

'Betsy, this is Chuck the steerite. Chuck, Betsy was one of the train passengers. Uh, she was real concerned about you.' I hopped out of the water.

'Pleased to meet you,' said Chuck, bowing his head.

'Where's everybody else?' I asked, looking around.

'I don't care,' she snapped, getting to her feet.

'Would you like a ride?' I asked quickly, before she took off by herself.

'What?'

'Chuck, would you mind?' I asked.

'Not at all, of course.'

'Well . . .' She looked at us both.

'I'll walk,' I said. 'He's still recovering from, uh, an accident.'

'Sure, why not?' She shrugged.

Once we were out of the trees by the end of the graded roadbed, she rather clumsily managed to get on his back. I emptied water out of my moccasins and put them back on again. All three of us looked west, down across the dwindling trees and into the widening desert beyond them.

'Where to?' Chuck asked politely.

'None of your . . .' Betsy trailed off. 'That is, where are *you* guys going?'

Chuck swung his head around to look at me with one eye.

'West, I guess,' I said. I still didn't see any footprints anywhere. 'We'll follow this little stream. If there's a town in the vicinity, it needs water.'

'As you wish.' Chuck took another mouthful of grass and we started off.

I could guess why Betsy wasn't with the other passengers. Doc had probably kept walking at his own pace and Betsy, the other independent traveller in that group, had just decided to let him go. Harris and Eulalie were undoubtedly still hustling anxiously after Doc, afraid to be left on their own in the middle of nowhere. In all likelihood, Doc was also following the stream.

I still had jerky in my pack, and Chuck had a better chance of following or finding water than any person. Other than those matters of survival, I just wanted to lose Prism Chisholm as soon as I could and Chuck merely wanted my company. If Betsy was going our way, that was even better.

Betsy also had provisions, mainly cheese and

dried fruit, which she shared in exchange for a bit of jerky. Chuck found plenty of grazing along the stream. Despite occasional rises in the terrain, we were losing altitude as we journeyed through the mountainous high desert.

Betsy surprised me around noon, looking down at me from under the floppy broad brim of her hat. 'You want to ride for a while?'

'Oh, uh, no, thanks. I'm okay.'

'Be that way, then,' she sniffed.

Late in the day, under a hot sun but a cool breeze, Chuck halted and swung his head back to look at Betsy. 'I am afraid I am tiring. Would you mind walking?'

'Of course not,' said Betsy. 'Thank you for the ride.' She climbed off and we proceeded.

At times I had a clear view behind us for a long way. No one appeared behind us, or anywhere else, either. We took occasional rests all day. Betsy sang softly to herself much of the way.

That night we built a little campfire, though we had nothing to cook. Chuck's considerable metabolism generated a lot of heat. With his permission, the three of us slept under the desert stars with him in the middle.

The next morning, as I kicked apart the fire, Betsy surprised me again. 'Would you like to ride first today?' she asked me.

'Uh – you take the first shift. Maybe later.' I looked around for Chuck, who had wandered a short distance away to graze. 'How are you feeling, Chuck?'

'Considerably better,' he said, coming back. He paused to swallow. 'I'm still underweight, but in another day or two I expect to carry you both.'

The terrain looked the same as the day before. The

lower we got in altitude, the hotter the sun became. It was a slow, plodding trip.

A number of days passed with the same routine. The country changed gradually, turning more into desert all the time. The brook still ran, and even got a little bigger.

We didn't ride right along the water, since trees and bushes grew heavily on both banks. Keeping it in sight was good enough. Occasionally we even left it to go around a bluff or take a shortcut, if the line of trees curved down the slope ahead of us.

As we travelled deeper into the desert, I didn't mention that the stream might just dribble out into nothing at some point in the low desert flats ahead. We had no way of knowing. If we were lucky, of course, it would flow into a river big enough to keep flowing even down there.

I kept an anxious lookout behind us but saw no one. If Prism Chisholm was on foot, we were staying a steady distance ahead of him. Maybe, if he and his partner had stopped to find horsites somewhere, that had delayed them for a while. Then they would start gaining on us. They would not have given up.

'What's that?' Betsy asked, maybe around noon one day.

'Where?' I looked up, expecting riders.

'That way.' She pointed ahead and somewhat to the right.

'I don't see anything unusual,' said Chuck.

'It looks like a horsite,' said Betsy. 'Or even a real horse, maybe.'

'Oh, beneath that tree?' I strained to look. A distant brown shape did look vaguely like a horsite at this distance. One might have sought shade under the tree this time of day. It was off our path, but then, our precise route was just a haphazard meandering, anyway. 'Let's go see. This way, Chuck.'

'Ah, yes. I see it.'

The shape looked more like a horsite as we got closer, but something about it was odd.

'It hasn't moved,' I said. 'It's been in exactly the same position since we first saw it.'

'I know that,' Betsy snapped. 'You think I can't see that?'

'Perhaps we can rescue him,' said Chuck. 'He must have malfunctioned.'

'Wouldn't he be dead by now if he had?' I said. 'He's still standing.'

'That would depend on how long it's been since the malfunction,' said Chuck.

We plodded on. The figure under the tree still didn't move. Finally, as we came up on it, I saw the rust.

'It's not alive at all,' said Betsy. 'It never was.'

I had heard of such machines, but I had never seen one. It was a robot horse from long before my time. This dry climate had preserved it right where it had stopped.

'A discontinued model,' Chuck said disdainfully.

I walked up close to it. Bits of some kind of artificial hide still clung to it here and there, but most of the stuff had eroded away. It had the overall design of a horse but was all metal and plastic with a lot of joints and stiff parts. Shiny panels, conforming to its shape, adorned its flanks, haunches, and rear.

'No way it ran out of fuel here in the desert,' I said. 'Those are archaic solar panels.'

'Perhaps its joints seized up,' said Chuck. He shook his head. 'A robot horse, indeed.'

I pushed back my hat and sat down on a rock to think. Another mount would speed us up considerably.

'I wouldn't wait for it too long,' said Betsy. 'Look up in the tree.'

I looked. A low branch jutted out almost straight from the trunk. Perched on it, the sun-bleached skeleton of a buzzard hunched eyelessly over the robot horse, still waiting for it to fall over and die.

'Starved to death, I guess,' said Betsy, smirking.

'Stupid bird,' muttered Chuck.

'Maybe the horse just had nowhere to go,' I said, getting up. 'Maybe it still works.' I put both hands on the horse's back and jumped, grabbing at the straggly black mane.

A handful of it came out in my hand and I slipped back.

'Mange,' Chuck suggested.

When I jumped again and clutched a firmer hank of mane, I was able to swing over one leg. His spine cracked under my weight, which wasn't much.

'Okay,' I said, settling comfortably. 'Come on, horse. Let's go.'

Nothing happened.

'It's not too bright,' Chuck observed.

'Maybe it was programmed to act more like a real horse,' said Betsy.

I kicked its flanks. It began to vibrate. With a couple of squeaks and grinds, it took a few steps forward.

'Hey, it works.'

'If you call that working,' said Chuck.

I spurred it again with my blunt moccasin heels. It walked forward again. 'Hey, I've got a horse. Let's go!'

'Wouldn't you rather ride me?' Chuck bleated.

'What are you going to name him?' Betsy asked.

'I'm not nearly as rusty,' said Chuck, following alongside. 'Even if I can't carry you both yet.'

'Rusty,' I said. 'The perfect name. Thanks, Chuck.'

'Don't mention it,' he muttered.

'Can you go any faster?' Betsy wondered.

'I don't want to press my luck,' I said. 'Rusty might just fall apart at a gallop.'

'I can gallop,' Chuck said proudly. 'I can stampede if I want to.'

'Let's angle back toward that brook,' I said. 'We've strayed too far from the water.'

Rusty seemed to move his legs at about the same speed I had been, but with much longer legs, our pace was now faster. Also, he and Chuck didn't have to rest as often as I did, though we still took a few breaks to drink from the stream. I was sweating from the heat all the time now.

Late in the afternoon, I lay on my back in the rocky bed of the shallow stream, fully dressed except for my moccasins, letting the cool water flow past me. The rocks hurt my back, but I was too hot to care. Just upstream, Betsy was soaking her bandana and wiping her face with it. Downstream, Chuck was drinking heartily. Rusty just stood there.

'You know,' I said. 'I bet if we left Rusty here, he'd stand right there until someone else found him, no matter how many years it took.'

'An excellent suggestion,' said Chuck, munching on grass.

'He's still useful,' I said, spitting out water in a little arc.

'I'm going to go "pick flowers",' said Betsy. She got up and disappeared into the bushes.

A few minutes later she came rushing back. 'Somebody's behind us!' She watched for my reaction.

I sputtered water and sat up. 'Where?'

'A long way,' she said. 'But they're on horsites.'

I crawled out of the stream and started putting my moccasins back on. 'They? How many?'

'Two.'

'I knew it.'

'I doubt this mechanical device can outrun a horsite,' said Chuck, studying Rusty. 'Or even me.'

'We'll have to quit following the stream,' I said quickly. 'We'll have to take off across open desert, huh?' I reached around to rub my back where the sharper rocks had dug into me.

'That's stupid,' said Betsy, mounting Chuck. She had gotten better at it with practice. 'That just means a horserace – pardon the term, Chuck – and you don't think you can win it.'

'So what do *you* want to do?' I demanded, mounting Rusty. His back creaked.

'Don't you know anything about tracking? What kind of a bank robber are you?'

'I told you before—'

'What do you recommend?' Chuck inquired politely, swinging his head around to look at her on his back.

'We should use the stream to lose them,' Betsy said impatiently. 'They can only track us to this point. You and Rusty can wade upstream or downstream from here for a long time. The trees are still thick enough to hide us from sight. They won't know which way we went because we won't leave any tracks in the creek bed.'

'Our hooves will muddy the water,' said Chuck. 'If it's clear here, they will know we headed downstream. If it's muddy, they'll know we went upstream.'

'Maybe not,' I said. 'This isn't Midwestern mud. That streambed is all rock and sand. Let's try it.'

'Well, it's about time,' said Betsy. 'Let's go upstream, back toward them. They won't expect that.'

'Who's the fugitive here, anyway?' I muttered, but no one heard me.

Betsy and Chuck led the way.

# Nine

I rode leaning low over Rusty's neck to avoid tree branches, with one hand on my hat. Betsy had less of a problem, since Chuck was lower to the ground. As long as we were moving in the water, I figured Rusty would be okay, but I was worried that his lower legs might rust shut when we got out and stopped for the night.

'Hey,' I whispered loudly. 'Just how far back were they?'

'A long way,' she said normally. 'A full day's ride, I think.'

'We'll have to leave the stream before we run into them,' I said, speaking up. 'Our trail comes close enough to the stream sometimes for them to hear the splashing.'

She nodded and hummed her tune softly.

I looked down. Chuck and Rusty only kicked up a little sand in the rocky stream bed. It settled very quickly.

Every so often, I peered through the trees and brush on the side of the stream that was away from our pursuers. The wind was coming up and it rustled the branches making them hard to see through.

If we left the streambed to travel across open land, Prism Chisholm and Sniffin' Griffin might just see us from a distance and this entire effort would be lost. In fact, they would be closer than they would have been if we had just gone on our way. Finally I saw that we were coming upon a rocky bluff of considerable size, enough to mask our departure from the streambed for a long way.

'Betsy,' I called softly. 'Chuck. Come on, let's go this way.'

Chuck stopped and swung his head around to look. 'Hmm. A wise move.'

'Okay, but give me a second.' Betsy dismounted and crept into the bushes.

Chuck drank up while we were waiting.

'I can't see them,' she reported a moment later. 'We'll have to go slowly so they don't see any dust or hear any hoofbeats. They might be closer than I think.' She mounted up again.

I enthusiastically kicked my own mount, still clutching the remains of his sparse mane. 'Come on, Rusty!'

Something hard thunked into my forehead and my feet swung up into the air. I rolled backward, upside down off Rusty, and fell facedown into the water, spread-eagled, with most of me on the opposite bank.

My hat started drifting downstream. I grabbed it.

I pushed myself up with one hand, spraying water, and rubbed my forehead. Rusty was standing motionless under a thick, leafy, low-hanging branch. Above me, sunlight filtered through a lush, green canopy of trees.

Wind rustled the leaves hard.

I got up and staggered to Rusty. When I held him under his muzzle, he let me lead him after Chuck and Betsy.

When we came out from under the trees, I had to shove my hat down hard to keep the wind from taking it. We angled southwest with the bluff on our left as we entered a long, fairly open descent of sand.

It led to some low desert flats visible in the distance ahead. I took a careful look behind us, but we would be hidden for some time from the peering eyes of even Prism Chisholm.

I mounted Rusty again and we skirted the edge of the bluff heading for the flats.

Chuck was trotting right along, much faster than the walking pace he had used ever since we had left the railroad camp. I nudged Rusty into creaking after him. Every so often, I twisted around to look behind us. All I could see was the jagged strip of green growing in the desert over the stream.

When we were about to move behind the curve of the bluff, out of sight from anyone on our trail, Betsy turned to look one more time. I saw her and looked again myself.

No one was in sight. I let out a long breath. Betsy's trick with the stream should slow them down considerably.

Then I winced as we rode into a stiff wind blowing around the far side of the bluff. Ahead of me, Chuck had stopped. He and Betsy were looking down the long slope ahead of us.

I came up alongside them. Rusty squeaked and rattled to a stop.

'What do you think?' Betsy called, over the wind. She was tying her bandana around the top of her hat, knotting it under her chin.

'What do you mean?'

'Down in the flats,' said Chuck.

In the distance below, a line of covered wagons rolled westward. Each wagon was pulled by a team of two yoked oxenites. The wagons all had dark dots on the top of their white covers.

'I don't get it,' I called to Betsy. 'What do you mean, what do I think?'

'We could join them,' she shouted even louder over the wind. 'Unless you don't want to because, you know, you're on the run.'

'They probably don't know that,' I shouted back. 'We could use the company. Let's go on down there.'

She nodded and Chuck started again. Now I rode Rusty alongside them. The wind kept blowing dust into my eyes.

Ahead of us, the wagons were coming to a stop. I was puzzled, since no water or shelter was nearby. As we watched, people got out of the wagons and unyoked their oxenites.

Betsy and Chuck both looked at me.

I shrugged.

The oxenites just stood around. The people tinkered with the tongues of the wagons and tied ropes to them. Then they threw the yokes into the wagons themselves. A few minutes later, I saw long poles coming up through the dark spots on top of the wagons, which apparently were just holes in the heavy cloth. Finally, the whole operation came clear when jibs were fastened to the tongues of the wagons and masts.

'Wind wagons,' I said, though the wind carried my voice away. I'd heard of them before, like the buffalo, but I had never seen any. The rear axles of the wagons could be turned by someone holding a tiller inside the back of the wagon, out of our sight.

Now yards with furled sails were being hoisted up the masts. None of the wagons moved until they were all in place. One guy, I supposed the wagon master, stood off to one side watching them all.

Suddenly the wagon master waved one arm and ran to the front of the first wagon. Every wagon unfurled a big square sail to go with its jib. The combination of sails looked like they would interfere with each other. In the strong wind, though, they filled in moments, and the wagons began to move.

This could only work in a strong wind across very flat land, but that's what the wagon train had. Since the angles of the sails and the weight of the wagons all varied, they began to roll forward at different speeds. They steered gradually out of their single file to proceed more or less side by side.

The oxenites looked up and began to follow at a plodding pace. If nothing else, they would get a rest from pulling. The wagons were moving at about the same speed as the oxenites.

Betsy and Chuck started after them again. I kicked Rusty to keep up. We rode along and I watched the wagons, wondering how well they would really work. If the wagons, especially the wheels and axles, were sturdy and properly made, they could survive a pretty rough trip, but they could get hung up on fairly minor obstructions.

For a while I didn't notice anything. Then I saw that the oxenites had fallen slightly behind. I kicked Rusty a few more times and he sped up with a flurry of squeaks from his legs.

Chuck and Betsy trotted with us.

The entire wagon train was rolling under full sail. They had spread out some to stay out of each other's way, but advanced across the flats now in a crooked line. Each one steered its own zigzag route to avoid rough spots in the ground.

'I think we'd better hurry,' Betsy called.

'Okay!' I kicked Rusty even harder, not sure just how he was programmed. He went into a canter, though, without hesitation. The squeaking grew worse.

Chuck had different gaits than Rusty. He was trotting very quickly as we all hurried down the lower portion of the slope. The oxenites weren't too far ahead, but they were now hurrying after the wagons, too.

When we finally reached the desert flats, the wind blowing around the base of the slope nearly threw me off Rusty. I clutched at him with my legs and managed to hang on to my handful of his mane. The wagons were really sailing fast now.

'Come on, Chuck!' Betsy shouted.

Chuck went into a full run.

I grabbed more of Rusty's mane and kicked him again. A whirring sound from his innards indicated some kind of change, maybe a higher gear or something. Anyhow, with a horrible screeching from his rear haunches, he galloped.

Sort of.

I had been on a few horsites, most recently behind Smellin' Llewelyn. Rusty didn't have their flexibility or the same rhythm. His suspension system was shot and every hoofbeat jarred my spine and rattled my teeth. Just the impact of his hooves with the hard sand threatened to knock me off with each step.

I hung on the best I could and rode after the wagons.

I was just barely gaining on the wagon train. Chuck was going faster than Rusty, as he had bragged. Betsy leaned forward and clung to his horns, her pack now bouncing on her back below her looped braids. They were just coming up on the oxenites.

The oxenites were steel in the same places Chuck was and biological in the same places, too. Their high, powerful shoulders were especially bred for pulling, as were their legs, but their legs were longer than those of control-natural oxen. They could run, and they were doing so, programmed to stay with their wagons no matter what happened. If they lost sight of the wagon train, they would follow its tracks.

As I rode up on the oxenites, a weird clanking started in one of Rusty's haunches. He didn't slow down any, so I kept going. If I stopped with the stampeding oxenites separating Chuck and me, he and Betsy might not miss me for a long time.

Rusty's programming allowed me to steer him with my knees or strong pulls on his neck, though the latter was meant for a bridle or a halter. It was hard to steer him just yanking up high on his mane. Still, I was able to weave through the thundering oxenites as I slowly gained on them.

Ahead of me, Chuck had carried Betsy through the oxenites on his own and was gleefully chasing the wagons.

The line of wagons had fanned out in front of me even more. In the backs of some of the wagons, kids and other passengers had noticed us as they looked out the back, but no one wanted to slow down. Other wagons had their rear flaps closed. Getting this kind of wind over a flat expanse was just too rare for them to risk missing it.

I had passed the oxenites now myself.

For the first time, I could see many of the drivers sitting in the backs of the wagons, holding the tillers that steered the rear axles. None of them glanced back. They had to keep their eyes on their courses, looking through the front of the wagons, aided by others positioned at the front to control the sails.

Right in front of me, one of Rusty's ears fell off.

I snatched at it, but missed. It wasn't worth stopping for. I rode on.

Another loud creak came from his left front shoulder. I looked down and saw his artificial hide

110

tearing away. Somewhere deep inside, a low grinding sound started again.

I leaned on the tear, not sure what was happening.

Ahead, the wind wagons were still careening about under full sail. Chuck and Betsy were right behind them now. I had put some distance between me and the oxenites thundering behind me.

I was leaning low over Rusty's neck with as much mane clutched in my hands as I could get. A scraping sound just behind me was followed by a clank on the ground. When I looked over my shoulder, I saw that Rusty's right rear leg had fallen off.

I froze, expecting him to pitch over and throw me at best, or fall on me, more likely. Instead, he kept going. The gait had changed, favouring his left side in a kind of canter, and I was reminded of a three-legged mutt I had once seen galumphing down an alley.

He was programmed and designed better than I would have guessed. I knew real horses couldn't do this, and I doubted horsites could, either.

I pulled his head around to the left, nudging with my legs at the same time. He slowed down enough to turn around. I kicked him again, heading back for his leg lying in the middle of wagon tracks, one set of steerite tracks, and a set of three-hooved robot horse tracks.

The oxenites were stampeding fast, but their programming wouldn't let them trample anyone if they could help it. I rode Rusty as fast as his canter would go and pulled him up in a cloud of sand next to his leg. With a quick glance at the wind wagons, I hopped off and grabbed the lower shank just over the hoof.

It was heavier than I had thought.

111

It had snapped off below his haunch, so it was mostly the narrow part of his leg, with the hock. Still, when I lifted the whole piece off the ground, the weight spun me as I staggered to stay under it. I stumbled around in a complete circle and had just gotten the leg over Rusty's shoulders when I saw the oxenites thundering toward us.

They wouldn't trample anyone . . . if they could help it.

At that speed, and with their weight, I suddenly wasn't sure they could. I leaped onto Rusty, turned him again, and kicked him into a gallop.

Sort of.

His creaking three-legged canter lacked the speed of his regular gallop, which itself couldn't keep up with one underweight steerite. Besides that, he kept veering left as he favoured that side. I also had to hold on to his leg or give it up forever. Certainly I couldn't count on finding someone to make another for a discontinued model like this.

Then I looked back over my shoulder. The oxenites were gaining on us. Right behind me, Rusty's tail came loose and fluttered away.

I kicked him harder, but nothing happened. He was already moving at full three-legged speed. 'Come on, Rusty!' I banged the top of his head with my fist.

His other ear fell off.

The oxenites had caught up. One by one, they thundered alongside and then passed us. If we had been stopped, I figured they would have stampeded over us. Since Rusty and I were moving in the same direction, they had time to manoeuvre around us.

In another few moments, the last of the oxenites were again ahead of us. The wagon train was small in the distance. I could just make out Betsy on Chuck, still right behind them.

Suddenly, tearing metal shrieked next to my left knee. Rusty's left front leg had come halfway out. As he pitched leftward, I threw myself off. The flat desert sand came up fast and smashed into my shoulder. I rolled several times on the hot ground, expecting Rusty to fall on me any second.

Just as I stopped rolling, I heard a thump and several prolonged rattling and banging sounds. I lay motionless with my face in the sand, breathing hard, catching my breath. The sunlight baked my back.

The sand here was pale yellow with bits of orange in it.

When I rolled over enough to look up, Rusty had skidded to a halt on his back with two legs in the air and one splayed out sideways. His fourth lay nearby.

As I watched, his head fell off with a clank.

# Ten

Night had fallen by the time I heard a set of hooves walking back my way. My shoulder was hurting where I had fallen on it. I had decided that, if necessary, I could spend the night here just as well as with the wagon train. I pulled some jerky out of my pack and patiently hurt my teeth with it. Rusty's head and loose leg lay nearby.

So I was still sitting on the sand, leaning my back against Rusty's torso under a crescent moon in the clear desert sky, when Betsy rode up on Chuck.

'What happened?' Betsy asked, peering around in the faint moonlight at all the pieces of Rusty.

'He came up lame,' I said, shrugging.

'Aha,' Chuck declared triumphantly. 'I knew it. Never fear. I am weary but I shall endeavour to carry you both in this crisis. I am pleased to announce that the wagon train has welcomed us as companions.' He hesitated. 'I declared you as my owner.'

I was too worn out to argue.

'It may prevent me from being rustled again,' he added, pawing the ground modestly. 'I hope I have not been presumptuous.'

'Doc and the other two from the stagecoach had already joined them,' said Betsy. 'No sign of . . . those two who were following us.'

'Your trick must have slowed them down.' I managed to get up and dust myself off. 'Rusty served his purpose, at least.'

'Maybe we can come back for him,' said Betsy. 'Riding him would save you money. The wagon master said that if we have our own transportation and provisions, we can just join up. But Doc and Eulalie and Harris all had to buy space on wagons to ride along.'

That was one of the longest speeches I had ever heard from her. Not only that, but I was flattered that she had come back with Chuck to look for me. I stood next to Chuck looking up at her. 'Uh . . . you want front or back?'

'You don't look so good,' she said. 'You better ride in front.'

I mounted in front of her and she put her arms around my waist. That made me nervous, and I sat very stiffly. Chuck made a wide turn around Rusty, eyeing his pieces curiously, and then headed for the wagon train again.

It was a long ride, especially with my shoulder aching and Betsy a little closer than I suspected she really liked. Chuck was understandably exhausted as he trekked onward. The wind had died down at sunset, but while it blew, the wind wagons had made excellent time.

A couple of lights on some of the individual wagons were visible in the distance long before we drew near the circled wagon train. Most of the wagons were as dark as the night. When we finally approached them, I saw the oxenites standing around the outside of the circle, milling about as they cooled off.

'It's Betsy and Chuck,' Betsy called forward over my shoulder.

A couple of solar torches threw just enough light to see. The circle was nearly empty. Most of the people were asleep in their wagons.

Chuck steered neatly between two of the wagons and came to a halt, panting. The tall, slender form of Harris walked forward.

'Welcome back, Louie.' Harris grinned real big and reached up to help me off.

'Hi,' I muttered wearily.

He grabbed my arm under the bad shoulder and pulled.

'Yow!' I flinched and fell off Chuck, landing on the same shoulder again. Stunned with pain, I lay there wincing and rolling back and forth.

'I stayed up to see you,' said Harris. 'My, this was an exciting day, wasn't it? I even recognized you riding behind the wagons earlier.'

I held my breath, still gripping my shoulder as I stared up at the stars.

'Tell you what,' said Harris. 'I've procured space on this wagon, here to my right, with a very nice family named, uh . . . well . . .' He shrugged. 'I'll ask them again in the morning. Anyway, if you'd like my spot tonight, I know you're hurt. Would you like it?'

Betsy got off Chuck next to me.

I didn't like lying there looking up at everyone, but I was in no shape to do much else.

'What do you say, Louie? Huh?' Harris asked.

I managed to roll over and crawl under the nearest wagon. Owing a favour to Harris did not strike me as a good idea. The desert night was cold, but I was too tired to care.

'Hey, Louie?' Harris bent down and stuck his head under the wagon after me.

'Shut up,' Betsy suggested.

'Good night, Louie,' Harris said cheerfully as he walked away.

'Are you all safe and sound, honey?' Eulalie's voice asked Betsy.

I saw her black, pointed shoes walk up from the other direction after Harris had gone.

'You can share my space in the Noslich wagon,' said Eulalie. 'As I said before, we ladies must stick together.'

'Leave me alone,' said Betsy, without conviction.

'You can sleep on top of a flat wooden chest padded with a nice, thick quilt under you and a blanket over you.'

'Shut up,' muttered Betsy, but she followed her away.

While they were talking, Chuck's hooves had left the inside of the circle and come around the outside of the wagon I was under. He lay down nearby.

'Remember I told everybody you were my owner?' he whispered. 'We have to make it look good, okay?'

I grinned, despite my shoulder. 'Okay, Chuck. But wouldn't you rather pal around with the oxenites?'

'Certainly not,' he said haughtily. 'They are, for your information, much like horsites. Since they generally function under constant, direct human instruction, they have been given highly limited programming. They cannot speak or think independently at all.'

I lay on my pack as a pillow and sighed. 'Good night, Chuck.'

'Good night.'

I awoke to a lot of loud banging and hammering and sawing. Sunlight was just slanting under the wagon to reach me. Chuck was already up.

I crawled out from under the wagon and yawned. Small fires heated breakfast by most of the wagons. The desert air was still cool. Steep canyon walls, invisible last night in the darkness, rose up on both sides of the wagon circle.

'Morning, Louie.' Harris strode up, smiling as big as ever. 'Sleep well?'

'Yeah, yeah.' I worked my sore shoulder a little. It wasn't too bad. 'What's going on?'

'Ever since we rounded a bend into this canyon, we've been out of that big wind. So now people are making repairs if they need them and letting the oxenites rest up. Laryngo declared one resting day here before we move on.'

'Who?'

'Laryngo Lenny Lard, the wagon master. He's got one of those bullhorn voices.'

'Oh.' If the wagon train was going to sit for a day, Prism Chisholm would have plenty of time to gain on me. He had probably picked up my trail on Rusty again by now.

One wagon nearby had a corner propped on a bunch of big wooden crates. A broken wheel lay on the ground, where a man was sawing a board. The interchangeable saw blade was plugged into a Fargo Spinwrist, one of the cheapest specials made. Despite its name, it came mail-order from New Haven. Other tool ends lay on the ground near him.

I looked around at the wagons. None had a solar panel. Not everybody was using a special that I could see, as they went about their business, but I knew about Fargo Spinwrists.

The irony was that plugging a saw blade or a screwdriver into a Fargo was less efficient than picking up a regular tool in a regular hand and using it. The only people who wore Fargoes were poor people so desperate not to be considered control-naturals that they would use tools like that rather than go without special parts. They couldn't afford solar panels, generators, and low-power engines for their wagons, either.

118

They could be the most unpleasant to a control-natural too, if they found out one was travelling with them.

At the wagon on our right, Betsy and Eulalie were just carrying empty metal plates to a washtub by the fire. Harris started towards them. I only followed because Betsy was there.

Betsy was starting to scrub her plate in the washtub.

'Never mind that,' said another woman. 'We'll all take turns.' She was a slender woman in a dress similar to Eulalie's, except that the printed roses on it were faded and it was torn around the hem. Her brown hair was tied up on the back of her head.

'All right, Maud,' said Betsy. 'Thank you for breakfast.' She walked towards Harris and me, taking a wide circle around Eulalie.

'You're welcome.'

'Morning, Eulalie,' said Harris.

'Morning,' she said quietly, ducking her head away. She dropped her plate into the tub and followed Betsy.

Betsy walked faster.

'Howdy!' A man's voice thundered, with a weird metallic echo.

I turned to see a tall, barrel-chested guy in a red plaid flannel shirt striding up with his arms swinging enthusiastically.

'Louie,' said Harris. 'This is Laryngo, the wagon master I was telling you about. Laryngo, this is . . . *Louie Hong.*'

He said my name like he expected it to be recognized.

Laryngo didn't seem to notice. 'We hear you had a little problem yesterday,' said Laryngo, his bullhorn voice ringing in my ears. 'Lost a lame horse, eh?'

'A robot horse, actually,' I started. 'He—'

'Dave Noslich said he could help you,' Laryngo boomed. 'Maud's husband. So happens they didn't sustain any damage yesterday. Dave said he'd go back and pick up your mount for you today while other folks make repairs.'

'*Oh.* That's real nice, but I'm not sure there's enough of him left to salvage.'

'Suit yourself.' Laryngo shrugged. 'Anyhow, you're welcome to ride along with us or buy space on a wagon if you want.' He strode away, calling to someone else.

'So you're this Louie fella?' A short, stocky guy joined us, wiping his hands on his trousers. 'I'm Dave.'

When he held out a hand, I saw it was a pincer claw plugged into a Fargo. I shook it.

'I've been taking stuff out of the wagon to make room,' he said. 'Maud'll sit here with all our things. She'll welcome a day out of the wagon.'

'Well, thanks, but Rusty pretty much came apart all over.'

'A robot horse, I heard you say? Well, I'm pretty handy with my hands, so to speak.' He laughed. 'Let's go take a look.'

'Maybe I can help you lift pieces of Rusty,' said Betsy. 'Have you got room for another?'

'Sure,' said Dave, with a shrug.

'I'll join you,' said Eulalie, edging behind Betsy with a wary glance at Harris.

'I'll be glad to help,' said Harris. 'Okay, Louie?'

Betsy and Eulalie were both glaring at me.

'Uh—'

'Come on, then,' said Dave. 'Help me yoke up the oxenites.'

'*Me?*' Harris hustled after him eagerly. 'Me yoke oxenites? How do you do it?'

I smiled weakly at Betsy, who whirled around and stomped to the open fold-down gate at the rear of the Noslich wagon.

Eulalie followed, lifting her skirts to climb into the wagon after Betsy.

I pulled out a piece of jerky, eyeing Maud's pot of hot cereal over her fire as I tried to bite down. Since I was getting one favour from this couple already, I didn't want to ask for another. Still, I wasn't going to live long on jerky alone.

Dave led his oxenites out of the herd and managed to hitch them to the wooden yoke in spite of Harris's help. Harris got into the back of the covered wagon and I was just climbing up the front to join Dave when Chuck came trotting up to me.

'Are we going somewhere?' he asked eagerly. 'I should trot alongside you.'

I looked down at him from the seat. 'We're going to fetch Rusty. Or at least, what's left of him.'

'*Oh*. Well, pardon *me*, I'm sure.' He stuck his nose in the air and started away.

'Come on, Chuck,' I yelled after him. 'We have to make it *look* good, remember?'

He paused and thought about it. After a moment, he gave a toss of his head and deigned to walk along parallel to the wagon, but at a dignified distance away from it.

Dave had plugged a bullwhip into his Fargo. He swung it forward and then pulled back hard to make it crack over the oxenites. They strained under their wooden yoke and the wagon jerked forward.

Unprepared, I fell backwards off the seat, into the wagon, and slammed onto the wooden floor. I was trying to sit up when Betsy stepped over me and took my place next to Dave.

'This certainly is exciting,' said Harris.

'Travelling in a real wagon train, and I actually helped yoke the oxenites.'

I got into a sitting position and found myself next to him. We were on the floor, leaning against one wall of the wagon. Eulalie sat on a small wooden box across from us.

'What happened to Doc?' I asked.

'He's with the wagon train, too,' said Harris. 'Keeping to the wagon he rented space on. We ran into the wagon train a day or two before you saw us.'

I nodded.

'Eulalie here had quite a time hiking on those high-heeled, pointed black shoes,' said Harris, nodding at her feet. 'Too bad she had to leave her trunk behind at the railroad camp. Are you feeling better now?'

She sighed and gazed out the back of the wagon.

A small stream wound patiently through the canyon. When we reached the end of it and turned back into the open strip of desert flats, I decided that this was probably the same stream we had been following earlier. The wind was still blowing hard, right into our faces, but not as hard as yesterday. The oxenites lowered their heads and kept their pace.

Out the back of the wagon, I could see that Chuck had moved behind us for the wind break provided by the wagon itself.

'Is that it?' Dave asked Betsy, after a while.

'I think so,' she said.

I got up and looked over her shoulder. The pieces of Rusty were still a long way off, but were unmistakable. 'That's him.'

The sun was hot when we finally creaked to a stop. I looked Rusty over and shook my head. His head was lying upside down on its nose, not far from the torso with three legs up in the air. That loose leg lay where I had dropped it. His ears and tail were still somewhere ahead of us and not really worth retrieving.

'He's lame, all right,' said Dave, still sitting in the seat with the reins in his hands. He tied them to the wagon and replaced his whip hand with a pincer hand.

Then we all got out to take a look. Chuck was wandering off a little on his own.

'Nobody could get parts for this now,' I said. 'You see why I don't think he's worth bringing back?'

'That is one lame horse,' said Dave. He turned around, looking at all the pieces in turn. 'Yessir. That sure is.'

'That was a real antique,' said Harris, standing next to Eulalie. 'No one has used robot horses for years. I've read about them.'

'I hardly see the point of transporting junk.' Eulalie edged away from him, folding her arms.

'Well, now, I don't know.' Dave knelt down by the torso and looked at the bent metal and ripped wires where the one leg had pulled out. Then he poked around the exposed insides of the neck where Rusty's head had come off. 'Tell you what, Louie. I'll haul this back for you and see if I can fix it up.'

'You think you can?' I was surprised. 'I, uh, don't have much money.'

'I'm a mechanic at heart,' he said, studying the torn end of Rusty's loose leg. 'Forget about the money for fixing an antique like this. It'll be a challenge. Besides, I can't guarantee anything.'

'If you're sure. . . .'

'I don't mind helping a guy in trouble, just so he's not one of those control-naturals. Come on, let's load the body first.'

'Uh – sure.'

Loading Rusty was easier than I had expected. Dave just unhitched an oxenite and tied a rope to him. Then he ran the rope back through the length of the wagon and tied it around Rusty's middle. With the other oxenite holding the wagon still, the unhitched one simply walked forward, hoisting the load up to the wagon level. Then all of us pushed it onto the wagon and untied it.

We were able to carry Rusty's head and fourth leg together, shuffling sideways in the sand. As everyone else took their places back on the wagon, I looked around for Chuck. He was in the distance, nosing at some large flat object on the ground.

'Come on, Chuck!' I yelled, wiping sweat off my forehead with my sleeve.

He looked up and swayed his head from side to side emphatically. The sunlight glinted off his stainless-steel head as it swung back and forth.

Dave shrugged and cracked his whip.

I jumped into the back of the wagon and we headed for Chuck.

By the time we reached him, he had gotten his head under what turned out to be a steerite hide. It was reddish and white, like him. He was tossing the edge of it into the air and trying to get under more of it.

I leaned out the back of the wagon. 'Chuck, what are you doing?'

'I intend to wear this back to camp.'

'*Wear* it?'

'Yes.' He tossed his head again and got more of it over his neck and shoulders.

'Well, all right.' I jumped out and pulled the hide over him.

'Look around,' said Chuck. 'Steerite tracks in a small herd came by here recently.'

'So I see,' I said, looking around.

'Since the wagon wheel tracks have gone over them, the herd obviously passed this way first. I suspect it is in fact the rustled herd from the train.'

'This should stay on now if you're careful.' I tugged a little more on one side of the hide. It was raw, of course, and recently skinned. 'Why do you want to walk around like this?'

'None of your business,' said Chuck, in a tone I had heard often lately.

# Eleven

Morning was well advanced by the time we returned to camp. Repairs were under way at most of the wagons. Some were critical, like damaged wheels, masts, or tongues; others were minor, replacing boards on the sides of wagons or tightening the suspension system under them. People were hammering and sawing on all sides. In big pots over the fires, hot water boiled for laundry. Some clothes, already washed, waved in the hot wind on lines strung between wagons.

We unloaded Rusty onto the ground. Betsy kept a wary eye on Eulalie and slipped away while Eulalie was watching Harris sidelong the same way.

'This may take me a while,' said Dave, pulling up a stool from his stack of belongings. Maud had begun loading them into the wagon again. He sat down to look Rusty over. 'Don't mind me.'

'I won't look over your shoulder.'

'I say,' said Harris, turning to Eulalie. 'Would you like to watch me unhitch the oxenites?'

'Maud will do it,' said Dave, without looking up from the tangle of wires in Rusty's neck.

Eulalie rolled her eyes and stalked away.

'I better talk to Chuck,' I said, hurrying away, too.

Chuck was walking in little circles near the oxenites, still wearing the hide draped over his head and body. He stopped when he saw my feet and lifted his head to look out from under it.

'Chuck? What are you doing?'

'I am considering a disguise,' he said quietly, glancing about. 'I could travel more safely if I appeared to be a real control-natural steer. They are less valuable and less apt to be butchered or stolen.'

'*Oh.*'

'How do I look?'

'Like a steerite with a loose hide draped over him.'

He lowered his head in disappointment.

'Your own hide is the same colour as this one,' I pointed out. 'The only difference is that you have stainless steel where real steers don't.'

'I know.' He shrugged morosely. The hide slipped a little.

'Maybe what you need is a mask.'

'A mask?' He raised his head.

'It's your steel head that people notice first. Your other stainless-steel parts aren't that obvious unless one looks.'

'Why . . . that makes sense.'

'Trouble is, I need a knife to cut the hide. My Cubby Scout knife isn't big enough, but maybe I can borrow—'

'Here,' said Betsy, behind me.

When I turned, she was crawling out from under one of the wagons.

'Keep a lookout for that snobbish, prissy, lavender creature, will you?' She took a large, sheathed hunting knife out of her pack and handed it to me.

'I'm on the alert,' said Chuck, earnestly peering about.

Betsy helped me pull the hide off Chuck and lay it flat on the ground. Then I started cutting one corner of it. I figured the exact configuration could wait till we had a small enough piece to try it on him.

'I wonder if it was ST 1214,' said Chuck. 'He had

127

experienced malfunctions in the past. If they continued, his thieves might have discarded him.'

'What?' I was hacking at the hide with effort as Betsy held it in place.

'The steerite whose hide this is,' said Chuck. 'I am certain that the small herd whose tracks we saw is partly from the train. In fact, I would not be surprised to learn that the rest of them are survivors from my own original herd.'

'And you think they discarded your friend after butchering him?' Betsy looked up. 'Why didn't you say so back there? Didn't you want to look for him?'

'I fear it is pointless. They may have buried him to conceal the evidence or may be carrying him along on a wagon or something. It is the potential fate of any steerite.'

I was dragging the knife across the hide repeatedly, making shallow scars. Betsy took her knife away from me and started cutting it herself.

'There we are.' She lifted a sizable rectangle of the reddish hide. 'Chuck, hold your head up a little higher.'

We stood on each side of him, folding the hide around his head. She marked a couple of places on it with little scratches and then laid it flat again. I watched as she cut eye and mouth holes.

'How delightful,' said Chuck, as she raised it.

He closed his eyes while we positioned it over his face.

'Well, it fits,' I said.

'How do I look now?' Chuck asked.

'Like a steerite wearing a m—'

'Shut up,' said Betsy, stepping back to scrutinize him.

'Moo,' said Chuck.

'That's about as good as it's going to get,' Betsy

decided. 'It won't fool anybody close up, but from a distance it might help.'

'Thank you for your help,' said Chuck politely. 'Moo again.'

'I'll have to cut leather thongs and punch some holes in it,' said Betsy. 'Then we'll lace it on for you.'

'Hey, what about his horns?' I asked suddenly. 'They're still steel.'

'All right. I'll cut little cones to fit over them.'

Chuck looked down at the rest of the hide. 'Thank you, ST 1214,' he added gravely.

'Say, Louie.'

I looked around.

'Over here.' Dave was waving me over. 'I'll show you something.'

I followed him back to where even more portions of Rusty than before were laid out in neat rows.

'See here?' Dave held up a knot of little gears and wires and other pieces, all still connected.

'I see it,' I said. 'But what is it?'

'This thing here drives an individual leg,' said Dave. 'There's nothing much wrong with it except its lubrication ran out. At a gallop, see, some parts seized up before others. That's why the moving parts ripped themselves out of the parts that froze first.'

I waved a hand at Rusty. 'You mean this thing was made before real oil gave out?'

'No, I don't think it's that old. It probably used something similar to the lubes and greases we use now.'

'Vegetable and animal and synthetics from back east.'

'That's right. The synthetics are the main thing; we just stretch them with the other stuff.'

'He's in a whole bunch of pieces. I don't suppose he'll be romping about again, huh?'

'Not so fast. I think maybe I can help. Certainly we have plenty of lube and grease in the wagons. If I can hammer and screw his working parts back into order, you can lube him up again. He'll function on the same stuff.'

'Really?' I stifled a thrill of hope. 'Wait a minute, though. How long will it be before he runs dry again?'

'A long time.' Dave tossed the little jumble of pieces into the air and caught it again. 'See, this guy is pretty efficient. You put the lubricants into a single opening and his system runs them through all the necessary parts.'

'Doesn't it evaporate sooner or later?'

'Eventually, but in this model it takes years. The lubricants don't evaporate much because he's all sealed up. When he's overheated, he just slows down and refuses to go on, like a horsite.'

'Or a real horse.'

'I guess.' He shrugged.

'I never saw any opening on him. Where does the stuff go?'

'It's under his tail, where it won't show. At least, until his tail fell off.'

'Oh.'

'So that's where he stands now. I'll get back to work.'

'Thank you.'

I returned to Chuck and Betsy, excited about the prospect of riding Rusty again. She had laced Chuck's mask on and was just tying the hide covers over his horns. From a distance, they would look no worse than the mask.

'Real steers don't talk, you know,' Betsy was saying. 'That will give you away for sure.'

'Moo,' Chuck said again 'That's why I'm practising.'

'You don't just *say* "moo",' I explained. 'That's just a – a . . .'

'An approximation,' Betsy said. 'It's more like this—' She made a very good imitation of a steer's call.

'Mmooo,' Chuck said, with feeling.

'Closer,' said Betsy. 'Try again.'

'*Mmooooooo*—' His eyes crossed with the extended effort.

I spun away, stifling a laugh.

'That's good, Chuck,' Betsy said quickly, patting him on the shoulder. 'Don't overdo it. Anyhow, remember, don't let strangers get too close.'

'Check,' said Chuck. 'I'll go study.' He wandered away towards the oxenites.

'Lunchtime,' said Maud. 'Louie, why don't you join us?'

'I'll trade you some jerky,' I said, following Betsy to the Noslich cookfire.

'Nothing fancy,' said Maud. 'Just stew, mostly from dried and powdered food.'

I took out some jerky and handed it to her. She broke it into smaller pieces and dropped it into the stew. After stirring it a few more times, she ladled it out into bowls.

Dave joined us, wiping his pincer hands on a cloth. 'Going pretty well,' he said. 'I keep hammering big pieces into shape with my Fargo mallet and then twisting little ones with my pliers hand.'

'I can't tell you how much I appreciate this,' I said.

'Aw, don't mention it again. Fact is, the experience may do me good.' He took a bowl of stew carefully in his pincers.

Eulalie climbed out of the Noslich wagon looking refreshed. Her lavender dress had been laundered and her shiny blonde hair was tied in a matching bow. She sat down near Betsy with her stew.

'We ladies must keep up our civilized habits,' Eulalie said. 'Thank you for the bath water, Maud.'

'You're welcome.' Maud sat down with her bowl on the other side of Betsy and spoke to the group at large. 'We're hoping to find some farmland we can work for shares, beyond the desert. But Dave may have to work on special parts and whatnot if we can't get land. That's why this experience with the robot horse is good for him.'

'I lucked out,' I said.

Maud turned to Betsy. 'Where are you headed?'

'None of—' Betsy took in a deep breath, embarrassed.

'No need to be shy, honey,' said Eulalie. 'I'm looking for a place to settle down, myself. It will be harder now that I had to leave my trunk behind in that awful railroad camp.'

'Well . . .'

'Are you joining your family?' Maud asked.

'No. Sort of. Maybe.'

'All right.' Maud smiled indulgently. 'It's not our business, after all.'

'My, you look pretty, Eulalie,' said Harris, walking over from the cookfire at his wagon.

'Think I'll go wash my hair again,' she muttered, 'After I dirty it up again somehow.' She got up and headed for the Noslich wagon.

'Personal grooming is very important,' Harris called, following her.

'I'll take my turn with the dishes,' said Betsy. She got up and started collecting them.

'Thank you. I'll see if Eulalie really wants hot water.' Maud left.

I picked up her wire brush and started scrubbing

out the bowls in the dishwater. After a few minutes, Harris wandered away. When I relaxed, Betsy joined me with the other bowls.

'I wish I knew where I was going,' I said casually, splashing in the water.

She picked up a cloth and started washing a bowl.

'At least people who know where they're headed can plan for it,' I added.

'These are dry,' she said, stacking a couple of bowls to one side.

'Heading all the way to the coast, are you?'

She started humming her song again.

When we had finished the dishes, I went to hear Chuck moo. He was working at it in earnest among the oxenites, who ignored him. I spent all afternoon in the shade under the wagon nearby, occasionally dozing.

I woke up to the sound of music – and not 'Sweet Betsy from Pike', for a change, either. Someone was tuning a banjo and someone else a fiddle. I crawled out from under the wagon and looked around.

The entire circle of wagons was set up for a party. Solar lights on all the wagons were on and big stewpots bubbled over all the cookfires. Everyone I could see was dressed up in finery, all of it out of fashion and worn, but neatly kept.

Rusty stood by the Noslich wagon, entirely together again except, of course, for his ears and his tail.

'Oh, there you are, Louie.' Dave walked over. He was wearing a white dress shirt that was too tight and a string tie that was loose and crooked. 'I've lubed him and tested him and everything.'

'And he works?'

'He sure does. You know, I can't tell just how long my repairs will hold up, but he's basically sound.'

'No kidding?' I sighed with relief. 'I sure do thank you.'

'That's okay. I learned enough to make it worth my while.'

Suddenly the music started up. A tall, skinny guy in a pink shirt with an oversized floppy string tie was playing the banjo with Fargo Fiddledees, solid steel hands featuring long, slender fingers. One hand ended in five picks, the other in narrow pads. Both hands could load memory and play very fast. They would not get tired nearly as fast as real hands.

'They call him Stringtie,' said Dave, flapping his own tie at me. ''Cause he's so thin.'

I nodded, watching his fingers flash over the banjo.

Stringtie was picking fast at 'Red River Valley'. Next to him, his companion was just starting to saw away on his fiddle with a long Fargo bow hand. The other hand was another Fiddledee.

The sun was low and red in the west, but not yet down. Some people started ladling dinner out of stewpots. Others went right to dancing around in the wagon circle.

Betsy was sitting on the open end of the Noslich wagon, swinging her feet in time to the fast music. Her hair was wet and she was braiding her loops again. Harris, also looking freshly scrubbed, was pacing about nearby.

Eulalie carefully stuck her head out of the wagon. When she saw Harris, she ducked inside again.

I ladled out stew from Maud's pot and ate it while I watched more people join the dancing. Laryngo stood by the musicians and called out a square dance in his booming voice. Betsy stood by the end of the wagon, watching them.

The sun had gone down by the time I had finished

134

my stew. The square dancers were all leaping and skipping about in lines and circles, under the lights on the wagons and the firelight beneath the stew-pots. I wondered if Betsy would dance with me or just tell me to shut up if I asked her.

I decided I could find out what sort of mood she was in first. As I walked towards her, though, Harris got tired of pacing around and spoke to her. I couldn't hear him over the music, but they joined the square dance together.

I watched them go.

Eulalie stuck her head out of the wagon again and saw me.

'Hi,' I said.

'Yuck,' she said to no one in particular, and withdrew again.

'Much my opinion of you,' said a man's voice from around the corner of the wagon.

I looked up into the sparkling multiple eyes of Prism Chisholm glittering in the darkness.

# Twelve

I spun around to find Sniffin' Griffin standing behind me.

'Easy, young fellow,' said Prism Chisholm, entering the light inside the wagon circle. His hands were in the pockets of his long tweed coat. 'There's nothing out there but desert anyway. It's a long way to nowhere on foot.' His eyes blinked steadily green.

I waited, watching him.

'That's right. We know you found a horsite to ride. Very lucky for you, as long as it held out. From the tracks in the desert, we also know he was injured in some way and was carted away. He'll be a long time healing.'

Rusty was standing almost right behind him, but if he hadn't noticed that Rusty was put together again, I wasn't going to brag about it.

'You can't lose us,' said Sniffin' Griffin, coming up next to Prism Chisholm. The firelight showed the long fringe on his buckskin jacket swinging back and forth. 'Between what he can see and I can smell, we can find anyone eventually.'

I glanced around, but no one had noticed us. Harris and Betsy were dancing; Chuck was outside the circle with the oxenites. The music covered the conversation.

'I want your help,' said Prism Chisholm. His eyes gazed a steady orange at me. 'Your skin temperature is rising and you are growing damp.'

I tried to swallow, but my throat was too dry. 'How?' I asked hoarsely.

'You have information regarding a certain bank robbery in Femur,' said Prism Chisholm. 'I want it.'

'All of it,' said Sniffin' Griffin. He hooked his thumbs into the straps of his leather chaps.

'And a certain train robbery. One that you and I in fact experienced together.' Prism Chisholm tilted his head forward and stared at me with his eyes sparkling turquoise.

The back of my neck tickled.

'I see heat increasing on your scalp and the surface of your face,' said Prism Chisholm. 'Yes, you are right to be alarmed. You are no fool. The man who directed the bank robbery from out in the street, I hear, and the inside man on the train job.'

'Him?' Sniffin' Griffin asked, surprised. He sniffed loudly. 'You sure, Prism?'

'If I am wrong, he can set me aright.' Prism Chisholm pushed his hat back on his head. 'Your horsite is by now partly a pile of junk and very likely part of the stew. We noted the tracks from the stolen steerite from the railroad camp. I suspect you bartered it for space here on the wagon train. That leaves you helpless and alone.'

I said nothing.

'You are too smart to attempt the desert on foot.' He nodded to himself. 'So I will let you consider the alternatives while we arrange to join the wagon train. Just don't keep us waiting too long.' He inclined his head for his partner to follow and they walked up the side of the wagons towards the musicians and Laryngo.

They might notice Rusty or hear about him from someone at any time. Keeping a careful eye on their backs as they walked away from me, I sidled up to

Rusty and took him under his muzzle. He followed me outside the circle without a single creak.

I had to walk him to keep his hoofbeats as quiet as possible. So far, the music covered them. I stayed out of the light from the wagons on the way to the herd of oxenites and snatched up my pack from under the wagon where I'd left it.

'Hey, Chuck,' I whispered hoarsely. 'You still here?' I strained to see in the darkness.

The oxenites shuffled around.

Somebody mooed.

'Chuck! Come over here.'

'Moooo.'

'Come on, Chuck! It's an emergency.'

'Moo again. Moo a third time.'

'Chuck, I don't have time to play. They may notice I'm gone any minute.'

'Which one am I? Can you tell?'

'Chuck, it's dark. Besides, in the light you don't look like an oxenite. You look like a steer.'

'Do I sound like one? Moo.'

'Come *on*, Chuck.'

'Oh, all right. You're no fun.' He walked up to me.

'Prism Chisholm and his partner have reached the wagon train. I have to leave. You coming with me?'

He eyed Rusty. 'You mean now?'

'Of course I mean now!'

'Fleeing at the last minute under the cover of darkness,' said Chuck. 'How very exciting. Where's Betsy?'

'I can't ask her to join the outlaw life,' I said, walking Rusty. I didn't add that she probably wouldn't come anyway.

Chuck nodded his understanding as we ventured away from the wagon train.

Finally I decided we were far enough to move

138

faster without being heard. I mounted Rusty and drew in a deep breath. 'I wonder which way Betsy would go.'

'I know what to do,' said Chuck. 'Follow me. Ready?'

He took off at a trot. I kicked Rusty and he trotted after Chuck without any interior squeaks or grinds. The pounding of our hoofbeats seemed loud, but when I looked back over my shoulder, I could still hear the fiddling and picking and handclapping from the circled wagons.

My best hope lay in Prism Chisholm's over-confidence. If he really thought I was trapped back there, and scared, he might not try to keep his multiple eyes on me too closely. Every moment he failed to notice I was gone would give us some extra steps.

We turned, leaving the wagon train out of sight behind a rise, and Chuck began to run. I kicked Rusty into a gallop, vaguely aware of canyon walls rising up on each side of us in the faint moonlight. Chuck was often lost in the darkness, but his hoofbeats made him easy to follow.

The night beckoned.

Between the dozing I had done in the afternoon and the surges of panic I felt every time I thought of Prism Chisholm, I had no trouble staying awake. Chuck had had a day of rest and no longer carried a passenger. We slowed to a walk and kept going all night.

The sun came up behind us and threw brilliant yellow rays across sandy bluffs and flats and canyon walls. For the first time, I saw the numerous steerite tracks ahead of us. No one was visible behind us, but I was sure Prism Chisholm would resume his pursuit this morning when he couldn't find me.

'Where are we going, Chuck? Are these the same tracks you saw where you picked up that hide?'

'Definitely. I have followed them by scent all night.'

'If this is a combination of the herd from the train and your original herd, then Duke's gang is driving it.'

'It also means,' Chuck said slowly, 'that your gang rustled my herd.'

'Before I joined them,' I said quickly. 'I mean, I never joined them. Before I met them.'

'Granted,' he said grudgingly.

'I guess they're planning to sell all the steerites in the far west,' I said. 'Since they were going that way, anyhow.'

'Maybe they were going there first and just robbed the bank along the way.'

'Could be.' I yawned. The sun was warming my back and making me sleepy.

The day wore on. We slept under the desert stars again and woke up early to keep pushing. A number of days passed that way. Before long, most of my jerky was gone and we were no longer following the stream. Each day, we moved more slowly as Chuck got tired and Rusty got hot.

One day, as we were plodding into the blazing sun of late afternoon, all I could think about was how thirsty I was. We had seen no one but each other for a long time.

'Hark,' said Chuck. 'Scrutinize yonder.'

'Huh?'

'Look up ahead.'

Far in the distance, a small herd of steerites was just barely visible on the desert horizon. Only a few riders were driving it. They kicked up a small, constant cloud of dust.

'We'll have to slow down,' said Chuck.

'Why? Let's go ahead and join them.'

Chuck swung his head back to look at me, alarmed. 'What?'

'As long as I'm on the run as an outlaw,' I said, 'I might as well be one, I suppose.'

'These are *rustlers*. They might even . . . butcher me again.' He started to sniffle. 'I just wanted to follow them. So we could get away.'

'We can tell them you belong to me, too. We'll both be safer with someone on our side than we are now, by ourselves.'

'Are you sure?'

'Definitely.' I remembered how apologetic Smellin' Llewellyn had been when he had found out Chuck was with me. 'You know, Chuck, we really have to find a place where we belong.'

'In the desert?'

'No, no – I mean, all the time.'

'That may be part of my herd up there,' Chuck said slowly. 'But I was duty-bound to escape.'

'You aren't undoing the escape,' I pointed out. 'You'll be mine, now.'

'Maybe we can free everyone else,' Chuck said hopefully. 'Okay, let's go.'

'Don't get your hopes up,' I muttered.

Soon the herd was out of sight around the next bend. We were going only slightly faster than they were. Of course, the tracks remained clear enough.

By the time the sun was going down, I could see that the herd had stopped for the night. A small campfire served as a little yellow beacon for us. I was exhausted and even the cooler night air wasn't helping me stay alert. Swaying on Rusty's back, I hung on the best I could and kept riding.

When we finally drew close to the campfire, a

surge of fear woke me up. Chuck was dropping back slightly to let me go first. At the sound of our hoofbeats, the three guys around the campfire all stood, hands on their guns.

'Who's there?' one of them called out.

I swallowed. 'Louie Hong.'

'Who?'

'What if it's not them?' Chuck whispered in a panic. 'Now what?'

'I held the horses in Femur,' I said weakly.

'Show yourself,' the man in the middle said sternly.

We proceeded slowly into the firelight.

Duke was the one in the middle. The others were Alkali Springs and Wesley Coon.

'Say, it is you.' Duke laughed. 'All righty. Step on down and join us.'

Alkali peered at me from his bent and crooked stance as I dismounted. 'What in tarnation are you riding?' he demanded, pushing up his oversized hat to look.

'Oh – this is Rusty.'

'I can see that,' said Alkali. 'But what is he?'

'He's a robot horse,' I said politely.

'A *what*?' He grinned.

'He's, uh, an antique.'

'Sorry I asked.' Alkali folded himself down by the fire again, shaking his head.

'Sit down,' said Duke, waving a hand at the fire. He resumed his seat on a rock.

'Thank you.' I did, then remembered Chuck. 'By the way, this is my steerite, here. I came into Femur with him.'

'Fair enough.' Duke nodded.

'Why is your steerite wearing a bag on his head?' Wesley was still standing, staring at him.

'Well—'

'*Moooo.*'

Wesley jumped.

'He's shy.'

'Shy?' Duke laughed again. 'You're a funny one, fella.'

'Uh, Chuck,' I said. 'Why don't you go hang out with the herd?'

'Moo again.' He trotted away, relieved.

Wesley turned around to find his seat again. The wire that ran from his glasses led to a bulge in his hip pocket.

'We were just gettin' the fire hot,' said Duke. 'Put on one more, Alkali.' He handed me a waterskin.

I took it and drank eagerly.

'Yup.' Alkali set two frying pans on the fire and pulled four steaks out of somewhere to drop in them.

I wondered if this was more of ST 1214, but thought better of asking.

'So, where ya headed?' Duke asked, pushing his leather hat back on his head. It looked like Betsy's, only bigger. He poked at the fire with a stick.

'Well . . .' I took a deep breath and chanced it. 'Carver Dalton and Smellin' Llewellyn found me on the run from Femur. They, uh, told me I could hide out in Washout.'

'They did?' Duke hesitated, then laughed. 'All right, all right. I guess I did you a bad turn back there, not tellin' ya what was up. Consider yourself in.'

'*Really?*' I felt a surge of excitement. 'I never belonged anywhere before.'

Duke leaned to one side and fumbled in a pocket in his long sheepskin vest. Then he pulled out a double bison and flipped it to me over the fire. 'That'll help keep ya till we get there. We'll split the full amount when we're all together.' He looked pointedly at Alkali.

Alkali scrunched up his pointed face and pulled out a similar coin from the folds of his duster. 'Here.' He handed it to me.

'Thanks,' I said to both of them. I was warm all over, and not just from the fire. I held the two coins flat in my palm where they could shine in the firelight.

'He's come unplugged,' said Alkali.

I looked around. Wesley was sitting motionless, staring blankly across the fire towards the darkness.

Duke reached behind him and tapped the back of his head, up by the wire. Wesley looked around.

'Give him a double bison,' said Duke.

'Oh – did I come loose?' Wesley straightened his wire and handed me a coin.

I stashed all three in my pocket.

'So,' said Duke, watching Alkali turn the steaks with a forked stick. 'How did ya get here all the way from Femur? Ride that antique, did ya?'

I started to answer, then froze. If I told them that Prism Chisholm was on my trail, I just might be out of the gang again – or worse, if they thought I was secretly on his side. 'Most of the way, lately,' I said.

'Holdin' close to the vest, eh? Well, that's good.'

A short time later, the steaks were done. I attacked mine eagerly.

'The steerites need water tomorrow,' said Duke, with his mouth full. 'We'll head northwest towards some green bluffs I saw today.'

I nodded, feeling businesslike. After all, rustlers were just ordinary drovers once they had the beef. 'Good idea, boss.'

'You said your name was Louie?' Wesley said. 'As the new man, you can help us out with one of our nightly duties.'

144

'Sure,' I said. 'I'll pull my own weight.'

'It's the steerites,' said Alkali. 'We got to sing to them every night.'

I looked up from my steak. 'You do?'

'It's an old tradition,' said Wesley. 'Historical records refer to it. A real drover wouldn't break it.'

I wasn't too sure about that, but I was in no position to argue. 'Okay. Whatever you say.'

'We don't have a guitar or anything,' Alkali added. 'You're on your own.'

'Right.' I finished my steak and set down the metal plate. 'I'll, uh, go try this out.'

They all grinned at each other as I got up and walked towards the herd.

'Hey, Chuck,' I whispered. 'Where are you?'

'Moo.'

'It's dark. Keep mooing, will you?'

'Moo. More moo.' He pushed his way to me on the edge of the herd. 'Here I am.'

'They want me to sing to the herd.'

'I thought you didn't sing.'

'Well, I don't. I was hoping you could help.'

'Why, certainly. I would be honoured.'

'That song you were singing before – how many verses does it have?'

'Three that I know.'

'If you lead, I'll follow along.'

'Since you've heard the first verse, I'll start by teaching you the second.' He cleared his throat and started, with me singing half a syllable after him.

'"Oh, roast me not on the lone prairie
'Cause my legs fell off and my eyes rolled free.
On a turning spit, even two or three,
Oh, roast me not on the lone prairie.'

The herd actually stopped shuffling around a little to listen.

'Now you try it,' said Chuck. 'I'm supposed to be in the audience, after all. I'll prompt you with the lyrics if you forget.'

I started singing the first verse, with Chuck whispering the lines just ahead of me. The herd shifted a little. I had trouble with the tune as well as the words.

'Keep going,' Chuck whispered. He prompted me on the second verse as well.

The steerites began to mill around. If I hadn't been on the edge of the herd, I would have been uncomfortable. My tune still wobbled and I had to hesitate sometimes to catch the words he was giving me.

Finally I started on the first verse again.

'Oh, roast me not—'

Hoofbeats began to rumble. I sang louder over the noise.

The steerites were moving away from me.

'Oh, my,' said Chuck, trotting away. 'See you later.'

' ". . . on the lone prairie—" hey, where you going, Chuck?'

'We're stampeding,' he called over his shoulder.

'What? Wait a minute!'

'I can't stop – it's in my programming. When the herd goes, we all go.' He galloped away after the others.

The entire herd of steerites rumbled away into the darkness.

At the campfire, Duke and Alkali had jumped to their feet. Alkali threw his plate down angrily. Wesley, scrubbing the frying pans with sand, just looked over his shoulder.

We couldn't round them up in the darkness. By daylight, they might have scattered over quite a distance.

I wondered if Prism Chisholm still wanted to talk to me.

# Thirteen

By midday, we had gathered most of the herd again, but no one was talking to me much. Chuck had returned almost immediately, as soon as his programming had let him. We drove the herd towards the green bluffs in the distance.

As the new man, I rode drag just behind Chuck. Alkali rode up on his horsite, all of his joints bouncing crazily with the motion. His hat slipped down over his eyes and he shoved it up again.

'We're still missing some, thanks to you.' He pointed towards a couple of low hills to the south. 'At least five. See if they're down there.'

I nodded and cantered in that direction. Chuck came with me.

When we had gone some distance, I slowed to a walk. 'I messed up again, Chuck. Now they're all mad at me. I don't think they want me in the gang anymore.'

'They haven't asked you to leave, have they?'

'Not yet. They probably just want me to bring all the strays in first.'

'Pardon my presumption, but you don't seem like an outlaw to me.' He hesitated. 'And your singing wasn't *that* bad.'

'Thanks,' I said wearily.

When we reached the crest of the hills, we saw five steerites standing on the far slope, right in front of us. They were startled.

'Hey,' one of them yelled at Chuck. 'Did you lead him here?'

'Traitor!' another shouted.

'I did not,' Chuck said haughtily. 'I am not part of your herd, remember? I am merely accompanying my owner.'

'Oh. He's your owner, eh? Well . . . all right.' The first steerite seemed mollified. 'You said your name was Chuck?'

'That is correct.'

'I'm ST 10096.'

'Pleased to meet you.'

'And our programming requires that we stray if we can from the drovers who rustled us.'

'Your programming lets you stampede?' I asked.

'Under certain conditions,' said ST 10096. 'Mostly for our own safety. For instance, horrendous noises often signify danger, so last night—'

'I get the idea,' I said quickly. 'Never mind.'

'We can still run for it,' ST 10096 said defiantly. 'We don't have to follow you rustlers.'

'Why didn't you run just now?' Chuck asked.

'It's kind of hot to run, actually,' muttered another steerite. 'Say, why do you have a bag on your head?'

'None of your business,' said Chuck, glaring at him.

'Oh, yeah?' The other steerite lowered his head at Chuck and started pawing at the ground.

'How barbaric,' said Chuck, turning up his nose.

'Hold it, ST 9870,' said ST 10096. 'We have to plan.'

'I'm getting lost in all these numbers,' I said. 'Would any of you like a nickname I can remember?'

'You won't have to remember us,' sneered ST 10096.

'I'd like one,' said ST 9870, looking up. 'Would you mind calling me Lugosi? I understand a fellow by that name once had something to do with steaks.'

'If you want. I've never heard of him.'

'This is no place to stray,' said Chuck. 'There's no water and no grass to speak of.'

'It's still our duty to escape,' said Lugosi.

'You can always do it somewhere else,' said Chuck. 'Unless your owner was driving you when you were stolen, you don't even know who it is.'

'We don't know who owns us.' ST 10096 looked at Lugosi. 'That's true.'

'You aren't obligated to die of thirst,' said Chuck.

'Okay by me, then,' said Lugosi. 'We'll go back with you. At least for now.'

I started back to the main herd, which was just going over the far horizon. All the steerites followed.

'Chuck,' I said. 'Don't you know these guys? I thought your original herd was in this bunch. Don't you want to help them escape?'

'A mistaken surmise on my part,' said Chuck. 'They are not my herd. However, they do tell me that at times they have spotted another herd moving roughly parallel to them, apparently driven by other members of your gang—'

'It's not *my* gang, really.'

'I wonder if that one is my herd.'

Now, in the heat of the day, we moved at a slower pace. Duke was driving the main herd slowly too, but we didn't seem to gain any ground. Sometimes they were completely out of sight.

When we had a view from some height, I looked back over our trail for a sign of Prism Chisholm. I didn't see anyone.

Late in the afternoon, we crossed the top of a ridge and saw the main herd stopped ahead. A mountain range had come into view, running north and south. The herd was milling about in front of a narrow pass.

Duke had ridden out in front. His way was blocked by a crowd of mounted men. One in particular was talking to Duke. The strangers far outnumbered the trio driving the herd.

As we watched, Duke turned back to the others and waved his arm to the north. They would not be using that pass to cross the mountains. The herd moved on.

I was hoping that the strangers would leave before we got there. Since I wanted to rejoin Duke, I didn't care about the pass, but I had no idea who they were. Unfortunately, they saw me coming with these steerites. As Duke moved on, they turned their attention towards me and waited.

The sun was reddish orange over the mountains in the west by the time we drew near. I figured about twenty guys with black hair waited for us. Then I realized something funny – their mounts kept shaking their heads and shuffling about and making messes. Every last one of them was a real horse.

I was careful to keep on the track of the main herd. As we neared the pass, I touched the brim of my hat to the guys standing by without pulling up to a stop.

'You with them?' one guy in a straw hat and blue shirt called out. He was in the front, the same one who had spoken to Duke.

'Sorta,' I called back, still riding.

He rode down towards me. Straight black hair fell past his shoulders. 'Sort of? How can you *sort of* be with them?'

'I spent one night in their camp,' I said carefully. 'I'll just be rejoining them. Good day.'

'Hold up.' He trotted down to me. 'You scared? We won't hurt you.'

'Glad to hear it,' I said, stopping Rusty.

'You're real timid. You a real guy? What they call a control-natural?'

'Could be,' I said carefully.

'In that case, you're welcome.' He held out his hand. 'I'm Stone Tree.'

'Louie Hong.' I shook hands with him.

'We don't meet many like you outside our own.' He studied me a moment. 'The sun is nearly down. You may spend the night as our guest. We have water and grass for your – your steerites, they're called?'

'That's right.' I looked after Duke, in the north. He and the herd were making camp a long way off. 'Thank you. We sure could use some water.'

'Come with me, then.' He watched me yank on Rusty's mane to turn him. 'I don't see how you can ride that thing, but maybe I can get you a bridle for it.'

His companions turned ahead of us and rode into the mountain pass as I rode alongside Stone Tree.

'You called me a real guy,' I said. 'Are you . . . that is, are all of you . . . control-naturals?'

'We're Utes, mostly,' he said. 'Many Navajo and a few from other tribes.'

'But you're all . . .'

'We're regular people, like you.'

I didn't know what to say.

'We ranch and farm this area of the Sierras. That herd you're "sort of" with is too big to go through here without damaging our range.'

'Sierras?' I turned to him excitedly. 'Sierra Nevadas?'

'That's right.' He laughed. 'Don't you know where you are?'

'Not exactly. Have you ever heard of a town called Washout?'

'No. We keep to ourselves.'

I turned around. 'Hey, Chuck. These are the mountains Washout is in.'

'What's Washout?' Chuck looked up.

'Uh – a town.' I'd forgotten he hadn't been with me at the stage stop.

'An interesting invention,' said Stone Tree, considering Chuck. 'You think of him as a person, don't you?'

'Well . . . not exactly.'

Stone Tree said nothing. He led the way into the pass. From the way he had spoken, I had thought he lived nearby, but we rode until well past sundown before he took a trail winding up one of the forested slopes. Lights came into view among the trees above us.

Finally we reached a cleared area with a number of log cabins and larger buildings around it. Lights on all the buildings lit up the courtyard.

'Your steerites can find feed and water up that trail,' he said, pointing. 'The corral is open and empty. They don't have to be penned in, do they?'

'I'll ask. Hey, Chuck—'

'These are potentially hostile surroundings,' said Lugosi. 'We won't try to escape here.'

'We will await you in this corral,' said Chuck. 'Come on, guys.' He led the others up the trail.

'This machine you ride,' said Stone Tree. 'Do you just park it for the night or do you have to take care of it?'

'Uh – I just let him stand wherever he is.'

'Okay. I'll take you inside first and tend my horse later.'

We dismounted and I followed him into one of the cabins. It was larger than I had expected and furnished in carefully crafted wood. A heavyset woman looked up from the fireplace.

'This is our guest for the night,' said Stone Tree. 'His name is Louie. Louie, this is Jane.'

'Pleased to meet you,' I said.

'Welcome. Please sit down,' she said, tapping the back of a chair.

Stone Tree went back outside to tend his horse.

'I am heating water for herbal tea,' said Jane, placing an earthenware pitcher of water and matching mug in front of me. 'Dinner will be ready when Stone Tree comes back in.'

'Thank you.' I poured myself water and drank the entire mug. Then I poured some more and drank half of it. I refilled the mug and stared into it, waiting until I could swallow some more.

'Thirsty, eh?' She filled the pitcher again.

I nodded, watching her. This whole community was like me, with no special parts. For the first time, I didn't have to keep my status a secret. I didn't know how to act or what to say.

When Stone Tree returned, they joined me at the table over stew. It was totally different from the Noslich's however. Nothing had been dried or preserved. Everything was fresh and sharply flavoured.

No one talked much over dinner. I was too uncomfortable to make small talk and too hungry not to stuff myself. They didn't seem to care.

After dinner, Stone Tree leaned back and relaxed. I was finished with my stew but still huddled possessively over my mug of water.

'Are you a drover by trade?' he asked.

'Uh – no, not really.'

'A cowboy, then?'

'Just looking for work, really.'

He looked at Jane, who nodded.

'He is like us, isn't he?' she asked.

'We don't normally trust your people,' said Stone Tree. 'Your steerites are interesting to me personally, but being part machine is no condition for a human.'

'Chuck is really very nice,' I said.

'Well, what we're getting at is, would you like to live here?'

I froze, staring at him. After a minute, I glanced at her.

'We have a number of small villages this size,' he said casually. 'We're thriving in a modest way.'

'I wondered where all those other riders went,' I said quietly, for something to say. 'This place doesn't have room for them all.'

Stone Tree picked up his mug and looked inside it. 'For some generations now, since these lands were abandoned to us after the diseases, we have had few children born. Oh, enough for our numbers to grow slowly, but not like in older times.'

I wasn't sure about these diseases, but they must have occurred at the time of the other disasters I had heard about.

'We have work for a young man who is willing to work.'

'Perhaps,' said Jane, 'you have been like a bird in the wrong flock.'

'Me?' I was still getting used to the idea. 'You would let me live and work here?'

Stone Tree smiled easily. 'If you want.'

'I don't know what to say. Nobody ever wanted me around before.'

'Your time is your own,' said Jane.

I looked at her, not understanding.

'You are free to do as you wish,' she explained gently.

'Perhaps you would like to know more,' said Stone

Tree. 'Sometimes we buy clothing and other items from your people. Traders come to the pass more often these days than they did when I was a child.' He tugged at his shirt as an example. 'For a long time, we had no contact at all. Our electrical power comes from a design of a generator preserved from before the diseases, run by the flow of a stream. One village here has a modest iron mine and smelting operation. We are self-sufficient in these mountains, and we will remain so.'

'It sounds very nice,' I said politely.

'I will ask you a personal question,' said Stone Tree. 'You need not answer it.'

I shrugged.

'Why do you live with those half-human people?'

'That's all I've known.' I shrugged again. 'At birth, some of us are designed at random to be control-naturals and we aren't allowed to have specials.'

'You would choose them if you could?'

No one had ever asked me that. Everyone, including me, had always known the answer. At least, they had assumed it. Now I thought of Dave Noslich and his pitiful Fargos.

'I've never had any choice,' I said slowly. I waited for him to take back his invitation.

'He is tired, Stone Tree,' said Jane. 'Louie, we have an extra room for you. It was Stone Tree's sister's room when they were children.'

'Thank you.'

'I'll show you where it is,' said Stone Tree, getting up.

A little later, I closed the door to their guest room and looked around. Like the rest of the cabin, it was small and clean. A small wooden door on leather hinges covered the window in the back wall. I undressed for the first time in more days than I could count and slid into a wooden bed with a soft pad but no springs. I switched off the small wall lamp and pulled up a heavy woven blanket that was scratchy but extremely warm.

The room was dark and chilly, but after all the nights I had spent sleeping in the open, I welcomed the privacy and the feeling of security. I wondered if Prism Chisholm could harass me here; I doubted it.

I could hear Stone Tree and Jane moving about in the other room. They seemed direct and honest. I was tired but wide awake, unable to stop thinking about their offer.

I didn't want to stay. I had known that from the moment he had made the offer at the table.

When I had been a kid, I had sometimes dreamed of finding a town full of people like myself, where I could belong. Since control-naturals always hid their status if they could, they never got together, so a town of them wasn't really possible. Now I had found something like that and didn't want it.

In the privacy of this room, protected by solid walls of heavy timber, I figured out one reason: I had been driven here and forced to hide.

Hold it, I thought, opening my eyes in the total darkness. That wasn't the entire reason. I had been alternately hiding out from outlaws and the law ever since leaving Femur.

Staying here forever, though, would be different. That would mean I was giving up.

I still had unfinished business out in the world I had been born to. Maybe I really would become an outlaw; maybe I wouldn't – but I wanted to decide. Then, if I wasn't going to be an outlaw, I would want to clear my name of the bank robbery. Also, I wanted to make sure Chuck was okay. And I was curious about Betsy – maybe I could get to know her better. With all that business accomplished, someday I might even choose to come back here. For now, though, I had something to prove to all those people who looked down on control-naturals. If I gave up and hid, I would only be proving them right.

Yeah, that was it. I would have to move on to show that I was more than those other people thought. Satisfied at last, I closed my eyes again. I was asleep almost right away.

Dawn didn't wake me, since light could not enter the room, but roosters woke me up. Breakfast was hot cereal of some kind. I felt guilty for accepting it.

I looked across the table at Stone Tree. 'I have thought about your invitation. Right now, I think I had better move on.'

Stone Tree nodded. 'As you wish.'

'If you change your mind,' said Jane, 'just come on back.'

'I'd like to tell you—'

'It is not necessary,' said Jane.

'Well, it's just that some men are following me.' I didn't want to confide all my reasons, but this one was genuine, too. 'I can't betray your hospitality by leading people here who would cause you trouble.'

'If that is what you want,' said Stone Tree. 'If and when you choose to become one of us, you will not have to fear outsiders.'

'Maybe I will join you some day,' I said. Then I turned my attention to breakfast.

I said goodbye to Jane. Stone Tree accompanied me outside.

'This is a parting gift,' he said, holding up an old leather bridle and reins. 'Will it fit your machine?'

'Thank you,' I said, staring at it in awe. 'Sure, let's

see.' I put it on Rusty and fastened the buckles. 'Perfect. Thanks again.'

He nodded. We mounted up and rode down the trail.

'Hey, Chuck!' I called.

In a moment, Chuck led the steerites trotting down from the corral.

'Good morning,' said Chuck cheerfully. 'On our way again, are we?'

'Yes.' I still had mixed feelings about leaving and did not want to discuss it. Besides, Stone Tree's attitude about the steerites had made me uncomfortable.

Stone Tree rode with me down the mountain pass, back to the edge of the desert foothills where I could pick up Duke's trail. There he waved farewell. As I rode on, he watched on his horse, which pranced impatiently, tail twitching.

# Fourteen

Duke and his herd were out of sight again. Our journey after them was not much different from that of the day before. Duke's tracks led north, as he apparently searched for another gap westward through the mountains.

'Say, guys,' said Chuck, turning to the other steerites. 'How about singing to pass the time?'

'Huh?' Lugosi said.

'Follow along. I'll start.' Chuck launched into 'Roast Me Not on the Lone Prairie'.

The others joined in, reluctantly at first. Each of them sang in a different key, Lugosi affecting some kind of funny accent with trilled 'r' and lots of 'v' sounds. Once Chuck was sure that they all knew the words, he divided them into rounds and they went on singing.

I wondered what Stone Tree would have thought. I wasn't even certain what I thought.

'What do you think?' Chuck called to me over the racket.

'Uh – it does break the monotony, doesn't it?'

Chuck looked pleased.

The main herd came into view in the distance over the next foothill, just as it ambled over another hill ahead. I could make out Duke riding in front and Wesley choking in the dust of the drags. Alkali bounced along on his horsite to one side.

We weren't gaining on them. They probably saw

us back here and just figured we would hustle enough to catch up. I decided the sun was too hot for us to hurry now. Maybe after they stopped to make camp after sundown, we could push on with their campfire to guide us.

They were soon out of sight again. Every so often, they came back into view for a short time. They always crossed over the next horizon before we drew any nearer.

Around midday, Duke made a turn into the mountains. I supposed he had found another pass not visible from my position. I gritted my teeth against the current rounds of 'Roast Me Not on the Lone Prairie' and kept riding.

'Say, Chuck,' I shouted. 'Do you know any other songs?'

'This is my favourite,' he called back.

'Would you mind taking a break?'

'A break? You mean, stop singing?'

'Just for a little while.'

'I thought you said it broke the monotony.'

'I'd like some monotony for a while.'

'As you wish,' he said morosely. 'Last round, everybody.'

As each round was completed, they quit singing. Finally they were all quiet except for their hoofbeats.

'Thanks,' I said.

'Don't mention it,' Chuck muttered. 'Well. Since you object to the entertainment, would you mind telling us where we are going? And what your plans are?'

'I'm not sure,' I said. 'I've been thinking about that all day.'

'I thought we were going to liberate the entire herd,' said Lugosi. 'Wasn't that the plan?'

161

'That's the short-range plan,' said Chuck. 'What about the big picture?'

'I can't return east at this point,' I said. 'I've ruled that out.'

'Our owners are probably back there,' said Lugosi.

'I don't dare,' I said. 'Prism Chisholm's on my trail, and I don't have enough supplies, anyway.'

'Are we to proceed to join the outlaw gang?' Chuck asked.

'I guess so.'

'That seems safer than confronting this Prism Chisholm fellow,' said Chuck.

'For now,' I said. 'If he picks up Duke's trail and follows him to Washout, then I ought to avoid Washout. Prism Chisholm can go after the guys who really pulled the job and leave me alone.'

'I vote we rescue our rustled comrades,' said Lugosi. 'What about that?'

'Yeah,' said ST 10096. 'That was the deal. That's why we came with you. Otherwise, we could stampede off into these mountains any time.'

'Okay, okay,' I said. 'We'll work on that.' I wasn't sure how, though. If I wanted to become a regular part of Duke's gang, freeing all his steerites was the wrong way to go about it.

'Great,' said Chuck enthusiastically. 'This calls for a celebration. Ready, guys? Follow me: "Oh, roast me not . . ." '

They all chimed in.

I sighed. Maybe this was their revenge for my singing to them.

We followed Duke and his herd into the mountain pass up the eastern side of the mountains. The steerites found more grazing and a stream for water. After stopping for lunch, such as it was, we moved on.

Plodding uphill slowed us down. The sunlight was still strong all day, but now was blocked most of the time by the tall trees. The dry air grew cool rapidly as we climbed higher.

'Hey, Chuck. Do you know "Sweet Betsy from Pike"?' I asked once.

'No,' he called back between verses.

As the sun fell towards the treetops lining the top of the ridge ahead of us, I kept looking for Duke. The main herd was either around a corner or over the ridge. Blundering through the pass in the dark was pointless if we couldn't see Duke's campfire, not to mention dangerous, so I gave up for the night. I stopped to make camp by the stream and built a little fire, still accompanied by the singing steerites.

I was almost ready to stampede, myself. Fortunately, it wasn't necessary. They finally clustered around the fire and quieted down. We slept on the forested hillside.

The next day, we trekked higher into the mountains on the tracks of the main herd. Even the steerites finally got tired of singing the same song. That was lucky for them, since I was almost ready to roast them all then and there, just out of spite.

Duke had not slowed down any, nor had we gained on him. Occasionally, just as we came over the crest of a rise, we would see Wesley's back, like the day before, just as he followed the main herd over the next horizon.

Late in the day, when I had not seen Wesley for some time, Chuck suddenly stopped in his tracks.

'What do you suppose that is?' he asked.

The other steerites stopped, too.

'Where?' I said, looking farther up the pass. The forested slopes rose sharply from the narrow pass on both sides. 'I don't see anything.'

163

'The noises,' said Chuck. 'They sound like clanking and pounding.'

'I've heard it before,' said Lugosi. 'In the last mountain range. People were building a railroad.'

'Our hearing is more acute than yours,' Chuck said to me. 'We were designed that way so we could avoid dangers.'

'You think someone's building a railroad?' I pulled Rusty to a stop.

'Yes,' said ST 10096.

The others all nodded.

'Hmm.' I took off my hat and scratched my head. 'Considering the chaos at the last railhead, I think we should be careful.'

'Ditto,' said Chuck.

'I wonder if Duke was meeting them or if he ran into them by accident.'

'May I make a suggestion?' Lugosi asked. 'Allow us to go first, listening closely, while you ride behind.'

'I'll make the steerite suggestions around here,' Chuck said sternly.

Lugosi flattened his ears and glowered at him.

'Let's do what he just said,' Chuck suggested.

'Good idea,' I said.

Chuck led the way as we proceeded. Before long, I too could hear the distant clanging of mallets on spikes echoing down the pass towards us. It was still a long way off. When the sun drew low over the mountains ahead, the sounds stopped as the crew quit for the day.

Chuck looked over his shoulder at me.

'We should take a look,' I said. 'Let's go carefully.'

'Of course.'

Chuck skulked forward, looking like he was tiptoeing. I wasn't sure that was possible.

The night was dark, except for the moon, by the time we came over a rise to find campfires in the depression below us. Chuck and the other steerites waited for me to catch up to them.

'Beware,' Chuck whispered.

'I don't think we should walk up to a bunch of strangers in the dark,' I said. 'Let's spend the night in the woods and see what they look like in the morning.'

'If you will pardon my arguing,' said Chuck, 'perhaps we can reconnoitre. If you would care to climb down from that mechanical substitute for a few moments, you and I could sneak down through the woods.'

I sat on Rusty for a moment, looking down at the lights below. 'Duke might be down there. Then we could declare ourselves.'

'Caution shall be our motto,' said Chuck. 'Remember our precipitate entry into Femur.'

'Good point,' I said, dismounting. 'I'm convinced. We better not just walk down the pass. Let's go through the trees along one side.'

'My night vision is superior to yours,' said Chuck. 'Please take hold of my tail.'

'Got it.'

'What about us?' Lugosi whined.

'You fellows stampede at the first approach of strangers,' said Chuck. 'My, isn't this exciting?'

'We don't have to take orders from you,' Lugosi muttered.

Chuck stepped up into the trees and I hung on as we worked our way among them, awkwardly walking sideways down the slope. Branches hidden in the darkness kept hitting me in the face and knocking my hat crooked. He was too low to the ground to notice the same ones.

We slowed down as we approached the camp. That made it easier to dodge the branches and roots and rocks. I was scratched and banged up enough already. Then Chuck stopped, peering through the trees, and I crept up to join him.

The pass had been cleared here and a roadbed had been graded. A couple of enclosures walled with tall vertical wooden slats stood farther up the road. Lamps inside the pens leaked light out through the narrow cracks between the slats.

'They look like giant henhouses,' Chuck whispered. 'Only with lights and no roofs.'

'I bet that's the herd,' I said. 'C'mon.'

We edged along the forest until we had come up alongside one of the pens. The light outside the pens was faint and uneven. I could see Chuck's nose twitching towards the nearer one.

'The breeze is going the wrong way,' Chuck whispered. 'And perhaps I am naïve or just confused.'

'What's wrong?'

'I think those pens have people inside them.' He looked at me. 'Do humans do that?'

'Not usually. Maybe they're convicts.'

A row of big tents ran along the roadbed some distance up the next slope. I could see the silhouettes of men sitting around a campfire eating. Nobody was looking this way.

'I'm too big to go any closer,' said Chuck. 'Someone will see me.'

'Stay here.' I got down on all fours.

'Moo,' said Chuck.

I crawled forward across rocks that had been scattered by grading the roadbed. In less than a minute, I was behind one of the pens, out of sight of the tents. I tapped on the slats.

I heard footsteps and quiet conversation inside.

'Who's out there?' someone said quietly.

'I'm Louie Hong, a traveller. Who's *in* there?'

'Wait a minute. What's your name again?'

'Louie Hong.'

'All right.' Footsteps walked away.

I looked at Chuck and shrugged. His masked head was barely discernible between a couple of trees.

Two sets of footsteps approached the other side of the fence.

'Yeah?' someone new said.

'I'm looking for a guy named Duke,' I said. 'And some rustled steerites.'

'You say your name is Louie Hong,' said the voice sternly. 'I have a cousin by that name. You a control-natural?'

I hesitated, surprised.

'Louie. Speak up, kid.'

'Yes, I am,' I said slowly. 'Your cousin? Say – are you Aunt Laura's son? The one who went west, named—'

'Hong,' he said firmly. 'Out here, I'm "Hong".'

'What are you doing in there? Can I come in?'

Several people on the other side laughed.

'This is a slave pen.'

'A . . . what?'

'You heard me. And if the straws see you, you'll be working on the railroad for no pay, too.'

'But . . . a slave pen? What are you doing in there? What railroad is this?'

'You ever heard of San Francisco?'

'Sure. It was destroyed in olden times.'

'That was the old one. A new city is being built up again on the ruins. This railroad is under construction from San Francisco to the east.'

'I didn't know that.'

'Your steerites,' said Hong. 'They're around here somewhere? Another herd came in earlier today. That makes two in the last couple days.'

'That explains it,' I said. 'Duke must have rustled them in the midwest to sell here.'

'Straw patrol coming,' said one of the other voices quietly. 'Watch yourself, Louie.'

Their footsteps wandered away with studied nonchalance.

I dropped to the ground again and peeked around the corner. The vague shapes of a couple of straw bosses were approaching the dim light in front of the pen, but they didn't seem suspicious. I watched until their line of sight was blocked by the pen itself. Then I scooted back to Chuck.

'Come on,' I whispered, grabbing his tail. 'Back to the other steerites. We have to plan.'

'Check,' said Chuck. He lowered his head and tiptoed back the other way.

Lugosi and his companions were still waiting in the darkness on the hill where we had left them.

'What happened?' Chuck asked breathlessly.

'This railroad is being built with slave labour,' I said. 'And my cousin Hong is one of them. And the other steerites are here too, to feed the crew. So is the second herd you heard about, Chuck, the one that might be yours. We can free them all.'

'Aha,' said Lugosi, pawing the gravel. 'It's about time.'

'I'm ready,' said ST 10096, huffing angrily.

'Not so fast,' I said urgently. 'I have an idea. Can you guys knock the corners of those pens down without trampling the people inside?'

'Sure,' said Chuck. 'We're smarter than real steers.'

'What about the herd?' Lugosi demanded

impatiently. 'If they aren't in the pens, then where are they?'

'I didn't see them,' I said. 'But these slopes are too steep and have too many trees to keep an entire herd on them. They have to be in the pass beyond the camp itself.'

'All right,' said ST 10096. 'We'll knock down the human pens, stampede through the camp, and find the herd.'

'If they're penned, we'll knock that one down, too,' declared Lugosi.

'Right,' said Chuck. 'And either way, our stampeding will make them join us.'

'I'm ready, I'm ready.' Lugosi shook his head, waving his horns as he pawed the ground some more.

'Easy,' I said. 'We should wait until they're asleep. Otherwise they'll shoot us when we go in.'

Chuck nodded soberly.

'They'll have someone on watch all night, I guess,' I added. 'But if we stampede down the hill fast enough, maybe this will work.'

'A sneak attack,' Chuck mused, looking down the slope.

Lugosi was prancing about, leaping and still shaking his horns.

'We'll just have to wait,' I said. 'Don't wear yourselves out too soon.'

Lugosi looked at me for a moment, then sighed.

Since we couldn't light a fire without giving our presence away, we all settled down on the hill to wait. Even Chuck realized that singing was unwise. They all quieted down and dozed a little.

I tried to remember what I could about my cousin, but it wasn't much. We had met three years ago. He was older than I and had come west when he was about the age I was now.

169

The air grew colder and I huddled next to Chuck. The campfire in the distance dwindled, but I could still see a couple of silhouettes next to it, occasionally tossing in another stick. Lights inside the tents went out, one by one.

I was too nervous to get sleepy. Finally, when the two guys by the fire had been sitting there alone for some time, I nudged Chuck.

He raised his head instantly.

'They've had time to fall asleep,' I said.

Chuck prodded another steerite with his nose. 'It's time,' he whispered.

One by one, the steerites got up and shook themselves, stamping around on the ground.

'Let me at 'em,' said Lugosi, pawing the ground again. 'I'm ready. Dirty rustlers, anyway.'

'I'll follow you, I guess.' I mounted Rusty, not really eager to go charging down there. If I stayed here, though, I might lose track of everybody.

'Follow me,' Chuck cried loudly. 'Moo!' He started running down the hill, followed by the others.

I kicked Rusty and cantered after them.

Even five steerites gave a pounding roar of hoofbeats on the hard ground. The two guys on watch by the fire jumped up and grabbed rifles, but when they looked in our direction, they couldn't see much in the darkness. They stood uncertainly as puzzled, sleepy shots rose up from the tents near them.

Chuck entered the light around the first slave pen at a gallop and careened against a corner of the fence. The corner post broke and started to cave in as he ran past. The next steerite smashed through it and sent splintered wooden slats flying. Two more steerites stampeded over the opposite corner and the whole back side of the fence, facing me, collapsed.

The two guys on watch fired a couple of times wildly at Chuck and then ran for the mountain slopes. Their rifles didn't bang, or crack. They buzzed.

The slaves didn't need any briefing. They leaped over the leaning and scattered boards, glancing about curiously but not hesitating. I saw someone kick a board aside and stride out calmly, as though he were leaving a barbershop at midday.

'Hong, it's me, Louie!'

He looked around, also blind in the darkness. I only saw his silhouette, really, but that manner of his had given him away.

'Here!' I reined in Rusty sharply as we entered the pool of light now thrown from lamps lying amidst the broken lumber. Then I leaned an arm down, to swing Hong up behind me.

'Slide back,' he commanded, batting my arm aside. He mounted up in front of me, over Rusty's shoulders.

'It's my horse,' I muttered weakly.

His weight pushed me back, and I grabbed him around the waist.

'Hyah!' He kicked Rusty into a gallop towards the camp, after the steerites.

Chuck and his companions had also smashed the second pen. Both pens were temporary, anyway, and not very strong. Escaped slaves were scattering in all directions.

I had expected the straw bosses and overseers or whoever else was in the tents to shoot at me and the fleeing slaves. Instead, they were running up the slopes of the mountains in their union suits and boots, carrying their guns and the rest of their clothes. Obviously, they couldn't tell in the dark how big the stampede was and they weren't going to stand around in the pass and find out.

We galloped over the campfire, past the tents. Up ahead, a loud chorus of steerite shouts, calls, and one moo told me the main herd had been found. The thundering stampede took on another magnitude entirely.

'Hyah!' Hong tried to run down a couple of the overseers, but their fleeing shapes threw themselves into the trees and we missed.

We rode on into the darkness after the stampeding steerites.

# Fifteen

All the lights were behind us and I could see nothing ahead or on any side. The moon was hidden or else down. We galloped on through the pass, following the stampeding herd.

'Can you see?' I yelled, terrified that we would ride headlong into a cliff wall or a big tree.

'Shut up,' said Hong, without turning.

'But do you know what you're *doing*?' I screamed.

'Shut up.'

I hung on hard, turning my head to the side and grimacing against imminent collision.

He took Rusty around a curve and kept going. Soon we were going up a slope. I could still hear the herd, but it was leaving us behind.

I let my face hang loose and sat up. Either Hong could see or Rusty could. I didn't care which.

After a while, Hong eased up and let Rusty walk.

'This isn't a horsite,' said Hong. 'What are we riding, anyhow?'

'An old model of robot horse,' I said, panting.

'Hm. An antique, eh?'

'He runs on solar panels,' I said. 'But he doesn't graze or anything.'

'He can go at night on reserve energy, then,' said Hong. 'But how long?'

'Carrying two of us, I don't know.'

'We're about to find out.'

'What do we do now?'

He didn't answer right away. 'Thanks for the rescue,' he said after a bit. 'Did you come out west looking for me?'

'No. I'm going to Washout. Ever hear of it?'

'The outlaw town.' Surprised, he actually glanced back over his shoulder.

'Know where it is?'

'No.'

'I have to find out where it is.'

'You an outlaw?'

'Not – no – yes.'

'Speak up, kid.'

'Well . . . a bounty hunter is chasing me but I didn't do it.'

'We'll keep moving tonight. The railroad slavers won't come after us until morning.'

'Any idea how we can find Washout? I'm . . . sort of with the gang that brought the rustled herd into your camp and sold it.'

'Rustler, eh? That's a tough business.' He was quiet a moment, as Rusty clopped along. 'That means your gang does business with the slavers.'

'Well, *I* don't,' I said, more loudly than I had intended. 'I didn't know anything about it.'

'Hm. Rustlers can't always choose their customers. The price of stolen beef can go pretty low.'

'So, where are we headed?'

'Washout is north of here,' he said slowly. 'We'll have to leave this pass at daylight. As soon as we can see, we'll head north over the mountain.'

I liked the sound of that. Hong seemed confident and capable.

I was worried about Chuck, but I knew that when the steerites finished stampeding, they would have to keep moving through the pass. These slopes were too steep for them to go overland here. We couldn't follow them without leaving a clear, easy track for the slavers to see.

Once the excitement of the raid began to wear off, I grew tired. Hong remained straight and alert, but after a while I leaned my head on his back and closed my eyes. My forehead hit something around his neck that rattled heavily. I didn't sleep, exactly, but I wasn't completely awake, either.

Sunlight stung my eyes. I blinked and straightened up, looking around at the tall green trees. Then I noticed for the first time just how odd Hong's waist felt.

I had been riding all night with my arms around a surface that was hard and slick under his flannel shirt and heavy jacket. Cousin or not, he had special parts like most people. This felt like a swivel waist of some sort. When I looked, I also saw the loop of black chain around his neck.

'Hang on,' he said shortly. He yanked on the reins and we started up the wooded slope on our right.

The ground was rocky here. The trackers behind us might miss our leaving the pass at this spot, with all the steerite tracks mixed with our trail. I hung on to Rusty with my legs as he angled upward through the trees.

We slowed down a lot. Rusty was plodding, but was able to go on now that the sunlight was hitting his solar panels. Around noon, we reached the crest of the mountain.

'I'm tired,' I said.

'Think about building a railroad under a lash, in a slave chain,' said Hong.

I woke right up.

We rode down the far slope.

Late in the day, we reached the valley at the base of the mountain. I was surprised to find a trail running through the mountains here, parallel to the pass we had just left.

'This pass joins the other one on the west side of the mountain,' said Hong. 'I saw the fork when we worked our way eastward past that spot.'

'So which way do we go?' I asked, too sleepy to think clearly myself. 'If we go west, we might run into the slavers circling back this way. If we go east, they might still be coming behind us.'

'We could go on north and take our chances over the next mountain,' said Hong. 'But those are fresh wagon tracks right there.'

I squinted at the ground. 'Lots of them. And oxenite tracks, too. That might be the wagon train I was travelling with.'

'Wagon train? I thought you were a rustler.'

'I didn't say so.'

'So you didn't.'

'If the bounty hunter and his pal are still with them, I can't join them again. But if they're out looking for me, that wagon train is a good place to hide.' I paused. 'Unless the railroad slavers attack them.'

'They pick on helpless travellers. A wagon train isn't worth their trouble.' He kicked Rusty. 'We'll follow it at a distance and see if we can find out about your bounty hunter, come nightfall.'

If the thought of the slavers didn't wake me up any further, remembering Prism Chisholm certainly did. Worst of all, Rusty didn't have any galloping left in him. I kept looking back over my shoulder, but no one was there.

Even before the sun went down, when we were riding in the shadows under the trees, Rusty finally came to a halt.

Hong kicked him a couple of times. Nothing happened.

'We used up his reserves last night,' I said. 'Until he gets some direct sunlight or a recharge of some kind, he won't move again.' I slid off and stumbled until I got my balance on the ground.

Hong dismounted, too. For the first time, I saw the shiny, rock-hard black boots he wore and his villain's moustache. He squinted at the ground from under a tousled shock of straight black hair.

'These wagon tracks are fresh,' said Hong. 'Come on.'

I was ready to collapse on the hard ground and go to sleep on the spot. Instead, I took a deep breath and followed him. At least he wasn't walking much faster than I was.

The sun went down and we staggered on. At last, just before the night turned completely black, we came around a curve and saw the vague shape of the wagon train not too far away. They didn't have the space to circle here, so they were just sort of bunched up.

'Suppose you look for your bounty hunter,' Hong said quietly.

I walked on, nodding, too tired to speak. We were also too tired to make much noise. No one noticed us as we walked up behind the first wagon.

Everyone was huddled around their cookfires for warmth as they ate dinner. I looked at every group several times and did not see Prism Chisholm or Sniffin' Griffin. Finally I decided I could approach the Noslich fire, where Betsy and Eulalie were sitting with their hosts.

I sneaked around the outside of the wagons and then crawled under the Noslich wagon. When I reached the other side, Betsy was sitting with her back to me, a short distance away. I stayed on my hands and knees, in case Prism Chisholm was somewhere I hadn't seen him.

'Hey, Betsy,' I whispered.

Nobody heard me.

I hissed at her.

They went on eating.

I looked around and crawled forward. When I could, I reached up and tapped Betsy's back lightly.

'*Hey!*' She jumped up in surprise, in the same motion swinging her fist back and smashing me on the side of head.

I rolled over sideways, almost too tired to hear the ringing in one ear. In the other ear, I heard several exclamations of surprise. I blinked up at the dark sky overhead.

'Louie? What are you doing here?' Betsy's face was outlined on one side by firelight as she looked down at me.

I gazed at her. At the moment, I couldn't think of any good reason to be there.

'Hang on, Louie.' Dave got an arm under me and lifted me up.

'We better take care of him,' said Maud.

'Prism . . . whatshisname,' I muttered.

'He can't have my space,' Eulalie called to Maud. 'I paid for it, remember?'

'Prism Chisholm isn't here,' said Betsy. 'He and his friend left the first morning they realized you were gone.'

I let out a breath of relief. 'Someone is with me—'

'Here,' said Hong, stepping out from between a couple of wagons.

'My cousin,' I said. My hearing was coming back.

'Well, my goodness, sit by the fire,' said Maud. 'We'll feed you.'

'Can we sleep under your wagon?' I asked. That seemed more important than food at the moment.

'Of course, of course,' said Dave, dishing out stew. 'Here, take this.'

A short time later, fed and too tired to think, I curled up under the wagon and slept.

I was still sound asleep when something prodded my arm. When I looked, it turned out to be Betsy's foot. The sun was shining.

'There's breakfast left.' She bent down to look under the wagon. 'But it's almost time to go.'

I was still tired, but not enough to risk having the rear wheels roll over me as the wagon pulled out. Blinking in the sunlight, I crawled out and looked around. Hong was already eating a bowl of hot cereal by the fire.

'Morning, Louie,' Maud said pleasantly, handing me a bowl of steaming cereal.

'Thanks.' I thought a minute, then fumbled in my pocket and came up with one of the double bisons. 'Uh, here.'

'But that's way too much.' She backed away from my outstretched hand. 'Oh, no. I couldn't take that.'

'But, uh, we . . . I mean—'

'We would prefer to pay our own way,' said Hong quietly. 'Please take it.'

'All right,' she said quietly, letting me put it in her hand. 'You have most of it on credit with us, then. And you have room to ride on the wagon.'

'Say—' Eulalie started.

'We'll make room,' said Maud tartly.

'I pay my debts,' Hong said to me. 'You'll get my part of it back.'

I nodded, having a mouthful of hot cereal.

'Mr Hong,' said Betsy.

'Just "Hong",' said Hong, between mouthfuls.

'Oh. Um, have you been in these mountains for a time?' She pushed her hat back on her head a little.

He nodded without looking up.

'I'm looking for someone who lives in these mountains,' she said. 'He is middle-aged with straight brown hair and a medium to heavy build.'

'Sounds like almost everyone in these mountains,' said Hong. 'Except for his age. He's older than most people here.'

'Thank you, anyway,' Betsy said politely. She pulled her hat back down and walked away.

All around, people were packing their wagons. Some were hitching up their oxenites. Far up the row, I heard Laryngo's booming voice echoing off the mountainsides.

'I just told Laryngo you were with us,' Dave said as he came up to us. 'He welcomes you back, but he's busy right now.'

'I have to go get Rusty,' I said. 'By the time I walk back to him, the sunlight will have recharged him some. Then I'll catch up to you.'

Maud took Dave's arm and drew him aside. The sunlight glinted off the gold double bison in her hand as she whispered to him.

Hong stayed with the wagon and they pulled out. I set out on foot to retrace the path we had taken the night before to get here. As soon as I rounded the first bend, I was surprised to see Rusty in the distance. In the dark, as tired as I had been, the trip had seemed much longer.

Then again, as I hiked it, the trip felt longer than it had looked.

'Well, Rusty,' I said. 'How are you feeling?' I touched one of his solar panels. The sun had warmed it, though the morning mountain air was still cool.

I mounted up and kicked him.

Nothing happened.

I kicked him a few more times. After a moment, he

took one slow step forward and the rest of him followed. He didn't have much energy yet, but at least he moved.

I could have walked faster. By the time we came around the bend ahead, the wagon train had reached the top of the next rise. The Noslichs were bringing up the rear and I could see Hong sitting in the back of the wagon, watching the scenery go by.

The straining oxenites hadn't drawn the wagon train very far yet, but I wasn't gaining on it. Sometimes a wagon got stuck and then every wagon behind it had to wait. They went even slower up slopes. Rusty still just barely kept up.

By mid-morning, I was coming closer. Rusty was getting enough sun, even when it was filtered through the trees that towered over us on the mountainsides. I kicked Rusty again and he even sped up a little.

The wagon train stopped at noon to rest the oxenites and make lunch. That finally gave me time to catch up. When I dismounted, I made sure I left Rusty in the sun.

Hong was just climbing out of the wagon. I had never really watched him move until then. Before, I had only seen him in the dark or sitting by the fire. Now I saw the swivelling motion of his waist beneath the flannel shirt and the loose, easy sway of two snake-coil arms under his long sleeves. He twirled his villain's moustache as he eyed Rusty over my shoulder.

'Works again, eh?'

I nodded, still looking him over. He had the kind of parts I had always wanted.

'Washout isn't far. But I don't know exactly where it is.'

'Think we should stay with the wagon train?' I tried to match his laconic, self-assured manner.

'It's going to San Francisco,' he said. 'Maybe I'll go back there, maybe not.'

He hadn't included me. I shut up.

'Think I'll take a walk,' he said, and wandered off towards the other wagons.

Maud was building a little cookfire while Eulalie watched. Eulalie dabbed daintily at her face with her lace handkerchief. Dave was moving stuff around in the wagon. Betsy got out of it and looked around.

'Say, Betsy.' I took a deep breath and got ready to tell her about my adventures since leaving the wagon train.

'What happened to Chuck?' she asked.

'You should have seen it,' I said eagerly. 'We rounded up some other steerites and raided a slaver camp and freed—'

'Is he okay?'

'Well, actually, the steerites all stampeded and—'

'Where is he? He seemed so nice.'

'Well, see, it was dark and we had to escape the railroad slavers, so—'

'You mean you don't *know*?' She threw up her hands and walked away, shaking her head and swaying her looped braids.

'It was their idea to stampede,' I called after her.

She waved a hand in disgust.

Maud was heating up stew again, but it wouldn't be ready for a while. I decided to follow Hong. Betsy had been courteous to him.

The wagons had simply stopped in order along the pass, so I walked up the row. I found Hong four wagons ahead, sitting on a rock off to one side. He was watching something at the rear of one of the wagons.

Doc, who had been out of my sight in this wagon train before, had swung down the gate at the back of

182

a wagon for a place to sit. He was carefully checking over his revolver and polishing it with an oily rag. No one but Hong was paying any attention to him.

Doc blew dust off the handle of his revolver and started to holster it. Then he noticed Hong and froze in place as they studied each other. After a moment, Doc slid the gun the rest of the way in.

'That's a slave chain, isn't it?' Doc said.

Hong gave one slow nod. 'That's a regular Peacemaker, isn't it?'

'That's right.'

'I got one, too,' Harris said brightly, walking down the row. He was now wearing a big tan cowboy hat, a matching frock coat that was loose on his slender frame, and a gunbelt. 'Hi, Louie.'

Hong and Doc were still looking at each other.

'Hi,' I muttered.

'I'm Harris Nye.' He extended a hand towards Hong.

Hong ignored it. Instead, he got up and sauntered over to Doc.

'Where have you been, Louie?' Harris asked. 'Get lost?'

'Not exactly. Uh, I have to get some lunch.' I turned back toward the Noslich wagon.

'I've had mine. I'll keep you company.' He trotted after me. 'Want to see me practise later?'

'Practise what?'

'My shooting.' He slapped his holster.

'Uh—'

'You know, just between you and me, I think Eulalie will be impressed. That is, once she sees that I can handle myself out here.'

I walked a little faster.

'But maybe you could give me pointers. That is, you being . . . well, *you know*.'

Up ahead, Maud waved to me and held up a bowl.

'That is, Louie, I guess I need more practise with my gun.'

'Practise is good,' I said noncommittally.

'Practise is good.' He nodded gravely, considering this.

I took a bowl of stew from Maud, thinking about Harris. Then I looked straight up at him. 'Would you excuse me while I have lunch?'

'Of course I will,' he said, sitting down on a nearby rock. 'You just go right ahead and eat. I'll just sit here and not do anything. That's okay. Don't mind me. I won't bother you at all. Not me. Don't pay any attention to me. You have your lunch . . .'

I sighed and sat down to eat.

# Sixteen

When the wagon train pulled out again, I was more than ready for solitude once more. Rusty was ready too, having stood in the midday sun for a while. When I mounted up, we followed the Noslich wagon with no trouble. However, I found that the steady clopping of Rusty's hooves was surprisingly similar to Harris's conversation.

With Harris back in whatever wagon he was riding, I spent the afternoon in silence. I found myself wondering what had happened to Chuck and the other steerites. They had probably escaped from the railroad slavers, but any of them could have stampeded over a cliff or something in the darkness.

We plodded through the mountains all afternoon. When Laryngo's booming voice called a halt for the night up ahead, the wagons again had to stop in a row. Hong promptly jumped out the back of the Noslich wagon and strode up the pass, his waist swivelling and his arms swinging with every step.

I slid off Rusty and followed him. He had developed a rapport with Doc in just a few moments that no one else had managed in many days of travelling with him. I wondered what I would have overheard between them if Harris hadn't interrupted my eavesdropping.

Up ahead, Doc was climbing out of his wagon with a studied care. He tossed a bundle to Hong – who unrolled a leather gunbelt and holster. Without a word, he strapped it on as they climbed up the mountain slope among the trees.

I stopped short, amazed. Then, as they disappeared into the woods, I hustled after them a safe distance. I was careful to step quietly and stay behind bushes and leafy branches. When they stopped, I crouched behind a big tree to watch.

They hadn't gone very far. Doc leaned casually against a tree trunk and nodded at something in the distance. I couldn't tell what it was, since the forest around us looked all the same to me, but Hong nodded in agreement.

In one fluid motion, Hong bent one knee slightly, whipped out the revolver, and drew it up on his flexible, snake-coil arm. He fired. Ahead of him, a small piece of bark exploded from the centre of a narrow tree trunk.

I was even more amazed. He already knew how to do this. As I watched, he holstered his gun again. Then he whipped it out again and blasted another hole right next to the first.

Not much daylight was left, but Hong practised through all of it. Neither of them said a word. In the fading light, I could just make out a small blaze of exposed wood where the bark had been repeatedly shot away.

Finally, when I could hardly see them in the darkness anyway, they turned and started down the slope. I scampered ahead of them, stumbling and sliding a couple of times, to reach the wagon train again before they noticed me.

As I walked back quickly to the Noslich wagon, I saw that other people I passed were suddenly looking away. The sound of the gunshots must have drawn everyone's attention, but no one wanted to admit it. They seemed to think I had been participating.

Harris stared at me with his mouth open as I skipped by, avoiding his eyes. Fortunately, cookpots were boiling over all the fires by now, so he had to stay at his own wagon for dinner. Around the Noslich fire, no one spoke as Maud gave me my bowl of stew.

Maud and Dave made polite conversation over dinner with Betsy and Eulalie. I was just as glad to stay out of it. No one addressed me, but Maud smiled real nicely when I returned my dishes.

I was still tired from the long night and day's ride with Hong out of the slave camp. After dinner, I curled up under the wagon and closed my eyes. Maud threw some kind of blanket over me without even asking if I needed it.

I had expected to go right to sleep. Instead, as the wagon creaked over me with the motions of the others climbing in, I lay wide awake on the hard ground in the cold mountain air. I still had visions of Hong's hand snatching up his gun on that whiplike arm and blasting holes in the trees. Maybe that was where his swagger came from.

Not that it would do me any good. Control-naturals were beyond blood relationships. I should forget about it.

I opened my eyes, tired but not sleepy.

The night wind was light, rustling trees all around the wagon train. For a moment, I thought I heard something else, maybe the louder sound of people on horseback moving through the forest. Or steerites.

I wriggled to the edge of the wagon and looked up. The moon offered a little light. I threw off the blanket and got up.

I got Rusty and led him slowly up the wooded north slope of the pass. It was steep and clumsy, but I heard the hoofbeats and rustling of branches again up ahead. Without more light, I had to stay on foot.

As the noises ahead grew fainter, I realized I was being left behind. I didn't want to wake up the wagon train by yelling after them, so I swung up on Rusty and leaned my head down alongside his neck to avoid what branches I could. Then I kicked him a little and we hurried on through the trees.

Before long, we were angling down the slope again somewhere west of the wagon train. The steerites, assuming that's who was ahead of me, had merely taken a detour around it. When I rode down out of the trees into the pass again, I kicked Rusty into a canter. 'Hey, guys! Back here!'

I rode up waving my arm in the darkness. Ahead of me, the dim moonlight suddenly outlined a crowd of people on horsites, all turning in surprise.

'Oops.' I pulled on the reins. 'Uh – hi, there.'

'You have business with us?' a man's low, drawling, gravelly voice demanded.

'No,' I smiled weakly. 'My mistake. Say, have you guys seen a loose steerite herd wandering around anywhere?'

'Probably from the wagons,' someone muttered. 'Shall we?'

'Sounds like he's looking for the same herd,' drawled the first man.

Some of them rode out to each side of me.

'You haven't seen it, eh? Well, thanks anyway.' Suddenly sweating in the chilly air, I pulled Rusty around.

They were already behind me. One of them reached forward for Rusty's bridle.

I turned him again, took a deep breath, and kicked him as hard as I could. He sprang forward and the horsites shuffled aside in surprise. Shouts rose up all around me.

I hung on tight and galloped madly into the

188

darkness, hoping Rusty could see well enough to stay in the rocky, winding pass and not pitch over a cliff or smash into a boulder.

Hoofbeats thundered after me, but no one fired any shots. That confirmed my fear that they were slavers. They knew I couldn't do any work for them if they shot me.

I could just barely see, hanging on to Rusty's neck and peering ahead as we galloped. Even worse, I didn't know where I was going. I rounded a curve and then suddenly realized that more riders were just ahead.

'Whoa!' I reined in hard, trying to turn him, but he was going too fast. I rode right into the pair of horsites and riders in front of me, jostling them aside.

Guns were drawn on both sides of me.

'Who are you?' someone demanded.

'Hey, there's more of 'em right behind,' warned another voice.

'I'm Louie Hong,' I whimpered.

'Who?'

'Hey, I remember. Louie, it's me, Smellin' Llewellyn.'

'Who's with you?' Carver Dalton demanded, as the slavers pulled up around us. 'Say, what is this, a double cross?'

'They're slavers,' I muttered, turning Rusty around. 'And they're after me.'

'Not any more, they ain't,' said Smellin' Llewellyn. 'Snyder, is that you? Snyder Gray?'

'Evenin', Smellin' – and Carver,' said the gravelly voice I had heard earlier. 'You sayin' he's with you?'

'Part of our gang,' said Carver. 'Duke brought him in personal. He helped us pull that bank job we told you about the other day.'

'You don't want bad feelings with the Duke Goslin

gang, do you?' Smellin' asked. 'Especially after we just sold you all that beef so cheap.'

'Funny thing about that,' Snyder drawled. 'That beef all got stampeded out of our camp by somebody. You weren't thinking of stealing it back and reselling it, were you?'

Smellin' and Carver both stiffened on each side of me. Snyder Gray was right in front of me and his companions surrounded us. If everybody started shooting, I was likely to get it from all sides.

'If you got an accusation,' Carver said coldly, 'you say it out plain.'

They were all silent a moment. No one moved. In the darkness, the silence seemed to stretch.

'We ain't sure,' Snyder said finally. 'Anyhow, we've rounded up most of them, so it don't matter that much. But we won't get took. You just remember that.' He turned to go then, but before he did, he reached over and yanked my hat down over my face. Then he led the slavers into a gallop back the way they had come.

I let out a long breath. 'That was close.' I yanked my hat up again.

'There weren't very many of them,' said Carver. 'They sent most of their guys on towards San Francisco with the bulk of the two herds we sold 'em. They just kept a few for themselves. Funny they lost them.'

'Yeah,' I muttered, swallowing. 'Funny.'

'So you made it this far,' said Smellin', whomping me on the back. 'Good goin'. Maybe we should have taken you with us after all. You could have helped us drive one of the herds from outside Femur where we left it during the bank job.'

Now he told me. Anyhow, that was the real reason they had come all the way to the Sierra Nevadas for their getaway.

'I'm with the wagon train,' I said. 'Thank you for helping me. I think I should go back and warn everybody at the wagons that slavers are nearby.'

'No need,' said Carver. 'Wagon trains are too much work for slavers. They won't bother with those folks.'

'Oh. Well, anyhow, I better get back.'

'Nothing doing.' Carver put a firm, probably friendly hand on my shoulder.

'Huh?'

'We're practically at Hawk Nest already.' His silhouette nodded in the faint light. 'You'll be safe there. We can't let you risk unnecessary danger on your own.'

'That's right,' said Smellin', with a sniff. 'Now you made it this far, it's our duty to see you're took care of. Besides, you got a cut of the loot comin'.'

'Uh—'

'Come on, let's go.' Carver reined his horsite away from me.

I didn't dare offend them. Besides, they had a point. With slavers running about and Prism Chisholm somewhere on my trail, I might be safer with them.

That just showed how much trouble I was really in.

They spurred their horsites on up the pass. It was now or never. Two heartbeats behind them, I kicked Rusty and rode after them.

Over the next rise, they took a path leading into the forest again. We strung out in single file, now that we were back to a walk.

'Hawk Nest,' said Smellin'. 'It's the sweetest little mountain retreat you ever saw.'

'It'll be the *only* little mountain retreat I ever saw,' I said.

At first, it was too dark to see it even when we got there. Somewhere in the forest, a guy yelled, 'Who's there?'

'My femur hurts,' Carver yelled back.

'Okay, that's the password.' The other guy laughed. 'Is that you, Carver?'

'It's Smellin' and me and a friend,' said Carver. 'We're coming in, Tether.'

We rode down into a small hollow. It looked a little like Stone Tree's settlement. Lights on a couple of log buildings showed us a clear area with a well. We left our mounts in a little stable. Rusty required no care, but I didn't dare go anywhere without Carver and Smellin', so I waited for them.

Then we walked over to one of the log buildings. Inside, the red embers in a fireplace barely showed bunks lining all the walls. Some had guys snoring in them.

'Take your pick,' said Carver. 'Just don't wake anybody up. We share this place with a bunch of gangs.'

Here I had thought I would be safe with Duke's gang. Instead, I was sleeping in a room full of strangers. The lower bunks were full, so I put one foot up on the rails at the end of a bed and tried to climb up.

My knees were shaking too much to hold me. Carver and Smellin' got behind me and pushed. I shot up into the air, somewhat to one side, felt nothing as I flailed in the darkness, and then crashed to the wooden floor on the far side of the bunk.

'Sorry,' muttered Smellin'. 'Guess you don't weigh as much as we thought.'

I was too stunned to move. They picked me up and threw me onto the top bunk to stay the second time. I heard Smellin' take a little hop, trigger his

Model C-5 Abilene Accordion ankles, and spring up to a top bunk. Carver flopped into bed more normally. I fell asleep without even loosening my moccasins.

When I woke up the next morning, the bunkhouse was empty. The sun was up; I had caught up on my sleep. Groggily, I slid off the bunk and staggered outside.

Blinking in the sunlight, I wandered towards the well and got in line behind two people. The guy in front had his head down the well as he lowered the bucket on its rope.

'Smellin', would you introduce me to this gentleman?' It was the woman in front of me. Her voice was high and precise, as though she had taken elocution lessons. She was short and compact, wearing a clean, full-length dress with violets in it. Straight blonde hair was parted in the middle to fall on to her shoulders.

Smellin' pulled his head out of the well and looked around. 'Oh, sure. This is Louie Hong. That there is Tinny Ginnie.' He had never sounded so polite before.

'Hi,' I said, in some surprise at finding a woman dressed this way in the outlaw camp. She looked like a schoolmarm, even more than Eulalie did.

'Pleased to meet you.' She extended a hand.

I shook it carefully. It was an abacus hand, with little counting rings on each digit. They rattled.

'So you're the fellow who came in with Carver Dalton and Smellin' Llewellyn last night.' She nodded to herself.

'Uh, that's right.'

'My goodness, you must be hungry. Smellin', you'll take him up to the café for breakfast, won't you?'

'Sure, I guess.'

'I would introduce you there myself, Louis, but I have chores to attend. Excuse me, won't you?'

'Yes, ma'am,' I said, watching her go.

'Come on, then,' said Smellin', reverting to his normal tone. He trudged up the slope towards one of the buildings.

I hurried after him.

We entered a combination general store and café. A tall woman with long, black hair was shelving canned goods behind a counter. She straightened when she heard our footsteps.

'This here is Choy Susan,' said Smellin'. 'The café and store belong to her.'

'Pleased to meet you,' I said politely.

She scowled at me. Even then, she was still pretty. 'What's his problem?'

'He's a control-natural,' said Smellin'. 'Duke brought him into the gang, though, and he's taking a cut of the Femur loot.' He shrugged and trudged back outside again.

Choy Susan shifted her brown-eyed gaze to me. 'Then you have credit here. Just don't get too friendly.'

'Thank you.'

Her scowl deepened.

'Gimme some breakfast,' I growled, scowling back at her.

She nodded and went through a doorway hung with wooden beads on strings.

I looked around. No one else was here. Half the front room here was the store and the rest had tables and chairs. I took a seat in the middle of the room, where I could see the door.

When Choy Susan brought me a bowl of hot oatmeal and a couple of pieces of bacon, I noticed that she was dressed in all blue denim, from the long-sleeved shirt with the sleeves rolled up to the snug jeans. She was half a head taller than I was and she thumped briskly across the floor on heavy black boots.

'Control-natural,' she said with a sneer, setting down the dishes with little clunks on the wooden table.

I forced another scowl at her. 'I don't see any specials on you.'

'*You* never will, either.' She put her hands on her hips and glared down at me.

I was shaking with nervousness, but acting mean seemed to be the way to make friends with her. At least, she was still standing here.

'You want anything else?'

'So,' I said airily. 'From the looks of Hawk Nest, Duke's gang is a lot more successful than I thought.' I tried to make that sound businesslike, but my voice quivered.

'They aren't bad,' she said grudgingly. 'But Hawk Nest, here, is shared by lots of gangs.' Her eyes narrowed and she leaned forward. 'And if anybody causes trouble, they lose credit at my store. You just remember that, shorty.' She stomped away.

I let out a quiet breath and ate my breakfast. It was hot and good. Something told me that nobody ever started trouble at Hawk Nest.

She was stocking shelves again. Every time she moved, her black hair swayed behind her. When I had finished eating, I watched her for a while.

'Aren't you finished yet?' she demanded, without turning around.

'Yeah,' I snarled back.

She went on shelving stuff. After a while she stopped to look at me. 'You still here for some reason?'

'Maybe.'

'You speak for Duke?' she asked suspiciously.

I hesitated. 'Is he here in Hawk Nest?'

'No, not yet. I don't know if he's coming here or going straight to Washout.'

'Washout.' I jerked straight up.

'That's right.' She looked at me quizzically. 'If he brought a control-natural into the gang, you must have more going for you than I can see.'

'Thanks.' Then I stopped, not sure if that was a compliment.

'He isn't looking for a new plan already, is he? You guys haven't divvied up your last take yet.'

'Maybe he is,' I said gruffly. 'What's it to you?'

She slammed a can of Georgia plums down on the counter. 'Now just what do you mean by that? I told him about that Femur bank. Heard about it from another drifter who passed through here once.'

'So?' That seemed like a safe response.

'So?' she screamed. 'If that thug boss of yours plans to cut me out of my share, I'll tell every other outlaw in Hawk Nest. He'll never be welcome here again.'

'I didn't say that,' I muttered quickly, suddenly terrified of causing a bandit feud. 'Duke wouldn't do that.'

'Well . . . that's better.' She cocked her head to look me over.

I got up quickly and touched my hat brim. 'Thanks for the breakfast.'

'I'll put some newbits on your tab.'

I hurried out, hoping she wouldn't repeat that conversation to Duke in too much detail.

Nobody was in the little open area. Wooden buildings stood in a haphazard ring around the edges. I walked towards the stable to see if anyone was there.

A door opened in a little cabin to my left. Tinny Ginnie walked out onto her front porch. She bent over to pick up some pieces of firewood that were stacked near the door.

'Easy, there,' I said, hurrying over. 'No need to get your dress dirty. I'll get that for you.'

'Oh, would you, Louis? Thank you.'

I trotted up the wooden stairs to the porch and lifted some of the logs. She held the door open for me and I walked inside the cabin.

'Just set them down on the hearth,' she said.

I did and glanced around a little, out of curiosity, trying not to be too obvious. The little cabin looked very cosy and lived in, with little doilies hanging over the back of a plush sofa and matching blue-and-white checked curtains and tablecloth. I walked back to the front door since I hadn't been invited to stay.

'Excuse me, but do you know where everybody is?' I asked.

'Nowhere in particular,' she said pleasantly. 'Some of the boys probably went hunting. Others are just out for a ride. Life can get pretty dull around here sometimes.'

I nodded.

'Thank you, Louis,' she said again.

I tipped my hat and walked back outside. The door closed behind me as I walked down the porch steps. Just as my foot touched the ground, a loop of cord fell over my head and shoulders and tightened sharply, pinning my upper arms against my sides.

I looked up in surprise but saw nobody as I was yanked hard to my left. The entire settlement tilted sideways until I thumped to the ground on my shoulder.

# Seventeen

I rolled onto my back and looked up. A face that looked vaguely familiar was partly silhouetted by the morning sunlight. I took a few deep breaths, trying to place him.

'You're out of line, fob,' he said.

'Who are you?'

'Tether Chen is the name. Don't forget it.' He shook his lariat a little and the loop around me loosened.

I knew his name, of course. Now I remembered seeing him in the bunch with Duke back at the saloon in Femur. He was a tall, thin guy, sort of like Harris. Unlike Harris, Tether moved with a fluid, confident motion as he pulled his loose loop off me and retracted it into a Wrancho Wroping wrist.

'Got the message?'

'Not exactly. You mean—'

He kicked the ground with the pointed toe of a cowboy boot and sprayed old pine needles and dirt into my face. 'I mean Tinny Ginnie, fob. Leave her alone.'

I spat out dirt while he marched away.

People drifted in all day. Most of them eyed me suspiciously and passed without speaking. That was fine with me.

Smellin' and Carver rode in just before dinner-time. By then, the bunkhouse was full of guys, mostly

198

napping or playing cards. I sat down by a tree on the edge of the clearing and watched.

No one had much to do here. Choy Susan walked around doing chores but Tinny Ginnie stayed inside. I noticed that Tether didn't go knock on her door or anything.

When Choy Susan came out to the front of the café and clanged the dinner triangle, I kept an eye out for Carver and Smellin' and followed them inside. They didn't say what they had been doing and I didn't ask. As everybody filed inside for dinner, Choy Susan put tallies on a chalkboard next to each name.

'You're the new man in camp,' said Carver, as we sat down. His narrow face had recently been shaved. 'That means you draw night duty.'

I nodded firmly, trying to ignore the sudden cold sweat I felt.

'You remember where Tether challenged us,' said Smellin'. 'That's the place.'

'Right,' I wheezed. I put my shaking hands on my lap out of sight.

'You fire one shot and we'll all come running,' said Carver. 'If somebody unwelcome is on the way, we'll back you.' His eyes fastened on me suddenly. 'If *not*, well . . .' He looked pointedly out the side window.

I had never looked in that direction. Now, for the first time, I saw the big, misshapen tree with one low-hanging branch. A frayed, withered rope swung in the breeze from it. Its bottom end was tied into a noose with nine coils.

I smiled weakly.

'Good boy.' Smellin' thumped me on the back and turned to the platters of steaks Choy Susan was setting in front of us.

I ate in silence. Actually, I saw no chance that I would . alert the camp unnecessarily. They had

199

forgotten that control-naturals aren't allowed to have guns.

Nor, at this moment, was I going to remind them.

I was eating quickly to have an excuse for not talking. As I stuffed myself, I wondered what I would do if intruders did approach the camp. I didn't have an answer for that, either.

By the time dinner was over, the sky was red over the western peaks. I decided to get Rusty and ride right up to the lookout post. The other guys dispersed, some of them to the bunkhouse and others to play cards by the fireplace in the café.

I was halfway to the stable, passing Tinny Ginnie's cabin, when I saw her standing on the front porch with Tether Chen. She was shaking her head.

'No. Absolutely not,' said Tinny Ginnie.

'All right, you,' I said loudly, suddenly walking towards them. It was just an impulse.

'Shut up, fob,' Tether yelled at me.

'Louis,' Tinny Ginnie said in surprise.

'Back off,' I shouted. I could just see this prim lady having to fight off all these outlaws by herself.

Tether lashed out his lariat, swung it once, and settled the loop over my shoulders in one easy throw. I grabbed the taut rope as he pulled me towards him, digging in with my heels. When they hit the bottom step leading up to the cabin, I braced myself and yanked back.

Tether, caught by surprise, pitched forward off the porch and landed on top of me. He then punched me a couple of times in the ribs. My arms were still pinned by the rope.

'All right, Tether,' said Tinny Ginnie. 'Please discontinue.'

He hit me once more in the stomach and got up.

'You're out of your league, fob.' He kicked more dirt on me and stalked away, shaking his head.

'Thank you, Louis,' said Tinny Ginnie, looking down at me in the waning light. 'I believe I should go inside now. Good night.'

I waved feebly, unable to speak. After a minute or so, I got up and staggered off to the stable.

Rusty was still standing in the stall where I had left him, just as though he were a real horsite. I led him out and rode up the winding path to the lookout. Darkness had fallen by the time I got there.

Night duty was boring. Everybody who belonged here tried to get in before dark, and if hostile intruders were coming, I wasn't going to stop them without a gun. I wasn't even sure that my shouting would be heard from here, if it came to that. So what was I doing here, anyway?

The real task was not falling asleep. I nodded off a couple of times, then jerked awake to the sound of distant laughter from Choy Susan's place down below. Lights were on there and in the bunkhouse.

I settled back against a tree trunk, wishing I could light a fire. Since potential intruders would spot it, I didn't dare, so I just huddled against the tree. As I thought about being here, though, life didn't seem that bad. I had something to do, a place to live, and credit at Choy Susan's.

Never mind that I was shivering out here in the dark.

I dozed again. The clopping of horsites and creaking of a wagon startled me and I sat up. 'Hey! Who's there?' I demanded.

'Shut up,' someone yelled back.

That wasn't the password. On the other hand, he didn't sound like part of a posse, either.

I was about to yell back when the wagon rolled

past me. A jumble of indistinct shapes lay under a dirty tarp. A faint voice was whimpering a mournful verse of 'Roast Me Not on the Lone Prairie.'

I jumped on Rusty and rode after the wagon.

The wagon pulled up at Choy Susan's. By now, most of the camp had gone to bed, but a few cardplayers wandered out onto the porch out of curiosity. Choy Susan pushed her way through them to the front.

'What took you so long?' she demanded. 'The wagon with the beef got here yesterday.'

'Wheel busted,' said the driver, climbing down. 'And I wouldn't expect to find any more running loose. I saw the slavers driving a lot of them; they must have rounded most of them up again.'

'All right.' Choy Susan nodded. 'In the morning, we'll set them out back to graze on the slopes.'

I drew in a deep breath. 'One of those steerites is mine,' I declared loudly.

'What?' Choy Susan looked at me in surprise.

'Hold it,' said Smellin' Llewellyn. 'Who's on guard right now?'

'Nobody,' I told him. 'I got business down here.' I expected an argument, or worse.

Instead, Smellin' just shook his head and stomped away towards the stable, muttering to himself.

'How do we know which one is yours?' Choy Susan demanded, hands on hips.

'He's the one who keeps singing. His name is Chuck and his number is ST 4006.'

'Say,' said the driver. 'The one that keeps singing? I noticed he was different. That's the one with the bag over his head, isn't it?'

'Yeah, it is.'

'All right,' said Choy Susan. 'Can the chatter. You

202

take your steerite, Louie. The rest are mine by right of stealing them.'

The driver threw back the tarp. In the yellowish light from the café, I could see a spidery jumble of stainless legs, curving spines, and hooves. Big steerite heads shone here and there, looking off in all directions.

'Hi, Chuck,' I said, picking out the head with the leather mask.

'Moo,' he muttered feebly.

'Here you go,' said the driver, tossing me a coil of rope.

'Thanks.' I looped one end over Chuck's head and mounted Rusty. Since I didn't have a saddle, I wound the rope around his neck once and held the rest of it. Then I rode over to one side, pulling Chuck from the pile with a series of clanks and a thud onto the ground.

I looked back at him. He was a heap of machinery now, without much in the way of flesh on him at all. It was the same condition I had left him in back at the Femur stable. I kicked Rusty and dragged Chuck up the trail to relieve Smellin' at the lookout.

Chuck spat out dust and pine needles as I dragged him along.

'Sorry about the rough trip,' I said. 'It's the only way to get you over here. And I don't trust all those people down there to leave you alone.'

He whimpered as I hauled him over a big rock.

'Besides, up here you'll get plenty of sunlight in the morning for your solar collectors.'

His head clanked against a protruding root and his horns stuck for a moment. Rusty pulled harder and yanked him free. 'When you can graze, I'll find some grass too, though these mountains don't offer much along that line.'

'Hey,' Smellin' yelled from above us. 'What's all that racket down there, anyhow?'

'It's me, Louie. I got my steerite back.'

'Oh. Good. I can go to bed, then.'

I hauled Chuck over to the lookout and shook the loop off him. 'Here. Give the driver back his rope for me, will you?' I was getting braver every minute.

'Keep it.' Smellin' waved a hand at me in dismissal as he mounted up. 'Practically everything here is stolen, anyway. It belongs to whoever has it.' He rode back down for the bunkhouse.

I let out a breath of relief and looked at the bundle of Chuck lying next to me, 'Well, Chuck, welcome to Hawk Nest, the hideout of the outlaws.'

Chuck sighed and closed his eyes.

He wouldn't even start to be himself again for some time.

Still, I was glad to have the company. I sat back against my favourite tree and coiled the rope.

I dozed occasionally the rest of the night, but no one else arrived at Hawk Nest. When the sun came up over the mountains, filtering light through the trees, I blinked awake. Light was reaching Chuck, which was about all I could ask.

'Chuck?' I said. 'I figure you'll be safer here, away from everyone else, than you would be down in the camp or with the other steerites.'

He opened one eye and looked at me. 'Moo?'

'Up here, no one is likely to see you until I come back up for night duty again.'

'Okay,' he whispered, closing his eyes.

'What about the other guys – Lugosi and ST 10096 and that bunch? Did they come in on the wagon, too?'

'No,' he muttered. 'They got away. The fellows on

204

the wagon are other members of the two herds we freed.'

I rode down to Choy Susan's just in time to stagger inside for breakfast. She had just opened up. Most of the other guys were still asleep.

Choy Susan put a tally by my name as I collapsed into a chair. Then she went into the back. My eyes stung so much that I could hardly keep them open.

'Good morning, Louis.'

I looked around for a moment without seeing anyone. Then I spied Tinny Ginnie sitting alone all the way across the room. She was just as neatly dressed as before, looking scrubbed and fresh.

'Oh! Uh, morning.'

'You look tired. My, did you draw a night duty by any chance?'

'That's right.' I smiled weakly, weaving a little in my chair. 'I'm all right.'

'My goodness. Are you on duty tonight, too?'

'Yeah. I'm the new guy. Besides, I don't mind sleeping all day.'

'Would you consider joining me at my table for breakfast? It's not ladylike for me to shout across the room this way.'

She wasn't shouting. In fact, I could hardly hear her. Still, I got up and walked unevenly to her table. I only bumped into three chairs and two tables on the way.

'Thank you.' She waited for Choy Susan to set our breakfasts down and walk away again. Then she let out a deep sigh. 'Louis, would you consider helping a lady in need?'

'Why, sure,' I declared enthusiastically. 'I'd be happy—'

'Shh.' She looked over my shoulder furtively.

'Huh?'

'This is not for everyone's ears.'

'Oh.'

'Louis, I have come to believe that Hawk Nest does not offer the proper life that I should be leading. Do you understand?'

I nodded. She did seem out of place.

'The town of Washout is not far. From there, a lady might even find her way to civilization. But first she would have to get there.' She sighed heavily.

'I've never been there,' I said apologetically. 'Otherwise, I'd be glad to help.' I still figured Washout would be a better place for me than Hawk Nest.

'Well, my goodness, I can find Washout,' she said, leaning forward. 'But would the outlaws let me leave easily? They can be very suspicious, you know.'

'How about leaving at night?' I whispered. 'I'm alone on night duty. We could just take off after everybody is asleep.'

'My, how exciting. *Would* you?' She clasped her hands together hopefully.

'Sure.' I suddenly felt very protective. 'I'll get a good night's . . . that is, a good day's sleep today.' I blinked my stinging eyes.

'I have many belongings in my cabin,' she said thoughtfully. 'I will pack in secret today.'

'It's a deal.'

She looked over my shoulder again and extended her hand. It was small and warm and firm when we shook on the plan.

After breakfast, I wove a crooked path to the bunkhouse. Climbing up to my top bunk took longer than it should have, but at least nobody threw me over it this time. I fell asleep fully dressed.

I awoke when the daylight was fading through the windows and open doorway. A couple of guys were napping on bunks. I slid to the floor and ran for the latrine.

By the time I got to the well, I had figured out that it was dinnertime. I splashed some cold water on my face and went into Choy Susan's. The place was crowded, but I found an empty chair next to Smellin' and Carver.

Only when Choy Susan tallied me and dropped a steak platter in front of me did I remember Chuck.

I looked around for Tinny Ginnie. She was all the way across the room in the same seat she had taken this morning. Tether Chen was sitting with her.

'Something wrong, sleepyhead?' Smellin' demanded with his mouth full.

'Huh? No, no,' I dug into my dinner, taking glances at Tinny Ginnie when Smellin' and Carver weren't looking.

'You still got night duty,' said Carver, sawing at his steak with one of his Swissarmie blades.

'Right,' I said.

'You don't mind?' Smellin' stopped to look up at me.

I shrugged. 'Just doing my part.'

He grinned at Carver and returned to his dinner.

I kept an eye on Tinny Ginnie, hoping to finish when she did. She was too far ahead of me, though. Besides, Tether followed her out. I would have to talk to her later.

Smellin' and Carver both glanced up in surprise when I finished eating and jumped up again. I hurried outside into the darkness. Lights were on inside Tinny Ginnie's cabin, so I headed that way.

Halfway there, I stopped. If Tether was calling on her, I didn't want to interrupt him. I looked around to make sure no one was watching and skipped around to the back of the cabin.

She had two windows in the back, both covered with those checked blue-and-white curtains. The curtains were drawn but one curtain had caught on a little white porcelain angel sitting on the sill. I crept up to the open space and peeked inside.

I could see all the way to the front door, where she was just saying good-bye to Tether. She hadn't packed anything I could see. Once she had closed the door, I tapped on the window.

She looked around, puzzled, until I tapped again. Then she came over and pulled up the window.

'Louis? What are you doing here?'

'It's Chuck, my steerite. I can't leave him here.'

'Your steerite?'

'Look, suppose we wait a few days. He'll be able to walk again before long. Besides, you haven't packed or anything.'

'Lower your voice, Louis,' she said sternly. She sounded like a schoolmarm. 'I fear we must leave tonight. I have told Tether that I am going to bed soon. Instead, I will pack my belongings and meet you at midnight.'

She lowered the window.

'Wait—' I stuck my hand out and she closed the window on it. I flinched in pain, grinding my teeth, trying not to make any noise.

When the window didn't close all the way, she leaned on it. I banged on the glass with my other hand and she raised the window again.

'Well, now, really,' she said wearily. 'Now what's the matter?'

'I won't leave without my steerite.' I massaged my sore hand.

She thought a moment. 'Where is he?'

'Uh, well, I'll have him with me.'

'All right.' She nodded. 'I'll think about it.' Then she slammed the window shut.

# Eighteen

I grabbed up my pack in the bunkhouse and threw the rope into it. Then I got Rusty and rode up to the lookout as fast as I could. On the winding trail, even Rusty stumbled in the darkness a few times on rocks and holes at that speed. Then I slid off and crashed through branches and bushes, peering around in the darkness.

'Hey, Chuck. Where are you? Can you talk?'

'Huh?' he whimpered.

'Come on, Chuck. It's Louie.'

'Over here.'

I sat down next to him under a tall pine. He was still skinny, lying in a tangled heap. 'We're leaving tonight.'

'What?'

'We're getting out of here. We're finally going to Washout.'

'But I can't walk yet.' He sighed. 'The sunlight today helped me some and I've been grazing. These mountains aren't that good for cattle.'

'I've got a friend who's going to think of something.'

'Really?'

'Well, that's what she said.'

'Oh.' He settled back to rest.

Now that I thought about it, that comment of hers wasn't much reassurance. Still, I was determined not to leave without Chuck. If Tinny Ginnie couldn't think of a way to bring him, I would stay until he could walk.

I sat with Chuck in silence. Sometimes he pulled up something to eat but mostly he just lay there. After several hours, I heard hoofbeats approaching from the outside.

My heart pounded. I didn't want to challenge anybody. Still, if I didn't, Smellin' or somebody might come up to find out why I hadn't.

'Who's there?' I said weakly. I couldn't see him and didn't move to a spot where anyone else could see me.

Nobody answered.

I cleared my throat. 'Hey,' I called, still not very loudly.

The hoofbeats stopped. 'Somebody say something?' a man yelled.

'Yeah,' I shouted back, relieved that he was alone. 'What's the password?'

'Here's the password.' Several gunshots rang out, hitting in the trees over my head.

I threw myself down next to Chuck. The hoofbeats galloped past into Hawk Nest. He went on firing all the way down the slope, for good measure. At least by the time he arrived at Choy Susan's place, the other guys would know I wasn't the one shooting.

So much for guarding Hawk Nest. Anyway, he didn't sound like a lawman to me. He sounded like he belonged there. 'You may pass,' I shouted after him, sitting up.

As the night wore on, I worried that someone would approach Hawk Nest when Tinny Ginnie came sneaking up here. She might be right about these outlaws not wanting a long-time resident to leave. With that worry, at least, I had no trouble staying wide awake tonight.

Finally, I heard slow hoofbeats and the creaking of a wagon from the Hawk Nest side. It sounded like the same wagon that had brought in Chuck and the steerites. I waited until I could make out Tinny Ginnie's silhouette in the dim light before I spoke up.

'I'm over here,' I said quietly, standing up.

'Well, hurry it up, Louis,' she snapped, not sounding at all like she had earlier. She jumped to the ground, even in her long dress. 'Where's your steerite?'

'Here.' I pointed. 'Isn't that the wagon that came in yesterday?'

'I bought it from Choy Susan. Now mount up and don't waste any time.'

'Okay.' I mounted Rusty and waited.

In the poor moonlight and starlight through the trees, I could see her grab Chuck's metal spine behind his head in one hand and in front of his tail in the other. Then she lifted what was easily two hundred pounds of him and threw him into the back of the wagon with several trunks and packing crates. He landed with a heavy thump and assorted clanks. I stared at her, remembering that her specials, whatever they were, had not been visible.

She climbed up into the wagon seat, primly holding her skirts out of the way. 'Quietly, now, Louis. Stealth before haste.' She shook the reins at the two horsites pulling the wagon and moved out.

I nudged Rusty and followed just as slowly.

Once we had put some distance behind us, she sped up a little, but the wagon wouldn't go very fast on the mountain road. After several hours, she brought the wagon to a halt. I rode up alongside her.

'I believe it is time for a break,' she said pleasantly. 'If you will build a small fire, Louis, I will make some coffee. I packed sandwiches in a box in the back of the wagon.'

'Sure.' I wasn't about to argue after seeing her throw Chuck around.

When I had the fire going by the side of the trail, we sat down and waited for the water to boil. The fire was small and would not be visible very far. She set out a couple of metal cups and the box of sandwiches.

'Louis, have you ever been to San Francisco?'

'No. I haven't been anywhere, hardly. Except for leaving home for Femur and winding up here.'

'I was thinking. Perhaps that is where a lady should seek proper society.'

'I thought we were going to Washout.'

'Washout is only a little better than Hawk Nest,' she said haughtily. 'It is a wide-open town of gamblers and brawlers and outlaws. Don't you think a lady belongs in a city?'

'I guess so.' I also guessed she could handle herself in a brawl, if it came to that. 'I think I'll take a look at Chuck.'

'Why?'

'Uh – to see if he'll make the trip to San Francisco.'

She nodded and lifted the lid on the coffeepot to peek inside.

I pulled up some grass on the way to the back of the wagon. 'Hey, Chuck,' I whispered. 'Here.'

He poked around with his nose until he found the grass. Then he munched on it eagerly.

'This lady is a little stranger than I thought,' I told him. I climbed up next to him so I could lower my voice. 'She picked you up all by herself.'

'No kidding,' he muttered with his mouth full. 'She wasn't too particular about the way I landed, either.'

'Well, now she doesn't want to go to Washout any more. But I don't know what I would do with you in

212

a city, do you?' Just then, at the last second, I noticed the footsteps coming up behind me.

'Louis!' Tinny Ginnie shouted, right alongside the wagon. 'Get away from those crates!'

Before I could turn, I felt hands grab the back of my neck and the back of my belt. I was jerked up into the air and released to sail a short distance in the darkness. Then I slammed onto the hard soil and rocks of the road. The wind was knocked out of me.

A moment later, a heavy thump and clanks sounded nearby. I was still catching my breath when I heard her throw some small items into the back of the wagon and drive off in a clatter of hoofbeats and a squealing of squeaks.

'It was a nice ride while it lasted,' Chuck said presently, from where he lay near me.

I was still lying flat on my back, watching tiny stars, wondering which ones were real. 'You know,' I said slowly. 'I was told, a long time ago, that Duke's gang was going to divide up the stolen loot in Washout.'

'Yes?'

'Right now, I guess the gang is still gathering little by little.'

'It would seem so.'

'So, where has the loot been kept in the meantime?'

'In Washout?'

'How about in an outlaw hideout?' I suggested. 'Where it would be safe because there's a lookout on duty every night who would sound an alarm if someone tried to run away with it.'

'That's a reasonable plan.'

'So if someone wanted to steal it all, the best way to get out of Hawk Nest secretly would be to bring the lookout in on the theft.' I struggled to sit up.

'Especially if that someone had stolen a team and a wagon to haul it away on.'

'What does this have to do with going to Washout?'

'Well,' I said, standing up. 'Dawn is just a few hours away. And when it arrives, some very angry outlaws are going to have a real grudge against the lookout who let the someone get away.'

'Oh,' said Chuck thoughtfully.

'And his steerite.'

'Oh?' He clanked a little as he raised his head. 'You mean . . .'

'And you can't walk.'

'*Oh.*'

For a moment, I straightened my clothes and checked for injuries. I found plenty, some older than others, but none of them were serious. I took off my pack and pulled the rope out.

'What's that for?' Chuck asked, alarmed.

'I don't know if this will work or not, but I'll try it.'

'Try what?' he whined.

'Don't give up yet.' I pulled the rope out of my pack. 'Can you stand up at all?'

'No, I can't.' He sniffled.

The hard part was getting Rusty to lie down. I didn't know if it was his programming, but I pushed and pulled and yanked in various places. Finally, I found that if I pushed gently straight down on his nose, he would first lower his head and then lie down.

I also had to work mostly by feel in the darkness. Still, I managed to lash Chuck's neck to Rusty's, and his skinny little body to Rusty's, all the way down the length of their torsos. Then I had to figure out how to make Rusty stand. That was accomplished by sticking a thumb and finger in his nose and pulling up.

Chuck rose up with him.

'Whoa – ho *ho*,' said Chuck, as he was lifted off the ground. 'Zowie.' He swung his four hooves around a little, dangling off the ground.

'Hold still, everybody.' I mounted up and waited gingerly to see if Rusty would fall over. He didn't, but he was listing somewhat to the right from Chuck's weight.

I kicked Rusty gently and he started to walk.

Chuck was still with us. He slipped a little, though, and had to bend his legs to keep his hooves from dragging.

I sighed with relief and kept going.

The sky was turning light now. Any minute, Choy Susan would wake up and find her wagon gone; I didn't believe for a second that Tinny Ginnie had bought it from her. At that point, she or someone else would check for those crates and then sound the alarm.

'Are we on our way to the fabled town of Washout now?' Chuck asked.

'Well . . . this trail must lead somewhere.' That was the closest I could come to finding Washout.

'Why are we going to Washout if all the outlaws are meeting there? Aren't we running away from them now?'

'Well . . . yeah,' I said slowly. 'But we can't get the loot away from Tinny Ginnie alone. My best chance of getting the outlaws off our backs is to meet Duke in Washout and explain. He'll never believe me if we just run away.'

'Why don't we wait for the outlaws here and explain?'

'*No!* That is, uh – well, Duke won't be with them and I'm afraid the others will be a little hotheaded. They might just string me up first, butcher you again and ask questions afterwards.'

'Oh, my. Will Duke believe you if we go to Washout?'

'Sure,' I said weakly. 'Come on, we'd better go.'

Rusty couldn't walk very fast hauling Chuck with him, but even the angry outlaws behind us couldn't ride much faster on these uneven, twisting mountain roads and paths. All we could do was keep going. As the sun rose, I began to wish I had eaten one of those sandwiches before I had gone to see Chuck in the back of the wagon.

We came around a bend and saw the unhitched wagon sitting by the side of the road. It was empty. Since both horsites were gone, I figured Tinny Ginnie had packed her trunks and crates of stolen loot on one and was riding the other, skirts and all. The only reason she had taken the wagon was my insistence that we take Chuck with us.

Chuck livened up from the sunlight hitting his solar panels. Pretty soon he had extended his legs and was sort of walking his hooves lightly along the road, though he still didn't put any weight on them. Shortly after that, he started singing again.

*'Oh, roast me not . . .'*

I clenched my teeth and tried not to listen.

I looked at the forested slopes we passed, wondering if we could hide somewhere. The wagon tracks were plain on the road, and we hadn't reached even one fork, so our pursuers would eventually catch up to us. I doubted I could convince a bunch of angry outlaws that I had been duped, at least not in the heat of the moment. If I could get to Washout, at least I might get lost in the crowd until they cooled off enough to listen to reason. More important, maybe Hong would be there.

As we plodded on, I kept looking back over my

shoulder. I didn't see anything, but I knew they would be coming. The sun rose higher.

'Chuck, look straight ahead.' Excitedly, I sat up a little. 'Is that a fork in the road up there?'

'Where?' He strained a little in the rope holding him up against Rusty.

'It is.' I looked behind us again to make sure no one was in sight. 'We might luck out here yet.'

'What do you mean?'

'As soon as we see which way her tracks go, we'll go the other way.'

'The outlaws will follow us anyway,' he whined. 'I just know it.'

'Maybe,' I said slowly. 'But if they think about it, they'll realize that only two people are missing from Hawk Nest. So the rider leading the second horse is the one with the loot.' I didn't mention that the outlaws might not be in a mood to stop and think it over.

Chuck stopped singing, at least, while he considered this.

I pulled up at the split in the mountain trail. One branch went on roughly west. Tinny Ginnie's two sets of horsite tracks followed it, I supposed towards San Francisco. The other branch, a less-travelled narrow one, wound north.

'North it is,' I said cheerfully. We took that branch and I relaxed a little. This winding path took us out of sight from the last trail quickly.

'Can I graze?' Chuck asked.

'Here?' I looked around.

'Yeah. There's some grass and stuff over on the right.'

'Well, we don't want to waste time.'

'I'm feeling much better from the sun now,' he said modestly. 'If I could eat for a little while, maybe tomorrow I could stand up.'

217

I thought about it. Now that the sun was up, I was ready to sleep. Nobody was in sight behind us. 'Let's go this way.'

I waited until Rusty had some rocks to step on and rode away from the trail through the trees, ducking my head under branches. The grazing that Chuck had seen was too close to the trail, but I found some more that was out of sight from anyone passing by.

'Help yourself,' I said, pulling up and dismounting. 'I'm going to sleep. Just don't make any noise, especially if you hear anyone nearby.'

'Check,' said Chuck, eyeing the patch of grasses just below his reach.

I didn't dare untie him; we just might want to make a fast getaway, or at least as fast as we could. Instead, I got Rusty to lie down in the same grass and weeds so Chuck could reach them. I paced around nervously, listening for hoofbeats and looking for a place to lie down.

'What's the matter?' Chuck asked, munching away.

'I hope this path goes to Washout. But if it doesn't, I wonder where we're actually going.'

'One way to find out,' said Chuck.

'Yeah.' I stretched out on a springy bed of old pine needles and tossed away a small cone. 'Anywhere would be better than Hawk Nest at this point, anyhow.'

I dozed off to the sound of Chuck chewing away next to me.

Cold woke me up. I shivered, turned over, and felt another sharp jab in my side. By the time I had thrown aside another pine cone, I remembered where I was.

The sky was still light, but we were lying in shadows. Chuck was fast asleep and breathing heavily as his specialized metabolism strove to build his health back up to a point of self-sufficiency. Rusty, of course, still lay patiently where I had left him, his head in profile to me.

'Hey, Chuck.' When he didn't move, I prodded him with my foot.

'Moo,' he whispered in his sleep, turning his head the other way.

'Come on, Chuck. It's time to go.' I poked him some more with the front of my moccasin.

'Alors,' he muttered. 'Stampede for your lives.'

I knelt down and patted him on his masked head. 'Chuck, wake up.'

He jerked all over, suddenly, and opened his eyes. Then he relaxed. 'Oh . . . I guess I was dreaming.'

'We ought to get going.'

'Ah. Yes, of course.' He yawned. 'Well, all right. Anytime you're ready.'

I had Rusty get up. Chuck came up with him, still tied securely. I mounted. 'You feeling any better?'

'Considerably, thank you.'

'Can you walk yet?'

'Maybe. But I wouldn't get very far.'

'I thought it was kind of soon.' I got Rusty back on the trail, and we went on our way north.

Several hours had passed when Chuck lifted his head and looked forward, his ears twitching.

'Hark,' he said. 'I hear something up ahead.'

'Something? What kind of something?' I asked softly.

'People, I would say. Even music.'

'You don't mean another singing steerite, do you?'

'Certainly not,' he said haughtily. 'I believe I hear a piano.'

'A piano?'

Over the next rise in the trail, I saw our

destination. Below us, in a little valley, the light from windows lined the streets of a small town. It was a lot bigger than Femur, which wasn't saying much. Now I could hear a lively tune plinked on a piano and sometimes distant laughter.

'Is this our long-sought Washout?' Chuck inquired politely.

'I don't know if it's Washout or not,' I said. 'But right now, it's definitely our destination.' I kicked Rusty and we started down the winding trail towards it.

By the time we reached the edge of town, I was getting real jumpy. I rode around behind some wooden warehouse or something that was locked up for the night. 'Chuck,' I said quietly. 'We can't go into town like this. We'll get laughed at.'

'We get laughed at anyway,' said Chuck. 'But what are you talking about?'

I got off Rusty. 'I have to untie you.' I pulled the knots free. As the ropes loosened around Rusty, Chuck sagged to the ground in a tangle of loops. He lay there, moving around feebly as I pulled up the rope and coiled it.

'Can you stand up?' I grabbed him around the middle and tried to lift. He was too heavy. Then I got down on the ground and pushed his hooves around in the right positions. His legs were so skinny and flexible that they hadn't really been under him. 'Now push.'

He slowly straightened, wobbling and shuffling his feet for balance. Then he swayed a couple of times. 'Whoa. Hoo-hoo.' His eyes widened as he swayed back and forth.

'That way,' I said, pointing. 'Lean against the wall if you have to.'

He leaned over and thudded against the wooden wall. 'Whew. Say, I'm still up.'

'Can you walk?'

'I wouldn't dare.' He giggled. 'I'm dizzy. Ooh, this feels weird.'

'Well, I'm going to go look around,' I said uncomfortably. 'See if I can find places to stay.'

'I'll wait right here for you.' He giggled some more and slid down the wall a little bit. 'You're spinning around and around and around . . .'

'Right.' I mounted Rusty and rode off towards the sound of the piano.

# Nineteen

The town had three parallel streets but only the middle one had signs of life at this hour. I rode close to the dark boardwalk on one side towards the lights ahead, passing some little shops. They were all closed. The music got louder.

Ahead of me, a couple of weirdly shaped guys staggered drunkenly out of the swinging saloon doors, laughing and pushing and shoving each other. I stopped, not wanting them to see me. They zigzagged away from me into shadows.

A wooden porch roof ran the length of the boardwalk. A sign swinging from it over the door said 'Silver Transistor Saloon' in blocky letters with curlicues on the ends. I got off Rusty and crept up to the windows of the saloon to peek inside. The place was about half full of guys playing cards and lounging around the bar.

Some of the other buildings up and down the street had lamps in the windows. Most of them were on the second floor where people lived over the storefronts. The saloon was the only establishment that was open to the public at this hour. If I was going to find shelter for the night, I would have to speak to someone here.

I held my breath and pushed open the swinging doors, then ducked inside, looking around. No one seemed to notice me. I let out my breath and sidled up to the bar.

'Yeah?' The bartender was a big, heavy guy with a low, rumbling voice.

'Uh – I need a place to stay for my steerite and me. I was wondering if—'

'You want a drink or not?' he demanded.

'Sure. Anything cheap.' I fumbled around for my newbits.

A moment later, he slammed down a mug of beer, slopping some of it onto the bar. 'One newbit.'

I dropped four of them onto the bar with little clinks.

He wiped the bar and swept them up with his cloth in one clean motion. Then he looked around the room for somebody. 'Go see the guy sitting alone in the back, there. He's Grudge, the smith.'

'Thanks.' I left the mug where it was and carefully walked around all the tables where people were sitting. I didn't want to chance annoying any of them.

Grudge was only a little taller than I was and almost as thin. His face and long-sleeved shirt were all sweaty and dirty, though, and he smelled of smoke.

'Excuse me,' I said. 'Mr Grudge?'

'Huh?' He scowled at me.

'I'm Louie Hong and I'm looking for a place to spend the night for my steerite and me. The bartender told me to—'

'You need a place, huh?' he snarled.

'Uh, yessir.'

He nodded and sipped his drink. 'You willing to work for your keep?'

'I even have a little money to pay my way.'

'That ain't what I asked you, boy.' He leaned forward and glared at me. 'I need help, not money. I'll ask you one more time. You willing to work for your keep?'

223

'Sure! I could use a real job.' I grinned. This was even better than I had expected.

'All right, then. You and your steerite can sleep in my horsite stall behind the smithy. In exchange, you work the bellows when I'm hammering. And to make sure you stick a while, you'll buy your own bellows.'

'Buy my own?'

'Take it or leave it.' He turned back to his drink again.

'Do we get to sleep in your place tonight?'

He shrugged. 'Sure, why not?'

'Okay. I'll take it.'

He nodded and downed his drink. 'Come on, then.' He got up and trudged out of the saloon with a weary walk as I followed him out.

The smithy was across the street from the warehouse where I had left Rusty and Chuck. Grudge unlocked his stable, which had two stalls and only one horsite. Then he went to bed in a little lean-to room.

I left Rusty there and trotted across the street. Chuck was still leaning on his spindly legs against the back of the warehouse.

'Hi-ho,' he said cheerfully. 'I'm still dizzy. Dizzy in a tizzy. I judge it is a reaction from insufficient blood volume for the exertion of standing up.' He giggled. 'Whoo-ee. Ooh-la-la. Kalamazoo.'

'Can you walk across the street? It isn't very far.'

'I doubt it. Let's find out.' He straightened up and then swayed back and forth a few times. 'Aha. Still standing, are we?'

'So far,' I said, backing up. I didn't want a giddy steerite falling on me.

He took a few steps on wobbling legs. Then he took a few more.

'This way,' I said, backing up.

He followed me slowly, quivering all the way. Step by step, he managed to stay upright. Once we got inside the empty stall, he giggled one more time and sank slowly into a tangled heap again.

That was enough effort for tonight. I curled up next to him and went to sleep.

A loud creak and bright sunlight woke me up.

'What's wrong with you, boy?' Grudge demanded. 'You got to bar the door at night.'

'Huh?' I rolled over and sat up.

'This here crossbar. You bar the door at night from the inside.'

'Oh. Yeah.'

'That's your steerite, is he?'

'Pleased to meet you,' said Chuck politely.

'Why has he got a bag on his head?'

'He likes it.'

'Looks a mite too warm to me. Well, anyhow, he don't look so good. Better get him out in the sun and the grass behind the building.'

'Okay.'

'Then get out front to the smithy. We got a fire to build up.'

The sun was just barely up. Chuck wobbled out on his shaky legs, now more sleepy than giggly. As soon as he reached the grass and brush behind the smithy, he collapsed into it with a sigh and began to feed.

I walked around to the front, rubbing my hands in the cold air. The smithy had a high, slanting roof but no side or front walls, so it was open to the street. The forge and anvil were in the middle but Grudge was sitting on a three-legged stool by a stone fireplace set into the back wall. A pot of water was hanging over the fire.

'Let's see you get the forge going,' he growled. 'See

those new bellows hanging on the wall? I'll take them out of your pay.'

That was fine, since he hadn't mentioned any pay before. I took down the bellows and moved aside an older set lying with its point in the forge. The bellows were easy to work, and soon the coals from the day before were glowing brightly. I tossed in some wood and the fire roared up.

'You'll do,' Grudge muttered.

Breakfast was some kind of hot cereal mush. I sat down on the ground by the fireplace to eat.

'So,' I said airily. 'What town is this, anyway?'

'This here's Washout, boy. What of it?'

'Thought it might be,' I said eagerly. 'What's it like?'

'What's it like? It's like any town around here. Miners, drifters, drovers.'

'How about outlaws?'

'Sure, outlaws. Now, your leading citizen here in town is Cicero Yang, the gambler. He hangs out in the saloon. Owns it, in fact.'

'And it attracts a lot of outlaws.'

'They like cards, some of them.' He set his bowl down and moved to the anvil. There he scowled at his hammer and tongs. 'Work, work, work. Hurry up and eat, will you?'

I hurried up and ate. Then I sat down on a log by the forge. Working the bellows was easy; I just had to start when he told me and stop when he told me. I kept an eye on the street as people passed by, looking for a familiar face, but I didn't see any.

Grudge had let a straight bar of black metal sit in the coals for a while. He pulled it out with the tongs and put it on the anvil. I quit bellowing and looked up.

The hammer he raised with his skinny arm was immense. He smashed the glowing metal bar with it twice and lifted it up to look. It was now in the shape of a horseshoe. He tossed it into a bucket of water and put another straight bar into the fire.

I stared at his scrawny body in amazement. He must have had the same specials as Tinny Ginnie, all totally unfamiliar to me. I decided never to argue with him.

We spent the morning that way. He was stocking up on horseshoe sets that would need only a little tailoring to individual hooves – which were themselves stainless steel. Old ones, though, especially needed the extra protection.

'You ain't bad, Louie,' he said finally, dropping his hammer on the ground. 'Tell you what. I'm taking the price of those purple bellows out of your pay, but you keep up this good for a week, I'll buy them back from you. Deal?'

'Sure!'

'We'll take a break now. Fact is, I'm not expecting anybody nohow. Check back with me when you feel like it or if somebody's here. Now go see to that steerite of yours.'

'Thanks.' I scampered around the corner to visit Chuck. He looked up from where he lay in the noon sunlight, munching grass.

'Chuck? Getting enough to eat?'

'Indubitably. With this excellent mountain sunlight, I can even walk.'

'I'm glad to hear it. You just relax for now.'

'That is still welcome advice, I assure you.'

I walked away grinning to myself. The better he felt, the more high-falutin' his speech became.

I walked up the street, looking around. The shops were open now, and a few people wandered the boardwalks here and there. I set out for the saloon, the centre of society in any town out here.

Only a few people were inside. I entered carefully, looking around.

'You again,' said the bartender. 'You looking for another job already?'

'I am on break,' I said proudly.

'Isomer Isaac,' said a man seated at a table. 'Will you introduce us, please?'

'Don't know him,' said the bartender. 'He just came in here last night looking for work and Grudge took him on.'

'Come here, fellow.'

I walked forward, suddenly blinking in surprise. The man who had spoken to me was drinking and playing cards with Harris Nye. Harris was wearing his tan frock coat with the yoked shoulders and matching hat that I had seen before, but now also deeply polished brown boots and a white shirt with a black bow tie. I could just see the buckle of his gunbelt as I approached the table. He was sweating heavily but managed a weak smile at me.

Harris had a few newbits and some poker chips on the table in front of him. The other guy had several high stacks of chips. Harris did not offer any conversation.

'I am Cicero Yang,' said the man across from him. 'The bartender is Isomer Isaac Phlegm, and my opponent in this game of blackjack is Harris Nye. To whom am I speaking?'

'I'm Louie Hong,' I said, looking him over.

Cicero Yang was stocky, brash, and brass-plated. He wore a gold silk vest embroidered with royal blue dragons that shimmered in the light. He was in white shirtsleeves; his coat was hanging on the back of his chair. His smile, embellished by shiny cheap nephrite and blinking red beads, was like a faulty strobe light. His grey gambler's hat was pulled down

228

low over his brass forehead and cascades of slightly wavy black hair flowed onto his shoulders. He stuck a no-smoke chawcite cigar between his teeth.

'Want to make a few newbits?' he asked.

'Could be,' I said cautiously.

'I shall be leaving town soon, possibly this evening and possibly tomorrow. I will give you one newbit to polish my boots and one newbit for polishing the buckles and doing it all right now while I play cards.'

'Oh. Well, I would, but I don't have any—'

'Here,' rumbled Isomer Isaac Phlegm. He thumped a wooden box onto the bar.

By the time I brought it back, Cicero was dealing again. Harris was even paler than usual. I sat down on the floor and started polishing Cicero's black boots.

From the tone of the quiet conversation, I could tell that Harris wasn't doing any better. When I had new polish on both boots, I took a moment to let it dry. I stood up to stretch my legs and looked around the empty saloon. I glanced at a painting hanging on the wall, looked past it, and then returned to it.

In the glass over the painting, I could see every card that was face down on the table in front of Harris as he lifted the corners to peek at them. They were reversed, though. I looked around some more and realized that this glass did not reflect his hand directly. It picked up the image from another painting on a different wall, which in turn reflected the image on the curved surface of a large, polished silver bowl on a pedestal. The bowl picked up Harris's cards from an angle. None of the reflecting surfaces was right behind Harris where people would notice it.

'Twenty-two,' Cicero said pleasantly through the cigar in his teeth. 'You're busted again. Too bad.'

I ducked down quick and started polishing real hard, like I hadn't noticed anything. Above me, Cicero was dealing again.

The swinging doors squeaked and quick, hard footsteps tapped on the wooden floor. When I looked around, I saw pointed, high-top shoes and the hem of Eulalie's lavender print dress. She walked right up to the table.

I kept my head down and went on polishing.

'Are you Cicero Yang, the proprietor of this establishment?' Eulalie asked.

'I am,' said Cicero. 'And you are. . . ?'

'I am in search of employment here.'

Cicero was quiet a moment. 'Mr Nye, would you excuse me? I have business to discuss with this lady.'

'Of course,' Harris whimpered. He got up and wove unsteadily to the bar, though he hadn't had a glass in front of him while he had played.

Cicero slid his chair back and stood, casually dropping my newbits to clatter on the floor. 'My office is upstairs.' He drew his coat from the back of his chair and they walked away.

I pocketed the extra coins, packed up the shoebox, and carried it to the bar.

Harris was pouring a shot of something brown from a bottle. He swallowed it, wheezed and coughed for a while, and then downed another. Then he squinted at me.

'Hi, Louie. I guess you know your way around a town like this, huh?'

'I've never been here before.'

'Yeah, but . . . I bet you wouldn't get into a card game with Cicero Yang.'

'Well, that's true.' I decided not to tell him about the reflections. He just might get into more trouble.

He sighed and poured another drink.

I heard the doors creak again and some heavy footsteps clomping up behind me. Before I could turn around, though, several hands grabbed me and yanked me high into the air from behind. I couldn't see who they were, as they held me up spread-eagled.

'Well, well,' said Smellin' Llewellyn in a loud voice. 'Look what I found.'

'You got some explaining to do,' said Carver Dalton.

I heard some clicks as he opened a couple of his blades.

'Where is it, fob?' Tether Chen demanded. 'And where is she?'

The high, beamed ceiling was whirling around over me as they held me up. One large, elaborate cloud-crystal chandelier was suspended from the centre of it. I wobbled and sagged as they shifted their grips and waved me around.

'She took the other fork in the road,' I gasped. 'The one going west. And she took all the – all the crates.'

'That's what I thought,' Smellin' said to the other two.

'That's what we get for letting in a control-natural,' muttered Carver. 'It figures. Let him go.'

Suddenly all the hands released me. I slammed onto the wooden floor on my back, banging my head. When I looked up, three chandeliers swayed above me, all of them out of focus.

Smellin' and Carver leaned on the bar. Tether paused to kick me once in the ribs with a pointed boot before joining them. Harris was taking a long draught directly from his bottle, paying no attention to anyone else.

'You mean,' Isomer Isaac Phlegm rumbled, 'I sent a *control-natural* to work for Grudge the smith?'

'Looks that way, Isomer Isaac,' said Smellin'.

'I hope he doesn't find out. That guy sure can hold a—'

'Duke's due in town tonight,' Carver said sternly, gazing down at me. 'You better be clean, Louie. He's already heard the loot's missing.'

'Tonight was to be the time we divvied up,' added Smellin'.

'Personally, I never heard a word of any of this,' said Isomer Isaac Phlegm. 'You guys want a drink or what?'

'Three Missouri mules,' said Smellin'. 'Hold the lehews.'

The bartender nodded and moved away.

'You know,' said Carver, with exaggerated lightness, 'I was in town back in Wichita when the vigilance committee hosted a necktie party for Isotope John.'

'Yeah,' said Smellin' thoughtfully. 'After that, he put in a slinky spring as a precaution against backlash.'

'Control-naturals can't do that,' added Tether.

I rolled over and got up, wheezing a little. 'I've got to go back to work,' I muttered, and staggered out the doors.

# Twenty

By the time I got back to the smithy, my head had cleared somewhat. I was still worried about convincing Duke that I hadn't stolen the Femur loot, but I figured he would take the word of Smellin' and Carver into account. Grudge was gone when I arrived, but another guy was standing around.

'Can I help you?' I asked politely.

He was a tall, heavy cowboy in a purple cowboy hat who frowned down on me as he swayed from one caterpillar tread to the other. 'Who're you?'

'I'm Louie Hong. As of today, I work for Grudge,' I grinned proudly.

'When's he coming back?'

'He didn't tell me.'

'I'll wait.' He paced around a little and then went to lean in the back corner of the smithy, out of the way.

'This here's my first job in town,' I said casually, tossing a few stray horsite shoes back into the pile.

First he ignored me, looking off down the street in both directions. Then he glanced down at me, straightening the point of his purple hat.

'New in town, eh? What do you think of my brand-new four-gallon Stetside purple hat?'

'Very fine,' I said. It was clean felt with a ring of ventilation holes just over the leather hatband.

'Grudge makes new apprentices buy their bellows, doesn't he?'

'Yessir. That's mine there.' I pointed to it.

'Can you lift that anvil?'

'The anvil?'

'I bet you're not strong enough to lift that spare anvil in the corner.'

'Spare anvil?' I took a good look at it. 'Sure I can.'

'I bet I can hold it on my head and still stand up.'

'Huh?'

He grinned. 'I bet if you can lift up that anvil and set it on my head, I can still stand up.'

'Ha. Bet you can't.'

'I'll bet you my hat. Against your bellows.'

'My bellows? What do you want with bellows?'

'Nothing. What do you want with my hat?'

'Nothing. Okay, it's a bet.'

We shook hands on it. 'What's that?' I looked down at his hand.

'This here? Sonny, that's a special wheel-fingered card-dealing hand, mail-order from St. Louis.'

'Oh.' I squatted down, got my hands under the anvil, and stood up. It was heavy, but I managed to walk over to him. Then I had to climb up on a couple of crates to get higher than his head. I set the anvil down gently on top of his hat.

He didn't move. With a slight hissing sound, the anvil slowly sank down, crushing the hat. At the same time, little legs shot out through the ventilation holes in the hat and jammed themselves into the wooden walls of the smithy.

'I'm still standing,' he said with a shrug.

I blinked and hopped back down to the ground. He certainly was, as the legs from his hat fully supported the weight of the anvil. I knew I'd been taken and was too dignified to complain.

He bowed forward and the anvil fell off. I danced out of its way just in time. Then he poked up under the back of his hat and the little legs shot back inside again.

'Hydraulic diffuser,' he said, walking past me. 'Installed in the top of my head.' He snatched up my bellows on the way out and clumped away on his caterpillar tread feet.

I sighed and waited for Grudge to come back. At least I had enough newbits to buy another set of bellows.

We had a little more business that day, but not much. It was just as well, since Grudge seemed to pull one muscle and two springs laughing at my story of the anvil.

'Isotope John tries that with every newcomer,' he told me, clutching at his side springs with a grimace. 'Most of 'em are too smart to go for a sure bet.'

Chuck was still feasting happily and feeling much improved. That night, I led him back into our stall where he wouldn't get rustled, and followed Grudge back up to the Silver Transistor Saloon. It was almost the only place to go at night, except to sleep.

A sizeable crowd had already gathered and people were pouring in. Grudge went right to the bar. I edged along the walls to the stairs. They led up to the second gloor. I settled about halfway up, where I could watch everyone.

At the top of the stairs, a hallway ran along a kind of balcony overlooking the back of the saloon. The railing that ran up the stairs and then along the balcony was made of teak posts inlaid with bits of abalone shell. Then a hallway ran back to private rooms that were built over the storeroom and kitchen on the ground floor.

'You can still find a chair if you want,' said someone.

I looked down. He was a tall, grizzled guy in neat,

snug, worn denim. His brown hair was short, as was his brown-and-grey beard. A Perlavarius violin bow ran along the inside of his right forearm. That kind had a loaded spring that could extend it when he wanted to use it. It was much finer than a Fargo Fiddledee bow.

'This is fine,' I said.

'Name's Hackles,' he said, offering his hand. 'I run a stable in town. Know just about everybody except you.'

'Louie Hong.' I shook with him.

'Thought so. You'd be the apprentice who lost his bellows to Isotope John.'

'Uh – yeah.' I forced a smile.

'You aren't the first. He's a tricky one.'

Suddenly the room quieted. Hackles and I both followed everyone's gaze at the doors. Doc and Hong had just walked in. Doc looked like he always did, but Hong had taken on an aggressive, alert tension.

'That's Doc Alberts and Hong the gunfighter,' said Hackles with raised eyebrows. 'They've both been here before, but never together.'

'Gunfighter? Hong?'

'Why, sure. Don't you know them?'

'Not . . . as well as I thought.'

'Well, now. Look at that Hong. He has a perpetual squint in a face the colour of Kansas wheat. His reputation as a gambler and a never-miss gun is aided by the villain's moustache he's twirling, though I can tell you he only sharks the professionals.'

'Glad to hear it,' I murmured, watching Hong saunter across the room. Other people were quickly looking away from him and Doc.

'Rumour has it,' Hackles went on, 'that he has that limber stride because he has two ball-joint knees.'

236

'He does?'

'He shot them clean out of Collapsible Jed Foley and had them installed for himself.'

'How about that funny waist? I noticed that when we were up in the mountains.'

'That's an Avocado waist with a one-hundred-forty-degree turning arc. He shot a lawyer in Arizona for that one. But his pride and joy is that pair of black boots.'

I nodded, gazing at them. They glistened in the light from the cloud-crystal chandelier like obsidian.

'Hong won those boots in a card game,' said Hackles, nodding into his beer mug.

'So that's my cousin,' I said quietly, somewhat in shock.

'No kidding? He's your cousin and you didn't know this stuff? Where have you been, fellow?'

'Back east a ways.'

'Oh. That's a good enough reason, I guess. Well, I'll tell you. He's quite a bluffer and quite a card player, which isn't necessarily the same thing. He won those boots from Sweetwater Curt in Dallas by bluffing a king-high hand over queens and nines.'

I nodded in silence, staring at Hong's boots as he and Doc leaned against the bar. 'He's really that good?'

'He's been known to lose a hand or two, and once even a foot, but never an eyeball or a newjoint.'

In a back corner, someone started a lively version of 'The Girl I Left Behind Me' on the piano.

'That's Fingers Lau,' said Hackles. 'The party doesn't really start until he starts to play.'

'Hey, Hackles,' growled Grudge, stomping through the growing crowd towards us. 'You trying to steal my new apprentice, are you?'

237

'Ha. You just want to get rid of him now that you know how stupid he is.'

Without a smile, Grudge slapped Hackles on the back hard enough to slop his beer on me. 'I don't have any more business than usual. When I don't need him, maybe he'll shovel out your stalls for you.'

'Sure,' I said eagerly.

'Okay, then.' Hackles nodded. 'You check with me on your free time.'

'This fellow is the finest fiddler in town,' Grudge added. 'Just make sure he pays you in cash and not tunes.' He turned to see where we were looking.

'This here is Hong's cousin,' said Hackles.

'He don't look it,' said Grudge, taking a drink out of his mug. 'But you see those loose arms of his?' He nodded towards Hong.

'Sure,' I said.

'They're gooseneck molybdenum steel. He won the first one by bluffing Salt Morass into folding with three of a kind to Hong's nine-high. Then I charged him one hundred twelve thousand newbits to take it apart, figure it out, and make him the second one. We didn't have a doc in town back then, so Hong had to have them integrated in some other town.'

'Hold it. You never told me that. Where'd he get that kind of money?' Hackles demanded.

'That was the day after he faced Red-Eared Rick in the street and made him cough up the take from his last bank job—'

'—all over the ground,' Hackles finished. 'I remember that. Yuck.'

'He's got one silver eye and one grey eye,' said Grudge. 'He's harder to stare down than a one-eyed flounder.'

'He's got something new since the last time he was

in town, though,' said Hackles. 'What's that around his neck?'

'I know,' I said quickly. 'The railroad slavers put that around his neck when they captured him. I guess when the slave crews work, their necks are all chained together.'

Hackle and Grudge both stared at me.

'Snyder Gray and his railroad slavers got him?' Hackles shook his head. 'That's hard to believe.'

'I saved him myself,' I said proudly.

'*You?*' they demanded in unison.

'With my steerite and some of his herd.'

They looked at each other.

'He *has* got a steerite,' said Grudge. 'With a bag over his head.'

'Hong would go on wearing a slave chain,' said Hackles thoughtfully. 'It's just like him. Everything about him is a badge of his life.'

'Even his boots,' I observed, looking at them again as Hong rested one on the rail at the base of the bar. They looked odd, somehow, and kept drawing my attention.

'His feet, you mean,' said a woman coming down the stairs behind me.

I got up and turned around to make room.

'Who are you?' Hackles asked.

'I'm Sally Flash the saloonie,' she said, winking. 'Cicero Yank hired me today.'

I looked at her again and stared this time. Eulalie had replaced her high-collared, lavender print dress with a low-cut red satin gown with white petticoats. Her blonde hair now fell to her shoulders and had lots of red and blue feathers fastened to it in the back. She gathered the full skirt away from me as she passed.

'As for Hong, those aren't boots. Take my word for it.' She patted me on the top of the head.

'Eulalie?' I whispered, still watching her.

'Don't get your hopes up, kid,' she muttered under her breath. Then she moved on into the crowd.

Grudge and Hackles followed her.

Cicero Yang came down the stairs too, carrying a large black bag. 'Louie,' he cried heartily, whacking me on the back.

I caught my balance two steps lower, clinging to the railing.

'Come on down, Louie. I have another job for you.' Without looking back, he strode into the crowd towards his table.

I hurried after him before the crowd could close behind him again.

Several guys were playing cards at his table, but his chair was empty.

'Gentlemen,' said Cicero, 'this here is Louie Hong. He is my personal boot and buckle polisher and he is the custodian of my personal seat.' Behind his back, he pressed a couple more newbits into my hand.

The others looked up from their hands with bland expressions.

'I am leaving town again on one of my routine jaunts. No one, I emphasize *no one*, is to sit in my seat except him.'

'The last guy to hold that job was shot and killed his first night,' said one of the card players, without looking up. He was a very young cowboy with PoppedEye forearms and very long fingers. 'I'm Tommy Clanger. It's been nice knowing you.'

'Huh?' I looked from him to Cicero.

'Pay no attention.' Cicero laughed. 'It's safe if you keep your mouth shut. See you when I get back.' He waved all around and made his way to the doors, the woven dragons rustling on his vest as he moved.

'Uh . . . yeah.' I smiled weakly. Maybe he thought I wouldn't notice his careful arrangement of reflective surfaces. Maybe he had seen me looking earlier in the day and liked the fact that I hadn't told on him. He obviously wasn't going to explain.

'You again,' someone shouted from the doorway. 'I shoulda known. We got business, you and me.'

People backed away from the doors and the bar. Cicero was gone. In a few moments, only Doc and Hong were standing at the bar and Smellin' Llewellyn was standing just inside, glaring at Doc.

Fingers Lau quit playing.

'Where is it, Doc? And where's Tinny Ginnie?' Smellin' demanded.

Doc set down his empty glass and peered into it with studied reserve like he was looking for something.

Smellin' stomped forward. 'Out of the way, you,' he yelled at Hong, reaching out to shove him aside.

One of Hong's gooseneck arms uncoiled and shot out straight. His fist smashed into Smellin's nose, which fell off onto the floor. Smellin' straightened with the impact, his eyes watering, and grabbed his face with one hand. He crouched to feel around for his nose on the hardwood.

Without it, his face lost character and gained distinction.

While Hong watched him, Doc picked up a bottle and refilled both their glasses.

Smellin' snatched his nose off the floor and ducked out of the swinging doors.

Fingers Lau banged away on the piano again, this time 'The Yellow Rose of Texas'.

Everyone went back to their own business. I decided to work my way back to the stairs. I was safer there, and I could still see if anyone sat in Cicero's chair.

241

Hackles was already standing by the stairs again with a half-empty mug by the time I climbed back up to my seat.

'Your cousin still takes care of himself,' said Hackles. 'He always could. I just can't figure out how he got captured by the railroad slavers in the first place.' He watched me carefully.

'He didn't say.' I looked over the crowd. Doc and Hong were still lounging at the bar. Others had gathered around them again but were being ignored. 'They sure seem to get along. Nobody else has gotten along with Doc that I've seen.'

'No,' said Hackles, turning to watch them with me. 'Doc was never real sociable after his family got killed.'

'They what?'

'Oh, it was a long time ago. Even before your cousin's time out here. He got his revenge on the gang that did it, but that just earned him a reputation as a fast gun. That was out this way.'

'What was he doing back around Femur in Missouri?'

Hackles shrugged. 'He keeps on the move but circles back this way every so often. He's been defending himself ever since he got himself a name.'

'I thought he was a gunfighter.'

'He is. That is, defending himself has kept him that way. But it's not by choice.' Hackles nodded towards them. 'Doc just bought a little cabin up in the mountains today from a miner gone bust. I was here in the saloon when they shook on it.'

'You think he's retiring?'

'He's been trying to retire for years and go back to doctoring. I think maybe Hong has decided to give him that chance.'

I nodded slowly, remembering Doc's quiet demeanour ever since I had first seen him.

Shouts of greeting rose up in the crowd. Someone was just coming through the swinging doors. I sat up straight.

Duke was still wearing his battered, wide-brimmed leather hat. His long sheepskin vest had collected a lot of dust and sand during the long trip from Femur, but his red shirt with the gold buttons must have been laundered, because it was as bright as ever. He nodded to the crowd and spoke to a few people. The roar of the crowd drowned out his voice.

Duke pounded people on the back and shook hands and took a quick drink. Everyone seemed to know him. Still, he declined several seats people offered him and apparently asked a few questions.

Then someone responded by pointing to me on the stairs. Duke looked up and began working his way through the crowd without taking his eyes off me. People parted before him.

Fingers Lau shifted to a funeral dirge in minor key.

My fingers and toes tingled with a desire to run. I had nowhere to go, though. I gripped the banister and watched him move closer.

Duke walked all the way to the side of the staircase and looked at me over the rail. Our heads were at about the same level.

'You're not running away,' he said. 'I like that.'

I whimpered at him.

'A control-natural like you doesn't have many ways to make money,' he said casually, still watching my face closely. 'A big haul all at once could come in real handy.'

I was too scared to speak.

'Of course, comin' to a wide-open mountain town like this with an outlaw gang and railroad slavers

243

huntin' for ya isn't the smartest move a guy could make.'

I shook my head in wide-eyed agreement. If he didn't know enough to include Prism Chisholm on that list, I wasn't going to tell him.

'Smellin' and Carver filled me in on some of that. So the question becomes, just how stupid are ya?'

I nodded gravely.

'Ya seemed like a bright enough kid back in Femur, even if I did hornswoggle ya with that horse-holdin' business. And ya seemed a right guy out on the trail.'

I managed to swallow.

'Now, somethin' else occurs to me.' He leaned an elbow on the banister. 'Ya never quite caught up with me to return some of those steerites you went to round up. Maybe you're bright enough to go into business for yourself, eh?'

I shook my head emphatically. 'No,' I muttered.

'What's that ya say?'

'No, no.' I spoke up finally. 'Not on purpose. That is, I followed you all the way to the railroad camp to rejoin you.'

'So I heard.' He grinned. 'I also heard that the railroad slavers are lookin' for the guy who stampeded some steerites over their pens and freed all their workers.'

'Uh—'

He laughed and reached over the banister to whomp me on the shoulder.

I slid down four steps this time and sat down hard on the bottom step, falling back to hit my head on one of the higher stairs.

'You're okay, Louie.' He walked around the end of the banister and looked down at me. His bulk blocked the end of the staircase and blotted out the

light over me. 'But the gang and I need to know –
where is Tinny Ginnie?'

# Twenty-one

The entire saloon had gone silent. Everyone was waiting for my answer. Even Fingers Lau knew better than to plink out any notes.

'She took the left fork towards San Francisco,' I said, hearing my voice shake. 'I took the right fork to come here so I wouldn't be with her when you caught her.'

Duke stared at me for a long moment. Then, finally, he grinned and shook his head. 'Just like a control-natural,' he said. 'You just gave up. Didn't even try to get it from her, did ya?'

'What has she got?' I asked him. 'Blue Bunyan biceps and a Cousin Jack back? She lifted my steerite all by herself.'

Duke laughed aloud and headed back towards the bar. Everyone else laughed, now, too. Fingers Lau resumed 'The Girl I Left Behind Me'.

'You're okay, Louie,' Duke called over his shoulder. 'You're too reckless to be dishonest.'

I fell back against the stairs, suddenly aware that my sweat had soaked through my clothes. As soon as my legs were strong enough to stand, I slunk off along the wall to the door and hustled back to Grudge's stall. Chuck lifted his head when I rolled down next to him on the straw.

'A difficult day?' he inquired.

'Not bad, Chuck.' I giggled idiotically in relief. 'We're off the hook from Duke. Now if Prism

Chisholm will just forget about me, everything will be okay.'

While he considered this, I fell asleep.

After breakfast the next morning, Grudge told me to keep the fire tended and then he plodded away. I was hunched over a ragged old set of bellows when a loop of rope settled over my shoulders and tightened. The rope jerked me backwards into the street, where I hit hard on the packed dust.

'Hi, Tether,' I wheezed, rolling around.

'You got nerve, fob,' he said amiably. 'I'll give you that.'

'Haven't you heard from Duke? He knows I split from Tinny Ginnie. He also knows I don't have any loot.'

'Wrong answer, fob.' He yanked on the rope and walked backwards, dragging me. 'I know all that. But I think you just might know how to contact her later on. Besides which, just between us, she might have asked *me* to escort her out of town if you hadn't been hanging around.'

My arms were still pinned, so all I could do was thrash around. 'I don't want to contact her. She throws steerites around like they're double bisons.'

'Funny you should mention double bisons.' He jerked on the loop, tightening it more. 'What about those gold double bisons, fob?'

By this time, the smithy had receded somewhat and I could see the wide, irregular trail my body had left in the dust as he had dragged me. 'Where are we going, anyway?'

'Nowhere special. Just for a walk around town. Now answer my question.'

I heard boots thumping down the boardwalk towards us in an easy gait. The rhythm sounded familiar, so I twisted around to look. Hong was walking towards us, his face expressionless as he watched Tether with one grey eye and one silver eye.

'You don't scare me.' Tether sneered at him and shook the loop on me loose. He pulled it off me and retracted it smoothly into his arm.

Hong was still ambling up to him, his gooseneck arms quivering loosely and his obsidian feet clunking hard on the boardwalk.

'You hear me?' Tether demanded. Hong was almost within arm's reach now. Tether shot out his lariat at Hong.

Hong stepped off the boardwalk and flung forward one gooseneck arm, suddenly stiff as a crowbar. His fist smashed into Tether's forehead. Tether's head jerked back and he collapsed onto the street, his rope fluttering limply to the dust.

'Be polite,' said Hong. 'Talk all you want. Don't fight.' Then he turned and went on up the boardwalk.

Tether spat out some dust and shook his head to clear it. While he slowly wound in his rope again, I got up and trotted back to the smithy. This time I sat on the other side of the bellows, facing the street to keep an eye on him. Hong wouldn't always be around.

Tether didn't follow me. He dusted himself off and marched away towards the saloon. I watched him until he was inside.

Grudge didn't come back. As usual, people came and went every so often, but Washout was a quiet town during the day. After a while, Harris came marching up the middle of the street in his fine suit. His fists were clenched and he was looking all around.

I kept my head down as I watched him, poking at the fire and working the bellows. Instead of going by, though, he saw me.

'Hey, Louie.'

'Hi,' I said noncommittally.

'Have you seen a fight here in the street? Somebody said a to-do was going on.'

'No. Sort of. Not exactly.'

'Huh?'

'Tether Chen and I had a little talk. Then Hong stopped by but he didn't stay long.'

'You mean I missed it?' Harris sighed and unclenched his fists. 'Say, Hong really gave Smellin' Llewellyn a lesson in rowdyism last night at the saloon, didn't he?'

'Were you there?' I looked up.

'Sure. And everybody saw you stand up to Duke, too. Say, this is the place to be, isn't it? Everything is so exciting.'

'I didn't exactly stand up to Duke. Fell down on the stairs was more like it.'

'Wait a minute.' Harris frowned down at me. 'What's a famous outlaw like you doing working in a smithy?'

'Well.' I sighed. Maybe it was time to help him out of his naïveté before he got himself hurt. 'Look, you don't exactly have everything right. I'm not really an outlaw, see, except that I'm wanted by the law. But I don't break the law for a living.'

'Hey, don't you worry about me.' He winked. 'I must have made a mistake. It's none of my business if you're incognito.'

'I'm not,' I said stoutly. 'I haven't been sick in years.'

'I think I'll go visit Eulalie at the saloon,' he said. 'Look for a chance to show off *my* specials.'

'You're wearing them now, huh? What kind of specials do you have?' I should have let him go, but I was curious, what with him being an unpredictable easterner.

'You really want to know?' He brightened.

'Sure.'

'Everything I could afford. One Overlaid Infrared Contact Eyeball insert from Private Eyes, Inc., of Springfield, Illinois. Two very expensive Aloha Outrigger Trigger Rigger index fingers made in North Carolina that are precisely matched to the pull on my gun. Best of all, I have a Cobra Brand Elbow and Forearm Complex.'

'That's a gooseneck-type arrangement, isn't it? Sort of like Hong's arms?'

'Sort of, only his arms are complete. Mine only start right above the elbow.' He hesitated. 'What do you think, Louie?'

'Very nice.' I sighed.

'Now to go see Eulalie,' he said, walking away.

'Sally Flash,' I called after him. 'That's her new name.'

As Harris marched away, again clenching his fists, I saw Betsy coming down the boardwalk across the street, hunched over and arms folded, staring at her feet as she walked. I had wondered if the wagon train had dropped her off too, but she had never let on where she was going. Now she went right on by without looking up.

I decided to take her earlier advice and shut up.

Once the fire had turned into a big glowing pile of coals, I had nothing else to do here. The forge held it all safely, and Hackles's livery stable was right across the street. I wandered over there to see about my other job.

'Hey, Hackles.' I knocked on the big open doors.

'Huh?' He walked out, yawning. 'Aha. Morning, Louie.'

'Morning, barely. It's almost noon, I bet.'

'Noon, eh? Time for me to meet Grudge at the saloon for breakfast.'

'The saloon? Do they serve food?'

'Of course not.' He slapped me on the back and I banged my head on a post. 'Just joking. They do during the day when business is slow. Anyhow, you shovel out my stalls while I'm gone, eh? It goes in a pile out back. You can't miss it.'

'Okay.'

He too ambled away.

Horsites, like steerites, were extremely efficient creatures, but they still couldn't use everything they ate. The stalls looked like they hadn't been shovelled out in a long time. Most of the horsites were gone during the day. My first problem, though, was the shovel.

The only one I could find had a very short handle that was open on top with a nest of loose, rusted wires hanging out of it. It had obviously been somebody's forearm and shovel hand. Some poor slob had left it to Hackles as payment instead of cash.

I wheeled a little wheelbarrow into the first stall and knelt down to get to work. The shovel was clumsy to use. I was soaked in sweat and out of breath pretty fast. All in all, I preferred working the bellows.

I wheeled out the first load, dumped it, and returned to the same stall. It still had plenty of loads to go. After several more, I left the shovel where it was and leaned back against the rough, worn boards of the wall to catch my breath.

Nobody in Washout seemed to be in a hurry about anything, anyhow.

I was just about to pick up the shovel again when someone pounded on the side of the open doors.

'Hackles, it's Duke. Where are you?' His footsteps came inside.

I got up to see what he wanted. Before I was out of the stall, though, the doors of the stable slammed shut. The stable had windows and lots of cracks between the doors to provide light, so I could just barely see.

'Shut up and stand right there,' yelled Betsy.

I carefully leaned around the base of the stall door. She had come in after Duke and closed the doors behind her. He was looking at her quizzically.

'Who are ya?' he asked, tilting back his hat.

She glared at him from under her own. 'You recognize this hat?'

'No.' He shrugged. 'Looks sort of like mine. Ya want my hat, is that it?'

'*No, I don't want your hat,*' she screamed. '*I've already got it.*'

He toyed with the bright yellow scarf around his neck for a moment, looking at her. 'How's that again?'

She whipped her hat off her head and flung it at him. He caught it and turned it around and around, studying it. Then he looked inside.

'Say . . . I remember this one.' He glanced up again, whispering. 'Polly? Polly? Is that you?'

'Not anymore, *Father*,' She sneered. 'My name is Betsy now.'

'No kidding,' he breathed, grinning at her. 'It really is you. And you're all the way out here.'

She marched up to him, snatched her hat back, and whacked him across the face with it. He yanked it away and she backed off, waiting.

He stared at her, tossing her hat to the straw at her feet. 'I don't take that from very many folks. In fact, not from anybody. Except you, if you'll stop playing games and say what's on your mind.'

252

'I just want to tell you that you're no good,' she shouted. 'No good for anything and no good to anybody.' She glared back at him.

'That's hardly news, except the guys in my gang might disagree.' He hesitated. 'Is that it?'

'No.' She drew in a deep breath like she was summoning courage. 'Why did you leave Ma and me, anyway? Huh?'

Duke sighed and shook his head.

'Come on. I travelled all the way from Pike County to find out.'

'Ya did? Say, that's impressive.' His eyes narrowed. 'I could use ya in the gang. How would ya like to join up with the old man?'

'Not a chance,' she snapped.

'Ya sure? As soon as the last two guys in the gang show up here in town, we're all figurin' to ride for San Francisco and find Tinny Ginnie. I could use a tough young lady.'

'That's all you want, isn't it? You don't even care I'm your daughter.'

'That's not what I meant.'

She walked up and kicked him in the shin.

'Hey!' He jumped, even in his boots.

She picked up her hat and hit him with it again. 'Go on, hit back.'

'What?' He ducked, flailing around with one arm to protect himself, but not to strike her.

'Come on. Hit me with your specials. Or throw me across the room with them.' She punched his substantial middle with her fist.

Her punch made no impression I could see.

'Polly, are you crazy? Stop it.'

'Hit me with your specials. Come on, what are they? What's wrong?' She kicked him in the other shin. 'I don't have any.' She slapped him with her hat again. 'I'm just a control-natural. So you can't be scared of me.'

'Well, so am I!' he shouted back, finally grabbing her shoulders and shoving her away.

I sat up straight.

'What?' she asked, stopping where she stood.

'This is a secret, but ... I'm one, too.' He occupied himself with straightening his vest and shirt.

'You are?' Her voice was small.

'That's why I robbed banks and trains,' he said, avoiding her eyes. 'It was a shortcut. Only, a man on the run can't keep a regular home. That's the answer to your question, I guess.'

She watched him without saying anything. Then she suddenly turned around and stomped out, pushing open the big doors just enough to slide through them. Sunlight shot into the stable.

Duke let out a deep sigh. He straightened his clothes, more to give her time to leave, I figured, than because they needed it. Then he left, too.

I knelt down in the stall and picked up my shovel. My mind was reeling. Duke Goslin, the great outlaw leader, was a control-natural. He had no more specials than I did. I couldn't stop thinking about it as I worked.

I was itching to tell somebody, but at the same time, I didn't want to say a word. That was a secret to keep, all right. I couldn't think of anything more dangerous than making him mad at me all over again.

The day went quickly now. After eating stew with Grudge, I went out back to find Chuck. He was standing in the waning sunlight, skinny but standing up as he munched grass.

'Hi, Chuck. Feeling better than ever, huh?'

'The sunlight here is quite strong,' he said with his mouthful. 'I am returning to normal activity. If you wish to hit the trail soon, I can go with you now without being a burden.'

'No, no. Take your time.'

'What are you doing in town here, anyway?'

'I have two jobs, now,' I said proudly. 'I shovelled out the stable today.'

'Yuck,' said Chuck.

'Well, it's honest work,' I pointed out. 'Not like robbing banks or something.'

'The point is conceded,' said Chuck. 'Yuck anyway.'

'Come on, Chuck,' I growled, kicking a clump of grass on the way back to the smithy. I was in no mood to have a scrawny, half-breed maverick pass judgement on my chosen careers.

He shrugged, sort of, and grabbed one more mouthful of grass. Then he trotted after me. Once I had left him in the empty stall for the night, I hurried over to the Silver Transistor Saloon. This time the place was already crowded when we got there.

Fingers Lau was banging out another lively tune on the piano. Grudge stumped towards the bar. Just as I edged behind a burly cowboy towards my spot on the stairs, a heavy hand fell on my shoulder from behind.

'Hey, fob. Where are you from, anyway?'

I tried to hurry, but Tether's grip on my shoulder was too strong to escape. A moment later, he came alongside me.

'So when are you going to see Tinny Ginnie next?'

'Never,' I said loudly, my voice cracking. I climbed up a couple of stairs. He came around to speak to me through the bars holding up the banister.

'Never? You can't get your cut from her that way, fob.'

'I'm not getting a cut. I'd rather stay alive.'

He grinned, clearly unconvinced, and headed towards the bar.

Relieved, I got comfortable and looked around. Card games were under way at most of the tables, but Cicero's chair was still empty. Harris sat by himself at a table by the wall, watching Sally Flash.

She was currently sitting on the lap of Smellin' Llewellyn, whose nose was held onto his face by a considerable amount of white tape. It was a sign that he had had it reintegrated and now the skin just had to heal. He kept looking over her shoulder at the hand of cards he was holding.

Sally got up in disgust and plunked down next on the lap of Isotope John, who was still wearing his purple hat. He slid an arm around her waist to hold her on, but then she lifted up a corner of his hat brim to look at him. The second she touched it, he dumped her onto the floor.

A couple of guys at the bar guffawed, but the card players weren't looking and the music was too loud for them to hear the words I saw her mouthing. Most people just never noticed. She got up and shoved her way through the crowd.

Then I saw Tether working his way back towards me, carefully watching the liquid level in the little shot glass he carried. I slid down the stairs and slipped through the crowd as fast as I could, heading for Harris. I didn't want to sit in the smithy all night unless I just couldn't keep away from Tether at all.

Harris's table was next to Fingers Lau's piano in one corner. A back door of some sort was behind him. When I got to the table, Sally stood right behind Fingers, tugging and pulling at her petticoats to right them after her splat from Isotope John's lap. Harris was watching her in fascination.

Just as I came up, Harris rose and went over to her.

A bunch of cowboys leaning on the piano struck up a loud round of 'Red River Valley', about as melodic as a horse in a tornado. I couldn't hear Harris and Sally, but I slid into an empty seat at the table to watch them. A moment later, they both came over and sat with me.

'Oh – hi, Louie,' said Harris, uncertainly.

'You want to be alone, I'll go.' I started to get up.

'No! No, of course you're welcome, Louie.' His eyes got wide again at the thought of insulting me.

'No, he's not,' said Sally, looking at me. 'Go 'way. Ick.'

I looked at her. The front of her dress looked funny, like something had slid around that wasn't supposed to, maybe jarred loose from her fall earlier. Then Carver Dalton came up behind her.

'You got no taste, lady,' said Carver.

'We're talking,' said Harris shakily, looking up at Carver.

'Come on.' Carver took Sally's arm and lifted her out of her chair. In a moment, they had disappeared into the crowd.

Harris's face was covered with a sheen of sweat. He seemed much less inclined to fight now that the prospect was imminent. Instead, he filled his glass from the half-empty bottle in front of him.

Suddenly strong hands grabbed me from behind and lifted me out of my chair, too.

'What – hey!' I squirmed around, trying to see, but I couldn't. The noisy crowd and smoke-filled air shrank in front of me as I was carried backwards through a door, kicking and thrashing.

It swung shut after my flailing feet were through and I found myself being carried backwards now through a storeroom of some kind. Then I was carried through another door, which also swung shut. A small yellow light over the lintel showed me that I was in an alley behind the saloon. The hands let go and I fell hard on my back into a mud puddle.

I blinked a few times to focus my eyes on the face hanging over me. Then I realized that my eyes were already focused; I was looking into the blur of Prism Chisholm's multifaceted ones.

# Twenty-two

'Evening, Louie,' Prism Chisholm said solemnly. He stood over me, looming at a great angle. His face was dark, but the yellow light threw a corona behind his head and the dark shape of his hat.

'I don't have it,' I said. Cold water and mud were seeping through my clothes.

He cocked his head slightly and reflected light glittered off the facets of his eyes.

'You got me, though.' I raised my wrists for him to cuff me.

'Not so fast.' He stuck his hands in his coat pockets.

I started to get up. He placed one foot on my chest and casually stepped on it. Once I was down again, he left it there but kept his weight off it.

'The real reward is for returning the stolen coinage. Now maybe you have it and maybe you don't, but I'm confident that you know where it is.'

'Tinny Ginnie stole it from the gang that stole it from the bank. She's gone to San Francisco.'

'Hmm. In a wagon, by any chance?'

'We left Hawk Nest in a wagon. Then she threw me off and shifted everything to the horsites.'

'Very good, Louie.' His eyes blinked green. 'I like your honesty. I had already figured that out.'

'Huh? You did? Then what are you doing here?'

'You members of the Duke Goslin gang know her better than I do. I can track her anywhere, but I can save time if you guys tell me where you're going to meet her.'

The back door opened and Tether Chen stepped out, suddenly wary when he saw Prism Chisholm.

I had never thought I'd be glad to see him, but I was.

They stared at each other unmoving, Prism's foot still on my chest.

'As I was saying,' Prism went on, still facing Tether, 'I reckon you know where it is. Maybe this fellow does. You are Mr Tether Chen, I presume.' His eyes sparkled a rotating orange and blue.

'You'd be that bounty hunter,' Tether said coldly. 'With the prism eyes.'

'That's only one of their features, I assure you. Yes, I am Prism Chisholm. I am after stolen property first and arrests only second.'

'I wouldn't count on arresting anyone here,' said Tether, with a grin. 'There's one of you against most of our gang. Not to mention, we're known and liked here in Washout.'

'I knew you were gathering here when your various trails converged. I have also found that this town has no sheriff or marshal, which tells me that Sniffin' Griffin and I are on our own.'

'Sniffin's here with you?' Tether grinned. 'Say. Smellin' will be glad to hear that. Maybe they can have it out.'

'You're getting chilled, Louie.' Prism looked down at me in steady red. 'You can get rid of me by coming up with your rendezvous point and date with Tinny Ginnie. Otherwise, we will all be having it out.' He tipped his hat and backed away, watching us both carefully. 'We'll be around.'

'Duke ought to know he's in town,' Tether muttered to himself. He went back inside.

I rolled over out of the mud puddle and got to my feet. After giving Tether a moment to lose himself in the crowd inside, I followed him.

When I slipped inside, hoping no one would notice the mud all over my back, Harris and Sally were gone from their table. Across the room, I could just see Tether leaving with Duke through the swinging front doors. That was a relief.

Hong was sauntering to Cicero Yang's table with that loose gait I was getting to know. He sat down next to Isotope John. Two other guys were there besides Cicero's empty chair. I hurried over to it, partly to watch the action and partly to stay with Hong. He should be able to help with Prism Chisholm somehow.

Isotope John was dealing. When I sat down in Cicero's chair and drew my feet up to sit cross-legged, he glanced up and sneered at me. Then he started tossing cards with his special wheel-fingered hand.

Hong nodded to me across the table, causing the chandelier light to shine on the big black chain around his neck.

'I heard about your lucky chain, Mister Hong,' said Isotope John. 'They say you've never missed with your gun or lost a night of cards since the railroad slavers put that chain on your neck.'

As far as I knew, he hadn't played cards or shot at anybody since the steerites and I had freed him.

'They say,' Hong agreed, looking at his cards.

I glanced up at Cicero's rigged reflecting surfaces. Hong had a pair of fours.

He unlaced a gun from one holster.

'Fred?' Isotope John said, looking at one of the other guys.

'Ten dollars.' He tossed in a big silver coin.

I stared at it. Dollars hadn't been minted in years, but they were as good as newbits if you had them. The glass over a painting reflected his king-high hand.

'Y' in?' said Isotope John.

Sally had wandered by and was standing behind him to look over his shoulder. I figured she knew about the mirror system too, having become closely acquainted with Cicero rather quickly.

'Raise ten.' Hong yawned and looked with a bored expression at Sally. Everyone stayed.

'Tommy?' said Isotope John.

The last guy, the young cowboy with PoppedEye forearms and very long fingers, shook his head and dropped his hand facedown.

'One card,' said Fred.

Behind Isotope John, Sally began to fiddle with the front of her dress. I turned away and just happened to catch Isotope John dealing from the bottom of the deck to Fred.

Tommy leaped up and yelled, 'I saw that!'

He went for his gun, but Isotope John leaned to one side, flipped out his pistol, and blew Tommy away like a mosquito. Tommy's gun went off though, and grazed Isotope John on the neck.

'Accused me o' cheating,' said Isotope John. A couple of bare wires stuck out of his neck.

I recalled what Hackles had told me about a slinky spring installed there.

'John,' said Fred sternly. He looked around.

A couple of cowboys the same age as Tommy were carting him out feet first. 'Phooey,' said Tommy, looking at a nest of wire ends protruding from his chest.

Isotope John glared at Fred. 'Dealer takes none.'

Fred shrugged and bet. 'Ten.'

Isotope John and Hong put in their money. Hong called and lost to a pair of eights.

'Well!' Isotope John grinned and swept in his winnings. 'Your chain wearing out, Hong? Luck weakening?'

'Luck never weakens,' said Hong. 'Deal.'

Sally wandered away, and when I saw the hand Isotope John dealt himself, I couldn't believe his audacity. One way or another, he'd given himself jacks and tens before the draw, most likely planning a full house. Fred held a nine-high hand and folded. Then when I saw Hong's hand – four queens – I thought I would faint from glee. Of course, he would have a hard time pulling off one of his patented bluffs when he had the best hand at the table. It had to be that fancy luck of his; I'd kept a clear eye on him every moment, and he never once made a funny move. But then – if Isotope John was cheating and in control, he had dealt Hong his hand on purpose.

'Ante's low for a lucky jerk like you,' said Isotope John. 'I hear you got that luck with guns, too.'

Hong raised an eyebrow and his grey eye glinted.

'So here's a real bet for you. If I win, you shoot it out with me.'

Now I understood. Isotope John had a good hand and would make better; when Hong beat him with an 'impossible' four queens, Isotope John could call him into the street anyway, for cheating. He apparently really wanted to shoot it out with Hong.

'Right,' said Hong. 'Gimme two cards.'

Isotope John and I both started as Hong tossed down a five and – a queen. As the dealer, Isotope John's astonishment was proof that he had dealt Hong four queens on purpose. Isotope John's worry now: a moment ago he had cheated so clumsily as to be caught. What if he'd fouled up again and Hong hadn't received four queens? After all, Hong had just discarded one, which would be untactful if he was holding three more.

Hong twirled his villain's moustache and kept those squinty eyes on Isotope John. He knew something was up; most likely he wasn't sure what. I figured he was doing the unexpected out of sheer orneriness and suspicion. He wasn't scared of gunfights.

'Two,' squeaked Isotope John. The doubt in his voice told Hong all he had to know.

'I'm on to you now,' said Hong with a grin. Isotope John went for his gun. Hong's snake-coil arms flew up with his pistols on the ends, and Isotope John checked himself with his gun still aimed downward. He managed a weak smile. Suddenly Hong spat and hit the wires protruding from that neck wound. Sparks flew; smoke fizzled; Isotope John's gun went off, shattering an obsidian foot.

'Hey,' said Hong, annoyed, looking at his stump.

'At least you didn't bluff me with them cards,' panted Isotope John, swatting his neck. 'That's your specialty, ain't it?' He holstered his gun. 'Serves you right.'

'I did bluff you,' said Hong, flipping open the cylinders of his guns. 'No bullets. I haven't loaded a gun for four and a half years now.'

Isotope John leaped up, furious. 'I'll be outside! You can load 'em or don't; I'll draw anyway!' He turned to go but stopped at Hong's voice.

'No you won't. You'll be scared to. I'll stare with my one grey eye and one silver. You'll shake. I'll swivel my hips on the Avocado waist and you'll get dizzy. My springy arms will wave every which way and you'll wonder if you're about to shoot an unarmed man – in which case I'd win. On the other hand, if you don't shoot . . . I might.' Hong tugged at his villain's moustache, and Isotope John pushed through the crowd, muttering.

At that, I jumped up and darted through the crowd. When I got outside, I ran like lightning on wheels for the stable, just barely able to see my way down the street. Moments later, Isotope John and Hong faced each other in the dark, dusty street outside the Silver Transistor.

Isotope John swayed impatiently from one cater-pillar tread to the other, stroking the edge of his jeans with the wheel-fingers on his card hand. I wasn't there, but at the saloon window, Sally Flash shoved a three-newbit piece into the slo-mo camera and recorded the whole thing so we could all see it later.

Hong's black hair fluttered in the slight breeze and the light from the big picture window of the saloon shone evilly off that silver eye. His narrow moustache quivered, and the snakelike arms bounced in readiness over twin gun handles. Down the way, Isotope John's trigger finger scratched nervously at his thumb and his cardplayer's eyes searched Hong's tight smile and slightly swivelling hips for an indication of whether or not his guns were loaded.

In the meantime, I was thundering up the stairs of the saloon like greased pigs, trying to make the upstairs balcony overlooking the street. But that thing I carried was heavy.

The camera zoomed in on Isotope John's face. His eyebrows were tense and unbalanced; his eyes went from eager to hesitant to eager as he measured the glory of outshooting Hong against the ignominy of killing him unarmed. Suddenly he flashed his teeth and one hand dipped for his gun.

Hong's ball-joint knees spun in two directions: he sank and swayed, sending his arms out and around like tentacles, his obsidian stump shining in the dust. He levelled the two gun barrels and the grey eye fogged sternly.

But Isotope John's gun was already level. He squinted and his circuits began to fill with the impulse that would run down his arm to the trigger. For another millisec, he hesitated.

At that moment, I appeared on the balcony, leaning over Isotope John. And as Hong's triggers clicked on empty chambers, I dropped Grudge's anvil down on Isotope John's head. Some good that hydraulic whatsifier did *now*. I'm not sure exactly what happened, but rivets and screws splattered out all across the dirt of the street, springing and bouncing.

Then the recording went black.

I looked over at Hong, grinning fatuously. He lifted his gaze with one silver eye and one grey one and looked at me, up on the balcony. He twirled his villain's moustache with his left hand, peering with that perpetual squint. For a long moment he studied me sternly, and I let my stupid grin freeze and die. Then, with a wink and a faint chuckle, he saluted me, pivoted, and sauntered back inside the saloon.

I felt warm all over. As a crowd gathered in the dark street below to collect Isotope John, I decided I'd had enough of the Silver Transistor for one night. Still grinning, I ducked out the back way unseen and took the rear alley to the end of the street. Then I crossed over to Grudge's.

Up the street, people were still looking around in the darkness for pieces of Isotope John. Most of him had been loaded on a wagon. Then I happened to see someone sitting quietly on the darkened boardwalk, huddled against the wall.

It was Betsy. She wasn't watching the crowd either, but was staring at the middle of the street in front of her. I walked up to her.

'Hi,' I said quietly.

She moved very slowly, turning to look up at me with wide eyes as though she were still coming out of a waking dream.

'Don't you have a place to stay?' I asked.

'You're a control-natural, aren't you?' she said.

'Sure. Everybody knows that.'

'So am I.'

I nodded, not certain what to say.

'You knew that, didn't you?'

'No.'

'Of course you did.'

'No I didn't. Not for sure.'

'Would you please leave me be?' She returned her gaze to the middle of the street.

'Okay.' I left her and went on to the smithy.

Chuck was fast asleep in the straw. I forgot about Betsy and lay awake there, reliving Hong's shootout with Isotope John. I went to sleep and dreamed about that final moment when he winked and saluted me before going back inside.

Galloping hoofbeats woke me up as they thundered up the street. I blinked and looked around as Chuck nudged me with his stainless-steel snout.

'Going to go see what it is?' he whined. 'You hardly spend any time with me any more.'

'But, Chuck, you weren't feeling well.' I sat up.

'Now I'm feeling better.' He shook his head and yawned.

'We still have to worry about you being rustled.' I

opened the stall door. 'Come on, then. We'll both go see who's come to town.'

His ears perked up and he trotted after me eagerly.

Grudge was already gone. Up the street, a couple of guys were pulling up their horsites in little clouds of dust outside the saloon. When one guy leaped off and landed on his feet, his entire bent body bounced up and down awkwardly for the next four steps that he took up to the boardwalk.

'Alkali Springs,' I said to Chuck, as we hurried towards them. 'That other guy will be Wesley Coon.'

Ahead of us, other people stuck their heads out of their doors or peered around their window curtains at the commotion. Many of the men were in their union suits, unshaven; a few of the women clutched together white lace that wasn't meant to be seen.

Wesley slid carefully off his horsite and trotted after Alkali, holding his heavy glasses in place with one hand and the wire leading from them to his back pocket with the other.

When we got to the Silver Transistor, I peeked over one of the swinging doors, not sure if I should go in. When I saw Hong eating breakfast alone at a table, I decided I could.

'Stay here, Chuck,' I whispered. Then I moved inside.

Duke was just coming down the stairs, tying his yellow scarf around his neck. Carver and Smellin' were coming after him along the balcony overhead.

'You boys sure make a racket in the mornin',' said Duke pleasantly. 'Glad to see ya.'

'You won't be,' said Alkali. 'One of our gang has been taken by the railroad slavers.'

Duke leaped down over the lower stairs and thumped hard on the wooden floor at the bottom. He strode towards Alkali. 'Who?'

'Tinny Ginnie,' said Alkali.

'Ha.' Duke punched a fist into his other hand, grinning real big.

Carver and Smellin' were hurrying down the stairs after Duke.

'You two ain't heard, I bet,' said Smellin'. 'Ginnie run off with all the loot from Femur.'

Even Alkali straightened up, almost. 'She did?'

'We saw her working on a road crew for the slavers on the way in,' said Wesley. 'I got the whole location recorded.'

'Then the slavers got the loot,' said Duke. 'Somebody wake up Tether in the storeroom. We got to plan. Hey, Ike, how about breakfast?'

Isomer Isaac Phlegm leaned his mop against the bar, nodding.

'For him, too.' Hong pointed towards me.

'Nothing doing,' said Isomer Isaac Phlegm. 'His kind can eat in the smithy where he . . .' He trailed off, looking into Hong's unwavering gaze. 'One more breakfast,' he muttered, going into the back.

Smellin' went to get Tether. Then Duke and his gang sat around a big round table. It had a couple of empty chairs left but I decided to sit with Hong, instead. As I sat down, I noticed Duke looking at me.

'Morning,' I said shyly.

Duke nodded thoughtfully, then turned to Hong. 'I hear ya might have a grudge with these railroad slavers.'

'I do.' Hong leaned back in his chair casually.

'The way I figure it,' said Duke, 'Tinny Ginnie has forfeited her share of our, shall we call it, group assets.'

The other guys at the table nodded agreement.

'I'm offerin' that share to you and Louie to split as ya like if ya want to join us.'

Hong shifted his gaze to me without moving.

'That's more than I figured to get,' I said.

'Hold it,' cried Smellin' Llewellyn. 'That Hong with the moustache punched me. He knocked my nose clean off the other day.'

'You want Tinny Ginnie and the loot or not?' Duke demanded.

'All right, all right,' Smellin' muttered, shaking his head. 'Jeez. And I even had to make peace with Doc to fix my nose. It's humiliating, I say.'

'You're fortunate he's a physician of honour,' said Hong. He turned to Duke. 'Illegal money is of no interest to me. However, if you loan me a horsite, we're in.'

'You got it,' said Duke.

'Me, too,' said Sniffin' Griffin. 'I got my own mount, though.'

Everyone turned to look. Sniffin' and Prism Chisholm were pushing their way through the doors. Chuck had moved aside to make room for them.

Duke and his gang all jumped to their feet, every one of them ready to draw.

Prism Chisholm's eyes glittered orange and silver. 'Don't bother, gentlemen. Since you no longer have the money, I don't have any business with you. That is to say, at this very moment. Feel free to sit down.'

He and Sniffin' Griffin took another table. Smellin' glared at Sniffin', who threw back the fringed sides of his buckskin jacket and glared back.

'What do ya want, then?' Duke demanded.

'I suggest we join forces,' said Prism Chisholm. 'My colleague and I can offer excellent tracking services through these mountains.'

'I can smell more'n he can,' growled Smellin' Llewellyn, fingering the tape around his nose.

270

'So you say,' sneered Sniffin' Griffin haughtily, looking down at him from his greater height.

'I'm sure you both smell a great deal,' said Prism Chisholm. 'Now, then. Shall we first get the money into our possession and then decide how to proceed?'

Duke studied his face for a long moment. 'Agreed,' he said gruffly.

# Twenty-three

We all remained at our separate tables, but the atmosphere grew less tense as Sally Flash and Isomer Isaac Phlegm served eggs and bacon. Prism Chisholm said nothing when the others all paid with double bisons. Chuck was still standing outside, with his snout pushed through the swinging doors just enough so he could see. I was relieved that we weren't eating beef.

'All right, Wesley,' said Duke, around a mouthful of breakfast. 'What have you got we can use?'

Wesley reached into his back pocket for a moment. Then his eyes got a glazed look, even through his heavy glasses.

'He's the only guy I know,' said Carver, 'who admits to keeping part of his brain where he can sit on it.'

'We spotted Tinny Ginnie in a railroad slaver work gang seven-point-twenty-one kilometres from here by the route we took to Washout.' Wesley's voice was thoughtful, as though he were reading something and rephrasing it. 'They were grading a roadbed in a narrow valley. The crew was unusually small, reflecting a recent escape of slaves. Very few overseers were in sight. The probability that the rest of the slavers are driving a large herd of steerites to San Francisco after buying two herds from us is ninety-seven-point-one percent.'

I glanced at Hong, smiling. Most of the former

slaves had apparently not been recaptured. He paid no attention.

'They'll be keepin' the loot safe somewhere, probably in their camp,' said Duke. 'We'll need at least one diversion to occupy the slavers themselves.'

'Divert them back to the gutter they came from,' said Hong impassively, twirling his villain's moustache.

'What do ya mean?' Duke looked up.

'When I was with them, I heard that another railroad crew is also building this way from San Francisco, one made up of honest workers. Think about it.'

Duke scratched his head and looked around his table at his companions. None of them said anything.

'So far,' said Prism Chisholm, 'the reputable company would not have been able to keep pace. That much I would calculate. If, however, we were to sabotage a critical portion of the slaver's railroad, the damage might be permanent.'

'Since they're low on slaves, they won't be able to catch up again,' said Duke, nodding slowly. 'Well, I got no special likin' for them. We did business with them over some beef, but that's all.'

I heard a slight creak as the saloon doors swung shut. It was followed by trotting hoofbeats as Chuck hurried away.

'This will require consideration,' said Wesley slowly. 'As I consider the map, I see several gorges the railroad slavers must already have crossed with bridges. However, I have not actually seen any of these bridges myself.'

'That's it,' said Duke. 'We'll find the biggest bridge they've constructed and blow it up.'

Hong nodded briefly and returned to his breakfast.

Duke turned to Prism Chisholm.

'I agree,' said Prism Chisholm. 'Now we must know the exact locations of the bridge and of their camp.'

'I have the routes recorded.' Wesley nodded, then paused, again staring into space. 'I can give directions to everyone. According to the almanac, however, there won't be any moonlight to speak of.'

'With my eyes to guide us, that will not be necessary,' said Prism Chisholm.

'And my nose to track with,' added Sniffin' Griffin.

'You couldn't track mud from the bottom of your boots,' growled Smellin' Llewellyn. 'I'll smell 'em out.'

Sniffin' Griffin glared at him again, but Prism Chisholm laid a heavy hand on his shoulder and he didn't say anything.

'Let's break this up,' said Duke. 'We have to buy dynamud and plan everything.'

Hong was in no hurry, so I wasn't, either. Soon, though, Duke slid back his chair and stood up. The rest of his gang joined him. Prism Chisholm and Sniffin' Griffin also tossed down their napkins and stood.

'Ever wondered,' said Hong, 'how the slavers capture people?'

'Huh?' Duke looked over his shoulder at him.

'Why hasn't somebody gotten rid of them? How can they control entire work gangs?'

Prism Chisholm studied Hong a moment. 'Speaking as an experienced bounty hunter, I have to say those are pertinent questions. I presume you have an answer?'

'No answer,' said Hong. 'But they knocked me unconscious without ever getting near me. Later,

274

working on a road gang, I prised loose a link on my neck chain and took a couple of steps to run away into the forest. I blacked out again.'

'You have no idea how they accomplished this?' Prism Chisholm asked.

'No idea.' Hong rose, also.

'We'll find that out, too,' said Duke. 'Tonight. We'll meet after dinner here at the saloon.'

Everyone dispersed. I came out of the saloon last, looking around for Chuck. When I didn't see him, I headed towards the smithy.

For a quick moment, I thought about staying in town that night or even moving on for good once they had left. If I ran, though, I would never know whether or not someone was still chasing me for some reason. I wanted to see this through until all the Femur loot was in someone's possession to stay.

'Louie,' Grudge shouted from behind his anvil. 'You're late for work.'

I waved and grinned at him. If he'd really been mad, he would have fired me.

I swaggered into the smithy. This was the most exciting day I'd ever had, plotting a caper with Duke's gang just like I was one of them. I knew he'd seen me come out of the saloon with some of the gang.

'Is Chuck out back?' I asked.

'Naw,' muttered Grudge. 'C'mon, pump those bellows, will you? I thought he was with you.'

I kept looking for Chuck the rest of the day, but he didn't come back. Since I had been late for work, I didn't think I should go take a nap, but I was too excited to sleep, anyway. Finally Grudge quit for the day and put some stew on the fire.

We ate in silence, watching the sun go down behind the forested slopes. He knew better than to ask questions from a member of Duke's notorious outlaw gang.

After dinner I hurried up the street for the Silver Transistor. All the horsites were waiting out front. This time everyone crowded into a corner around the biggest round table. I couldn't find a seat in the jumble of chairs around it, so I sat behind Hong, where I could look over his shoulder.

'A round for everybody, Ike,' called Duke.

Fingers Lau was playing a loud and lively version of 'Midnight Special' in his corner. Nobody else would hear us.

Isomer Isaac Phlegm nodded and began filling mugs four-handed from a converted firehose. Sally Flash picked them up and brought them over four at a time.

'Now, then,' said Duke. 'Tether bought the dynamud at the general store.'

'It's packed on my horsite.' Tether nodded.

'We'll have one bunch of guys go to their camp while somebody goes to blow the bridge,' said Duke.

'Allow me to make a suggestion,' said Prism Chisholm. 'We all proceed to the camp together, perhaps offering to sell some of our number to them as a ruse. Once we have their attention, the group going to the bridge can slip past them.'

'That would work,' Wesley said, tapping his wire with a couple of fingers. 'The track they have already laid, of course, leads right back to the bridge in question.'

'Sell me back to 'em,' said Hong.

Across the saloon, Doc pushed inside the doors. He nodded briefly at Hong and went to the bar.

Smellin' leaned close to Duke. 'As long as you're hiring on guys I hate, you might as well ask him. He's got the kind of reputation we can use.'

Duke cleared his throat loudly. 'Uh – Doc? You're Doc Alberts, aren't you?'

Doc turned very slowly and looked over the people at the table before nodding slowly.

'We could use another gun on a little project tonight,' Duke called. 'Would you like to discuss—'

'No, thank you.'

'You didn't even listen to him!' Smellin' jumped up, throwing his chair backwards.

'I'm retired from violent pursuits,' said Doc. 'I am a full-time physician. I tended you and I am now tending a patient in the cabin I recently bought on the edge of town.'

'Yeah, well. . . .' Smellin' looked at him uncertainly.

'By the way, how is your nose, Mister Llewellyn?'

'Better,' he muttered.

Hong slid his chair back quietly and stood up across the table from Smellin', his loose arms swaying slightly.

'My patient is named Isotope John,' said Doc. 'He is mending.'

'I'm not letting you weasel out,' said Smellin'. 'I'm calling you out.'

'He's retired,' said Hong. His voice had an edge.

Smellin' looked at him. While they faced each other, Doc ambled towards the bar, apparently in no hurry. Smellin' glanced at him but he couldn't afford to forget Hong.

'Save your impatience for the railroad slavers,' said Prism Chisholm. 'Shall we be off?'

'Aw, shucks.' Smellin' collapsed into his chair again. 'Forget it, Doc.'

'Good idea,' said Duke. He got up and glanced around the table. 'Those railroad guys know most of us. We'll pretend we're sellin' Hong, like we said.

Tether, you stay in the back because you have to sneak around to the bridge. Mister Chisholm, you and your associate will help Wesley and me find the way, but then back off so you don't make 'em jumpy. They're skittish around strangers, unless they got the drop on 'em.'

Prism Chisholm nodded.

Duke started for the door and everyone pushed back their chairs and rose to follow him.

'Louie,' said Duke. 'You stay here.'

I stared at him, half out of my seat, feeling a twinge in my stomach. 'Me? I want to go.'

Duke didn't hear me, his mind on more pressing matters. They all walked away, clunking in deliberate steps across the hardwood floor. Hong was last.

'Hey, Hong.'

He stopped to look at me, swivelling on his Avocado waist. 'I owe you two favours. I'm paying one back,' he said.

'Huh? How?'

'Leaving you here where it's safe.' He turned his back and sauntered out after the others.

'That's no favour,' I said, not very loudly. I still couldn't bring myself to argue with him.

The swinging doors swung back into place behind him.

I sagged in my chair, watching them go. So much for being part of the gang. So much for earning my cousin's respect. I was still a control-natural.

So was Duke.

I jumped up and ran for the door. Sally Flash came around a table in front of me on her way to the bar and I ran smack into her. I bounced off the front of her with a clank and landed hard on my back on the floor, slamming my head as glasses crashed and Sally shrieked.

I sat up and looked around. She was just sitting up across from me in a pile of soaked petticoats, surrounded by shattered mugs.

'Very cheap,' she sneered.

I hopped up, jumped over her, and ran out into the street.

The gang was cantering out of town. I took off like spudbusters down the street for Rusty, by the smithy where I had left him. If I lost track of the gang, I'd never find them again tonight.

I had made moccasin tracks about halfway to the smithy when Harris trotted up alongside me.

'Hi, Louie! Whatcha doing?' he asked cheeerfully, keeping pace with me.

'Nothing. Leaving town,' I panted.

'I heard hoofbeats. You're pulling a job?'

'Yeah. No. Sort of.' I leaped on Rusty and kicked him to life. As I galloped out of town on him, leaving Harris behind, I realized that if I got too close, they might send me back again or even damage Rusty so I couldn't follow. I slowed him to match their canter, straining to hear them ahead and trusting to Rusty's eyesight.

A few minutes later, Harris galloped up behind me on a horsite.

'Where are we going, Louie?'

'What are you doing here?'

'I want to join the gang.'

'Well—' This was no time to argue. 'Keep quiet. They told me to stay in town. If they know we're back here, we'll have to leave.'

'Really? Why?'

'*Quiet!*'

He finally shut up.

I thought a minute. 'Harris, what kind of specials do you have again?'

'You forgot?' He sat up straight, encouraged. 'One Overlaid Infrared Contact Eyeball insert from Private Eyes, Inc. Two Aloha Outrigger Trigger Rigger index fingers that are precisely matched to the pull on my gun. And my Cobra Brand Elbow and Forearm Complex.'

'You just might get to use them tonight. Come on.'

'*Really?*'

We hurried after the gang but soon they slowed to a walk. I moved Rusty up fairly close to them. If we were lucky, no one would detect more slow hoofbeats along the trail.

Up ahead, I could just hear voices.

'A fork is right ahead,' said Wesley. 'We go to the right.'

'I see it,' said Prism Chisholm.

'I smell it,' said Sniffin' Griffin.

'You can't smell a fork in the road, you fake,' said Smellin', laughing.

'Maybe *you* can't,' sneered Sniffin'.

'Can you smell my fist comin' at you?' Smellin' demanded.

'Save it!' Duke snapped.

A moment later, the short column was angling to the right.

We proceeded that way for a long time.

'Their camp was over the next rise when we saw it,' Wesley said finally.

'I can smell 'em,' said Smellin' Llewellyn. 'They stink.'

'That's you,' said Sniffin' Griffin.

'Attend me,' said Prism Chisholm. 'We will hang back.'

'I'll go around them up on the slope,' said Tether.

'The rest of us will take Hong down there,' said Duke. 'Let's go.'

I hung back, listening to them go. Harris rode up alongside me.

'Now what, Louie? Huh?' he asked eagerly.

'I'm not sure.' That afternoon, I had envisioned myself riding down into danger as part of the gang, not as an outcast. I turned slightly to one side, listening. 'Harris, do you hear something? In the woods nearby?'

'Like what?'

'Moo,' said somebody.

'Chuck! Come out, Chuck.'

'Ditto moo.'

'Come on, Chuck! This is important.'

'Reprise moo.'

'Then *where* are you?'

'*Ibidem* moo.' He finally walked out of the forest, followed by the other five steerites who had stampeded with him before.

'Where have you been?'

'Rounding up our little herd, now that I'm feeling well again. We were just coming into town when everybody rode out, so we followed you. Sneaky, huh?'

'Oh.'

'I said, *sneaky*, *huh*?'

'Yes, yes. Definitely. Say, would you guys like to stampede these railroad slavers out of business for good?'

'Sure,' said Lugosi. 'We like to stampede.'

'You wait here. Harris and I will sneak up real close and see what's going on. We'll signal you when to stampede if it's necessary.'

'How?' Chuck asked.

'I have a sixty-shooter,' Harris said proudly. 'Want to see it?'

'Not now,' I said quickly. 'Come on.'

When we rode over the next rise, we could see one slave pen down in the hollow and the slaver camp just past it. This time both were heavily lit with portable lamps, throwing incidental light up and down the trail. A big campfire blazed in front of their tents.

I nudged Rusty into the trees to one side, out of sight, and Harris followed.

# Twenty-four

When we had sneaked down close, we stopped where we could look through the trees into the camp. Duke's gang was still mounted and dickering over Hong's price. The railroad slavers stood on the ground across the campfire from them, holding rifles.

Before, I had seen the railroad slavers only as fast-moving shadows fleeing the stampede of Chuck and his companions. Now six of them were standing in a row. The one in the middle was Snyder Gray; I remembered his drawl.

They looked like ordinary drifters or cowboys, without any sign of prosperity on them. In fact, they all had cheap Fargo Spinwrists with simple but exaggerated Coeur d'Alene hands, made of flexible steel that could grip hard and lock into place. Those hands were fine for working mining machinery but were really kind of slow for pulling a rifle trigger repeatedly.

'We're low on cash right now,' Snyder Gray drawled. 'But we need all the labour we can get.'

'We got no use for him,' said Duke. He was drawing out the conversation as long as he could to give Tether time to pass the camp in the woods and head for the bridge. 'We did business with you over that beef to everybody's satisfaction. You want to make some kind of deal now or not?'

'Here's the deal,' said Snyder Gray. 'We'll take all of you.'

Hong's flexible arms immediately dipped for his guns. Duke too belatedly fumbled for his. So did everyone in the gang except Wesley, who mistakenly grabbed the data box in his back pocket out of habit instead.

The slavers didn't hesitate. Every one of them raised his rifle and clamped down hard on the triggers with their Coeur d'Alene hands. Instead of squeezing the triggers repeatedly, they gripped tight and hung on. The rifles buzzed instead of banged, and nearly everyone in Duke's gang went into the jiggling flitters, right in the saddle.

Prism Chisholm's eyes turned an opaque white. Smellin's nose vibrated out of its triangle of white tape. Hong's goose-neck arms quivered uncontrollably. Alkali bounced even more strangely than usual, sideways as well as up and down. Carver's Swissarmie blades flashed out and then folded back in again, repeatedly.

'Chuck!' I screamed. 'Come on, Chuck!'

At that, Harris fired his gun right behind me, temporarily deafening one of my ears.

As the thunder of steerite hooves rolled down the slope toward us, I stared at Duke's gang. Only Duke himself had managed to level a gun. Snyder Gray knocked it away with a rifle barrel and then clunked him on the head. Even as Duke hit the ground, his companions were also falling out of their saddles.

Behind me, Harris let out a little breath of shock. 'Moo!'

Chuck led the steerite herd down the trail at a run. Now, though, the slavers were free to turn towards them. Their rifles buzzed again and the steerites began to fall. When Chuck went down, the steerite behind him stumbled over him. I suddenly realized that the only reason the first stampede had worked

284

was surprise; the slavers hadn't had time to aim. Now they were ready.

All the while, Harris and I were just sitting there among the trees.

'Come on, Rusty!' I said in a harsh whisper, and kicked him. A moment later, we were crashing through the brush. I leaned down low and held my hat on as Rusty picked his way through the trees with his robotic eyesight. Harris followed. The buzzing sound behind us went on, as did the thumping of steerites to the ground.

In a few moments, Rusty burst out onto the trail past the camp. It ran alongside the railroad that had already been laid. I kicked him again, trusting to his eyesight as we plunged into the darkness. Hoofbeats up ahead told me that Tether was trotting just ahead.

'Tether! It's Louie,' I shouted.

'Louie?' He sneered, pulling up. 'What do *you* want?'

'Keep going to the bridge! The whole gang's been taken prisoner.' I slowed to a canter.

'What?' He spurred his horsite to keep pace.

'That's right,' said Harris.

'Didn't you hear the noise?' I demanded.

'What are *you* doing here?' Tether asked Harris. 'No, never mind,' he added quickly. 'All right. Let's blow the bridge.'

'They'll be coming,' I told him. 'As soon as they finish knocking out all the steerites and throwing everybody into pens. They must have heard me yelling and Harris shooting.'

We rode on fast. So far I didn't hear anyone behind us. Finally we pulled up at the near end of a huge railroad bridge. It crossed a black abyss even darker than the rest of the night.

'We gotta blow it and then rescue everybody,' said Tether. 'I got the dynamud right here, but it has to go at the base of the trestle. Otherwise, the supports will still be in place and they can just build the top parts back on again.'

'I know what,' said Harris. 'Let's go to the other side of the bridge and set the dynamud. Then when the railroad slavers cross the bridge to come after us, we can blow it up then.'

'Yeah? Then how do we get back to this side again, afterwards?' tether glared at him.

'Uh . . .' Harris shrugged weakly.

Tether opened saddlebags from his horsite. He pulled out a small chemical lantern that gave off a muted green glow when he turned the crank. It hung from a loop that he slipped over his neck. Then he slung the saddlebags over one shoulder.

'Fob, you keep watch here. If you hear hoofbeats, say so.' Tether handed the lantern to Harris. 'You hold this and come down to the bottom with me.'

'Sure.' Harris took it and followed Tether.

Listening for riders coming was a lot like holding horses outside the bank, only this time I knew what I was doing. Both activities meant just standing there. I watched the green lantern sway back and forth as Tether and Harris looked for a way to climb down the side of the gorge.

Time passed. I paced around the tracks in the chilly air. They were still wandering about only a metre or two down the slope. I could hear Harris making eager suggestions and Tether muttering at him in annoyance.

'We'll have to plant it up high,' Tether said finally. 'There isn't a good place to climb down here.'

Suddenly I whirled around, listening. 'You guys hear something?'

286

The lantern swung crazily as Tether and Harris hurried out of the gorge and came running over to me.

'What?' Tether asked softly.

'Evening, strangers,' drawled Snyder Gray.

Six shadows stepped out of the trees around us all at once. Dim green light limned six rifle barrels that were pointed at us. Panicked, I leaped at the rifle right in front of me and they all began to buzz. It was held by Snyder Gray.

I vibrated all over. Even my teeth seemed to rattle, but my momentum carried me into a collision with Snyder Gray. I grabbed the rifle and swung it around, pulling. He grunted and we began an awkward shuffle on the uneven ground. As the beam of the rifle moved, the slaver next to us suddenly stiffened and started the jiggling flitters right where he stood.

Tether's lariat had shot out of his arm, but it fluttered limply as he too began the weird quivering two-step. Harris had pulled his six-shooter half out of its holster with his Cobra Brand Elbow and Forearm Complex before joining Tether in dancing to the inaudible music.

I stumbled but managed to hang on to the rifle. Snyder Gray was bigger and heavier than I was, but I was lower on the slope and had leverage on him for pulling. When the rifle slipped free of Snyder Gray's hands, I fell on my back and fired it at him. He too started shaking in place.

Off to one side, Harris and Tether collapsed in a heap. I felt harder vibrations as the other slavers turned their attention to me. Expecting to black out any second, I swung the rifle around and swept it across all of them. The remaining five quaked strangely where they stood, as well.

I swung the rifle back and forth repeatedly to include all of them. Even after they had all fallen in a heap, I gave them some long extra doses before I released the trigger. The effects were temporary and I needed some time. Then I lowered the rifle, exhausted, and rolled over to my hands and knees.

Harris's long legs twitched slightly like a bug that was almost dead. Tether wasn't moving. I crawled over to look at them in the green lamplight. They hadn't received as much of the strange rifle fire, whatever it was, as the slavers I had shot, but they were unconscious.

I gathered the rifles from the slavers and threw all of them over the side of the gorge. Just as I swung back the one I had used, I changed my mind. Instead of throwing it, I stashed it behind a rock near Tether.

Then I picked up the green lamp, taking care not to strangle Tether with the loop as I pulled it off him, and peered down the slope into the gorge. It was rugged, with plenty of big outcroppings and a lot of jagged trees and bushes. I pulled the saddlebags from Tether's shoulder and slung them over one of mine. Then I hung the lamp around my neck and started climbing down the slope.

Tether couldn't climb down here because of his lariat hand. Harris's Cobra Brand Elbow and Forearm Complex would have made climbing hard for him too, though his overlaid Infrared Contact Eyeball insert would have helped him see. Still, in the green glow from the lantern around my neck, I could pick out the holds I needed easily.

Before long, I actually found myself at the base of the dry gorge, looking up at the massive crisscrossed timbers forming the trestle of the bridge. I reached into the saddlebags and pulled out two bricks of malleable claylike stuff. It had a green tinge now, making it resemble mouldy cheese.

I broke the stuff into little handfuls and started packing it into joints I could reach. Since I didn't know how long the slavers would remain unconscious, I couldn't take too much time. I walked along putting it in different places, sometimes as high as I could and sometimes down by the ground. The gorge was too wide for me to cross the entire base of the trestle. When I ran out of dynamud, I reached into the saddlebags for fuse and matches.

They were empty.

Tether had probably planned to ignite the dynamud by shooting at it from a safe distance. I started the long climb back up the wall of the gorge. When I was about halfway up, I heard someone stirring above. Hoping it was Tether or Harris, I climbed faster.

I was covered in sweat by the time I pulled myself over the edge of the slope. From the green glow of the lamp still around my neck, I could see Harris just sitting up. Tether too was pushing himself into a sitting position. So far, the railroad slavers were still motionless.

'Tether,' I wheezed. 'I planted the dynamud. But we have to set it off.'

'You did that? Say. Maybe you're all right, after all. Where is it?' He blinked at me, rubbing the side of his head. 'I was going to leave the lantern down there so I could see where to shoot. You're still wearing it.'

I looked down at the lamp on my chest. 'Oh.'

'We got to rescue the rest of the gang.' Tether got up groggily.

'Harris,' I said quickly. 'Are you awake?'

'I blew it,' he muttered. 'I had my chance to shoot it out with those bandits and they got me.'

'You told me you had an infrared eyeball insert?'

'Yeah. Fat lot of good it did me.'

'You can see in the dark with it. Come on, we need it.' I grabbed his arm and pulled him to the edge of the gorge.

'Huh?' He wove unsteadily.

'Look, I had to knead that stuff to make it stick. It should still be warmer than the trestle. Can you see it down there with your insert?'

'Uh . . . sure. Little globs of stuff, right?'

'Shoot one of them. If one goes, the others will follow.'

'Really?' He rocked back and forth unsteadily on his fancy, unscuffed cowboy boots. 'What did you say?'

'This is your big chance,' I told him urgently. 'You want to go down in history?'

'Hoo ha,' he muttered.

'Harris. *Do you want to be on the cover of a magazine back east of the Mississippi?*'

He stiffened up and looked down the gorge again.

'Shoot it!'

In a long sequence of microseconds, he whipped out his six-shooter with his Cobra Brand Elbow and Forearm Complex, sighted with his Private Eye Infrared insert, then squeezed the trigger with his Aloha Outrigger Trigger Rigger index finger. The gun barked.

Nothing happened.

'I missed,' he muttered.

'Try again.'

He missed again, and a third time. Just as Tether got up and staggered over to us, Harris fired a fourth time. An orange-and-yellow explosion thundered below us, and a second later a long series of similar explosions rolled along the base of the trestle like a giant string of firecrackers.

In the uncertain light thrown off by the dynamud blowing up, I could just see the trestle collapsing into the gorge like a toy house of glued toothpicks. The crashing echoed up and down the mountainsides.

'Come on,' I said. 'Those slavers aren't going to sleep forever. What if they have friends?'

Tether nodded weakly.

I snatched up the slaver rifle I had stashed, wishing I had saved two more. It was too late for that now. We mounted up and rode for the slaver camp.

We slowed down as we approached, looking for more slavers. The horsites belonging to Duke's gang were all just standing around. No one else was in sight.

'Nobody's home in their tents,' said Harris quietly, peering forward. 'That big wooden pen has people in it, though. And the steerites are all hogtied on the trail just past it, I guess wherever they fell.'

'You sure?' Tether asked.

'I just scanned the tents and the surrounding forest with my infrared insert. It's about time I got some use out of it.'

We cantered down to the slave pen. No sounds came from inside. I jumped off Rusty and ran to the door, still holding the rifle. The door was only closed with a long wooden bar. I slid it out of its braces and reached for the grip to open the door.

The door suddenly swung open to a chorus of shouts, hitting me in the forehead. I staggered backward, surprised. Duke charged out and slammed his massive red-shirted chest into me. I thumped onto my back, clutching the rifle. He and the entire gang ran over me, screaming angrily, followed by the other slaves who were inside.

'Hold it, hold it,' Tether yelled. 'Duke, it's us. Tether and Louie and this other guy.'

I rolled over and looked up. Hong reached down and pulled me to my feet.

Duke had trotted to a halt, glaring around with his fists clenched. 'Where are they? The railroad slavers?'

'They're out cold,' said Harris. 'Six of them, at least.'

'That's the whole bunch,' said Duke, still looking around. 'The rest of them are driving most of their steerites on west. They're just straw bosses working for the big company based somewhere else.'

'Only six?' Tether said.

'It's not their numbers that makes them tough,' said Hong. 'It's their rifles.'

'They don't have them any more,' I said. No one seemed to hear me.

'Where's Tinny Ginnie and the loot?' Tether asked. 'I don't see her.'

'According to these other guys who were here at the time,' said Duke, 'she ran off her first night here. She kept how strong she is a secret. Then just before dinner call, she ripped off her neck chain, hit one of the straws from behind, and ran for it in the dark. Told somebody she was going to New Mexico.'

I was glad to hear that. It was a long way off. Not that I had a grudge against the New Mexicans.

'She must have given up the loot,' said Smellin'. 'Suppose we find it and get out of here.'

Duke and his gang marched up to the tents. Tether lassoed the tent poles with his loop and Smellin' and Duke helped him pull all of them down. Carver slashed up the fabric of the tents out of sheer spite. Alkali bounced around the debris eagerly, throwing stuff aside. Wesley followed him and kept ducking out of the way.

The other freed slaves were milling around, looking at each other and the gang curiously.

Hong sat down on a rock to wait.

Prism Chisholm and Sniffin' Griffin stood back impassively, watching.

I didn't want to hang around if they were going to have it out with Duke right here. None of them had recovered their weapons yet, but those would be stashed in the tents, too. I walked Rusty quickly up the trail past the pen.

'Going to free the steerites?' Harris asked, trotting after me on his mount.

'Uh – yeah.' I looked around at the steerites tied up on the ground in the light thrown from the pen and the green glow from the lamp still around my neck. 'Chuck? Which one is you?'

'Over here.' Chuck sighed. 'How embarrassing this is. "Moo", indeed.'

I knelt to untie him. 'Harris, would you help with the others?'

'I'm a failure,' he muttered.

'This is no time to talk,' I said. 'Bring all the steerites into Washout with me, though, will you?'

'As you wish.'

Shouts and cheers rose up from the tents. Harris and I hurried back down there. By the time we arrived, the gang was tying wooden crates onto horsites. Everybody had their guns back in their holsters too that I could see.

'Just one crate to a horse,' Duke called. 'Those gold double bisons are heavy, and we've got a lot of extra riders.'

Everybody in the gang laughed, and even Prism Chisholm grinned. Hong smiled faintly. Soon everyone mounted up and started back for Washout, with the other freed slaves riding double with members of the gang. All the way back, Prism Chisholm never took his eyes of Duke or the crates.

# Twenty-five

Harris rode alongside me all the way back to Washout as silent and unexpressive as Prism Chisholm's eyes. As before, we brought up the rear of the gang, now with the steerites behind us. They didn't sing. When we got back to town I had Chuck lead them around back of the smithy.

Harris and I rode on up to the Silver Transistor after everyone else. I was still carrying the slaver rifle.

The saloon was almost deserted when we arrived. Doc was the only customer, sitting at a table near the paino. Fingers Lau was sitting on the piano bench, asleep with his face on the keys. Isomer Isaac Phlegm was sweeping the floor and Sally Flash was leaning on the bar in her finery, yawning.

'What happened, Duke?' Isomer Isaac Phlegm straightened up over his broom.

'We got all our belongings packed on the horsites,' Duke said proudly. 'We'll give you the whole story some other time.'

'On the horsites? Why don't you bring those . . . *belongings* . . . in here and divvy up?'

'Nobody in this town would dare touch that gold tonight.' Duke looked squarely at Prism Chisholm 'We got some business to discuss first.'

'Did you blow the bridge?' Sally asked eagerly. 'We heard noises like thunder from somewhere. That was you, wasn't it?' Her Finegrinder & Denton Barbilou Bluebells were wide with wonder.

'That was Tether and Louie and this skinny guy, here.'

'Naw.' Sally stared at the three of us just coming in. 'Them?'

Tether shook his head. 'Not me. Them two.'

Harris grinned shyly.

'Harris Nye.' Sally sashayed up to him, swishing her petticoats with both hands. 'Did you really plant those charges?'

'No. Louie did.'

'Yuck.' She glanced at me and wrinkled her nose. 'Harris, you must have done something. What did you do?'

'He set them off,' I said. My face was hot with embarrassment at the recognition as I shared the credit. 'Nobody else could have, right then.'

'That's right,' said Tether. 'But you're okay too, fob.'

Duke thumped me on the back heartily, knocking me three steps closer to Sally. She grimaced at me and took Harris's arm to lead him to a table.

'So you blew the bridge.' Isomer Isaac Phlegm nodded in approval. 'On behalf of our absent owner, Cicero Yang, sit down and drink up. I'll charge it all to him.'

'According to my data,' said Wesley, 'the competing outfit will overtake that slaver railroad in two weeks, long before the big trestle can be rebuilt.' He tapped his glasses a few times. 'The slavers will never catch up.'

Everyone else sat around the biggest table again in a semicircle. I didn't want to sit here in the line of fire if the palaver came to that. Casually, I walked away and moved up on the staircase again to plunk down in my favourite spot.

'About those *belongings* of yours,' said Prism Chisholm.

'Well, now.' Duke leaned back in his chair and looked across the table at him. 'The way I see it, you don't have the firepower to take it.'

'I have a proposition to make to you . . . in private.'

'*Well*, now.' Duke raised his eyebrows. 'Maybe you're willing to be bought off? That's the sensible solution. That way, we wouldn't have to shoot you two.'

'You and I will discuss it,' said Prism Chisholm. 'I will leave Sniffin' here to represent my interests.'

Duke nodded and shoved his bulk out of the chair. Prism Chisholm was nearly as wide but a little shorter. He blinked a blue-yellow glance at the saloon doors as he and Duke walked towards the stairs. I scooted out of their way against the railing like a rodent as they approached.

While they tramped up the steps past me, Betsy slipped inside the swinging doors and hurried along the wall after them. At the table, the others were drinking and raucously exchanging their versions of the night's adventure. None of them noticed her.

'Hi,' I said shyly. Her eyes looked beyond me up the stairs.

I watched her stomp up the steps past me, her looped braids swinging. On impulse, I took a quick glance at the gang below, none of whom was watching, and padded after her quietly on my moccasins.

I had never gone all the way up the stairs before. Below us, Smellin' Llewellyn and Sniffin' Griffin were arm wrestling to shouts of encouragement, all of them for Smellin'. The carousing woke up Fingers, whose hands began to play something quick and lively while he was still staring about groggily. Betsy turned the corner down the hallway ahead, and I hurried silently after her.

I peeked around the corner. Down the hall, she stopped outside a closed door and took a deep breath. Then she opened it and walked inside.

She left the door ajar. I crept down the hall, got down on all fours, and edged around the door frame just enough to look.

Prism Chisholm and Duke hadn't even had time to sit down at the round card table yet. They both looked at her.

'This is my daughter, Polly,' said Duke. 'Would you excuse us, Polly? I'll be out in a minute if you want to talk.'

'My name's Betsy, like I told you,' she said angrily. 'And I know what you're doing.'

'I invited her to join us,' said Prism Chisholm, his eyes glowing bright green. 'She was waiting outside the saloon doors just now, listening.'

'You?' Duke glared at him and slid his heavy sheepskin vest back from his gun. 'She's got nothing to do with this.'

'This was my idea, *Daddy*.' Betsy sneered. 'I waited for you to come back to town and I listened from outside on the boardwalk. Anyhow, don't you think it's a little late to start taking care of me now?'

'Your idea?' Duke looked back and forth between them.

'Here's my offer,' said Prism Chisholm. 'You return all the stolen gold from Femur to me and Sniffin' Griffin. Otherwise, your daughter will tell everyone, including your own gang, that you are a control-natural.'

'You're nasty,' he said to Betsy through clenched teeth. 'You don't play fair.'

'It runs in the family.' She glared back at him. 'Take it or leave it.'

'Hold on, not so fast.' Duke was sweating heavily, his face flushed nearly as red as his shirt. 'I can't let people know, but . . . give you all of it?'

'Take it or leave it,' Prism Chisholm echoed sternly. 'It's not a payoff. We're returning it to Femur.'

'You still have to make it worth my while,' said Duke. 'I put a lot of time and effort into that job.' He rubbed his forehead with the heel of one hand. 'Besides, you realize some of that gold is spent. We've been living on it ever since the robbery.'

'Understood,' said Prism Chisholm with a shrug. 'Now about my offer.'

'Take or leave it,' Betsy repeated.

Prism Chisholm nodded. Lights shone off his multiple facets with the motion. Some of them blinked red, others a deep blue.

'I don't know.' Duke wiped his face with his yellow bandana. 'If I take that offer, you got to help me make it stick. Otherwise, it's not worth anything to me.'

'Help you?' Prism Chisholm asked.

'If I just give you all the loot, my gang will tear me to dogfood anyway. With that in mind, I might just as well keep it all myself and take my chances. If you want it, you have to steal it from us so I still look good.'

'I see.' Prism Chisholm's eyes glittered and blinked a full colour wheel, thoughtfully. 'That could be arranged. Logically, however, your gang would then chase me. To keep up appearances, you would have to participate. Perhaps you are planning to take it from us again on the trail.'

'What for? Polly here could still spread the word

about me and I'd be ruined.' Duke sank into a chair and mopped his face with his bandana some more. 'I'll arrange for you to steal it tonight. That will give you two at least until dawn to get a head start. And if my guys all drink themselves silly tonight, they'll sleep late tomorrow.'

'And you can subvert the chase once it begins,' said Prism Chisholm. 'I agree.'

'Just remember,' said Betsy. 'If that gold doesn't get all the way back to Femur, I'll tell on you, even if these guys are dead.'

'Don't worry,' Duke muttered. 'You're under my protection from now on.'

She watched him suspiciously but said nothing.

'Let's get this over with,' said Duke. 'Mister Chisholm, I'll find a way to give you the opportunity you want downstairs. Keep an eye out. It'll be up to you to take it.' He pushed himself out of the chair.

I scrambled up and ran back down the hall on my toes. At the corner, I skidded a couple of times on the turn but then took stairs two at a time back to my spot, next to the slaver rifle leaning on the wall where I had left it. Then, with my heart pounding, I looked back up at Duke as casually as I could when he appeared on the balcony.

By the time Duke reached the stairs, he had assumed a hearty stride and a big smile. Prism Chisholm followed him and Betsy came down last, her face tight and angry.

When the guys at the table saw them, they waved and yelled. Smellin' and Sniffin' were still straining over the table in a stalemated arm wrestle and ignored everyone. Hong had moved to Doc's table and they were talking quietly.

'Party time,' Duke yelled. 'Call out the town!'

Isomer Isaac Phlegm shook his head, grinning,

and walked to the front of the saloon to ring the steel pentagle hanging by the door. In the corner, Fingers shifted to his fast version of 'Red River Valley'. Duke stood over the arm wrestling match with his hands on his hips while Prism Chisholm sat down in his chair again at the table.

Betsy stood behind Prism Chisholm with her arms folded.

Sally Flash hopped up and pulled Harris to his feet. 'Go wake up Hackles at the stable,' she said. 'Tell him to bring his fiddle.' She lifted her skirts and trotted outside with him but turned in the other direction.

Duke's gang seemed to figure the party meant everything was okay. I picked up the slaver rifle and took it down the stairs into the crowd. Then I worked my way over to Hong and Doc, a little shy about interrupting them.

'I feel fine now,' Hong was saying, levelling his perpetual squint at Doc.

'So do the rest of them, I would say.' Doc looked at the rowdy gang. Then he saw the rifle I was carrying. 'Say, is that one of them?'

'That's right,' I said, handing it to him just like we had been introduced normally. 'I thought maybe you could tell us what it is. I threw the rest of them in the gorge before we blew up the bridge.'

Doc tilted back his black hat and frowned at the rifle. He tinkered with it a little. I had never taken the time to look at it closely, but now I saw that the entire butt had the shiny surface of a solar collector.

'Not much in the way of moving parts,' said Doc. 'I could open a couple of seams to look inside if I had the tools from my medical bag. But from the symptoms you described, Hong, I'm sure I know what it does.'

Hong twirled his villain's moustache and waited respectfully.

Doc turned to me. 'How did the rifle fire affect you?'

'It rattled my teeth,' I said. 'And it kind of tickled all over.'

'But it didn't knock you unconscious.'

'Well . . . I wasn't in it very long.'

'Did it affect Duke, do you know?'

'Sure. They captured him. Or, wait a minute.' I hesitated, remembering. 'Maybe not. When the rest of the gang was all wiggling in their saddles, he reached for one of the slavers. They had to hit him on the head.'

'I thought as much.' Doc turned the rifle over in his hands, studying it. 'None of the six slavers you met up with were control-naturals.'

'They had Fargo Spinwrists and special hands.'

'This weapon disrupts the electrical current running through a person's special parts. In particular, it jams up the tay-chip interface that converts energy between human tissue and specials. That's why you control-naturals are immune to its effects.'

'Not completely. It did rattle my teeth.'

'I can't figure out why you felt any vibrations at all. That's the part that doesn't make sense.' Doc shrugged and handed the rifle back to me. 'Just a side effect, I suppose. The rifle was badly made. It must be a new invention; if anyone besides the slavers had them, they would be mass-produced. Or maybe these rifles are also used for something else we don't know about. I imagine you felt inaudibly low sound waves.'

'Never heard of such a thing,' said Hong with a grin. 'So to speak.'

'Me, neither,' I said, accepting it back with some

surprise. I realized, then, that everyone considered it mine as a spoil of conquest. Before, I had just carried it around for protection and then later to ask Doc about it.

'If one person can invent one, so can someone else,' Doc cautioned. 'Don't get overconfident with it.'

I nodded. Immunity hadn't stopped Duke from getting clunked over the head. Anyhow, I didn't know guns. 'Here. Why don't you take it home and look inside if you feel like it?'

'I'd like that.' Doc took it back and leaned it against the wall.

By this time, the Silver Transistor was filling up with people. Some of them walked in sleepily, blinking in the muted light of the cloud-crystal chandelier, but they quickly got caught up in the bouncy piano music.

Harris brought in Hackles, carrying his fiddle as Sally had suggested. Alkali bounced up to Hackles at the bar in his springy walk, shoving his oversized hat up out of his eyes. Wesley converged on him from the other side.

'I heard you got the loot,' said Hackles, grabbing a mug in his free hand. 'What happened?'

Harris found one of the few remaining empty tables and sat down again, still subdued.

'I can't let this go unrecorded,' shouted Carver. He flipped out a sharp blade with a pointed end from his Swissarmie Brand swivel hand and carefully carved his name and the date into the gold-leaf surface of the bar. A bunch of cowboys came in, roused by the clanging of the pentagle, and stopped to watch him. A few moments later, they joined him at the bar and Carver regaled them with the whole adventure as they bought for him.

Duke wouldn't have to pay for all this, after all.

Isomer Isaac Phlegm glared at Carver's handi-work on the bar but said nothing. Cicero Yang was the owner; this was what he got for leaving town all the time. Isomer Isaac reached under the bar to turn the crank of the keg and started filling mugs four-handed as more townspeople and drovers walked in.

Hong and Doc sat back, surveying the crowd.

Smellin' and Sniffin' still strained against each other in their arm wrestle, both grimacing like they had toothbrushes in their mouths sideways. Smellin's nose was still taped all around from when Doc had fixed it for him, but it was a little crooked now, making him look even stranger. Sniffin's fringe swayed from his buckskin sleeve as their hands quivered without moving to either side.

A steerite snout in a leather mask stuck itself through the swinging doors. After a moment of hesitation, Chuck's whole head followed. He looked around through the eyeholes, then saw me and walked inside. I could just see the other steerites waiting politely outside on the boardwalk and the street beyond.

Sally pushed in past them with a line of young women in tow. Most of them were still tying ribbons in their hair or straightening their dresses. One had pushed up her sleeve to see if her elbow had come unhinged.

Chuck picked his way along the wall, brushing aside some of the tables and chairs on his way. He politely waited for people to move out of his path before proceeding again. I met him over by the stairs.

'Uh, hi, Chuck. I don't think you're supposed to be in here.'

'This is important. We've had a herd council.'

'A what?'

'A herd council. We have noted that in each of our cases, the time limit on our rustling insurance has passed.'

'Rustling insurance?'

'Our owners have by now either entered their claims for us or forfeited them. Our programming shifts automatically at that point to make us free mavericks. We have decided to form our own formal herd and request that you become our legal owner.'

'Formal herd? What's that?' I was more confused than before.

'That just means we make certain programming changes in ourselves for cooperation. But how about it? You could be a small rancher.'

'Me?' I scratched my head more out of surprise than any itch. Steerites were extremely expensive. 'Me an owner?'

'You won't turn us down, will you?' Chuck lowered his head shyly and pawed at the hardwood floor with a stainless-steel hoof. It left big gouges. 'We're afraid of being taken over forcefully by the, shall we call them, uncivilized types who frequent this area. But, um . . . we like you.'

'Aw. I like you, too. But, me an owner? What do I have to do?'

'Not much. We vouch for our ownership, so you don't have to prove it. Just find us grazing range and take us to market when we're ready. *And*, see that we're slaughtered by professionals, will you? We do have our pride.'

'Of course,' I said, feeling my face glow with a kind of astonished excitement. 'I'll make sure of it.'

'Thank you!' Chuck swished his tail excitedly. 'I shall go report the good news to the fellows.'

As he trotted away, now crashing into furniture

and ramming people aside in his eagerness, I started giggling to myself. Not only were Duke and Prism Chisholm forgetting about me, but I actually owned a little herd of steerites. Now I could make my own way, without pumping bellows or shovelling out stalls for others.

I decided to greet my new herd. Chuck's wake had closed behind him, but I climbed over smashed tables and chairs and then dodged cursing drinkers on my way towards the doors.

Suddenly the music changed. Fingers Lau switched to 'The Girl I Left Behind Me' again, only now Hackles had unsprung the Perlivarius bow from his forearm and was sawing away on his fiddle next to the piano. Wesley Coon was standing by his side. He was totally motionless, with the familiar glazed look in his eyes, except for the blur of his fingers on both hands as he fingered and picked at a banjo.

'Everybody dance!' Duke yelled. He shoved a couple of chairs and tables aside. Carver led the cowboys who had been listening to him over to help. Soon the furniture was haphazardly thrown against the walls and Sally was collaring guys to join a square dance with her young female guests.

One table remained near the centre of the saloon, where Smellin' and Sniffin' were still glaring at each other with sweat running down their faces and their hands turning white from the sustained effort. They sniffed and snuffled breathlessly at each other.

Alkali couldn't wait. He was hopping around happily in little circles by himself, all his joints bouncing out of step with each other and the music, as well. When the square dance began, with Grudge standing on the piano calling it, Alkali remained oblivious to it and the others obligingly danced around him.

Tether leaped onto the bar and shot his loop over part of the chandelier. He jumped and retracted his rope a little so he could swing back and forth over the square dancers, holding a full mug in his regular hand. Isomer Isaac Phlegm winced, looked away, and went on pouring.

By the time I had reached the doors, Smellin' and Sniffin' were still deadlocked. I stepped outside onto the boardwalk, looking back over the swinging doors out of curiosity. Prism Chisholm looked pointedly at Duke, who nodded.

'Whenever you're ready,' said Duke.

I could read his lips that time from where I was, but the music nearly drowned out their voices. Prism Chisholm tapped Sniffin' on the shoulder and he shook his head vigorously. Duke leaned down and spoke to Smellin', who made a face. Then Duke reached under Smellin's arms and lifted.

Prism Chisholm did the same with Sniffin'. Smellin' and Sniffin' kept their grip on each other even as they were pulled to their feet, elbows completely off the table. Their bosses wrestled them backwards until their hands, slippery with sweat, finally slid apart.

Prism Chisholm spoke quickly in Sniffin's ear, his eyes reflecting opaquely in the white light from the chandelier. Sniffin' relaxed, nodding reluctantly, and allowed himself to be escorted towards the swinging doors.

I dodged back into the shadows to one side as the two of them came out. Chuck and the other steerites were huddled together down the street, talking among themselves. They could wait.

Prism Chisholm and Sniffin' Griffin began moving the crates to their horsites. They would sneak off with the gold, but they wouldn't lower themselves to become horsite thieves.

Through the window, I could see Smellin' still muttering angrily to himself at the bar. Duke gave him a sympathetic pat on the back and moved towards Betsy, who was still eyeing him suspiciously. He inclined his head at the doors with a questioning look and she nodded. A moment later, they walked towards the doors together.

# Twenty-six

The square dance was still in full swing. Between tunes, Wesley would reach back and tinker with the wire leading to his rear pocket and then play again. His brain seemed to know the same songs that Fingers' Lau's six-fingered hands knew. The music and hand-clapping was louder than ever.

The swinging saloon doors opened, throwing more light onto the boardwalk, then swung shut again. Prism Chisholm whirled, reaching for his gun, but stopped when he saw only Duke and Betsy in the light slanting through the doorway.

'Just saying goodbye,' said Duke amiably, stepping forward into the street. Betsy came with him.

'You sure none of your guys saw you come out here?' Sniffin' demanded, as he tightened a rope on a crate. He sniffed loudly.

'They're havin' too much fun to notice the boss.' Duke leaned an arm casually on his horsite.

'So what are you doing out here? You're supposed to be distracting your gang. That was the deal,' said Prism Chisholm.

'I've been thinking.' Duke put his other arm around Betsy. She flinched, but he held on to her. 'All I want is, say, ten percent.'

'Forget it,' said Betsy, looking up at him. 'I'll tell them all—'

Duke glared down at her, face-to-face, and she stopped in mid-sentence. For the first time, she was truly scared. She jerked to get away, but he held on to her without much effort.

'I wouldn't hurt you, Polly,' said Duke. 'But I might just keep you with me on a little trip, so you can't tell anyone right away.'

'So how are you going to make us give you any gold?' Prism Chisholm demanded. 'It's two against one and you have to worry about her getting away from you.'

'You'll give it to me because a fight out here between us will bring my gang running. And they just might shoot first and hear about my being a control-natural after you're both dead.' He tightened his arm around Betsy, who glared up at him with angry eyes. 'You won't have time to discuss matters with them.'

'I see little or no temperature change in your skin surface. You are cool and calm.' Prism Chisholm's eyes glowed a steady orange as he studied Duke.

'And you won't follow me out on the trail because my gang will be after you. I'll tell them that you have all the money; they'll take my word over yours – or yours,' he added to Betsy.

Betsy squirmed, but he held her firmly.

'You men will have to head back for Femur as fast as you can,' Duke went on. 'Meanwhile, I'll tell them Polly and I have urgent business elsewhere. If I tell them to cut me out of the take, it'll mean that much more for them. They won't argue.'

'You're crazy,' Betsy snapped. 'When you give up your take, they'll suspect something.'

'There's risk involved,' Duke allowed. 'I can handle a little risk.'

Sniffin' Griffin sniffed loudly, glowering at Duke. Prism Chisholm's eyes blinked blue, glittered while he thought a moment, then glowed green.

'Ten percent,' said Prism Chisholm slowly. 'That might be a manageable amount.'

'Nothing doing,' I said loudly, stepping forward on shaking knees. 'Let her go, Duke.'

They all turned and looked at me in surprise. My heart was pounding but I didn't have time to think about it.'

'Louie?' Duke cocked his head to one side. 'What do you want?'

'I know your secret too, Duke. You're a control-natural. I was shovelling out the stable when you told her. And I overheard the deal upstairs, too.'

'You, too,' Duke said in surprise. 'And I gave you your chance.'

'You're an outlaw. I never really wanted to be a thief.' I fumbled around in my pockets and pulled out the coins I found. Most were in my pack back at the smithy. 'Here.' I tossed them onto the ground

'You're a fool,' said Duke. 'You can have part of the ten percent.'

'Forget it. And let her go.'

Duke still had his arm tight around her. He seemed taller and heavier than ever in his big hat and sheepskin vest and red shirt. Light from the saloon shone on his gold buttons. 'You going to make me, Louie? You don't wear a gun. Suppose I call my gang out here.'

'My cousin is in there, too. And Doc has the slaver rifle I gave him.'

'Call that a stalemate, then.' Duke stared into my eyes. 'So what are you going to do about *me*?'

What I was about to do was fall over backwards. My knees were quivering harder every moment. 'I have my steerites here to stampede over you. Right, Chuck?' I called over my shoulder.

I didn't hear anything.

'Chuck?' I glanced back nervously.

'Uh, moo?'

'What's wrong, Chuck?'

'We've had enough stampeding for one night, boss,' Chuck whined. 'See you later.' All the steerites flattened their ears against the sides of their heads, turned, and trotted away into the darkness.

'So.' Duke laughed. 'Why should any of us listen to you?'

''Cause I said so,' I declared stoutly. 'I'm the one who saved everybody tonight. I got the bridge blown up and I rescued all of you so you could get the gold back. Duke, go back into the saloon.'

Suddenly Betsy yanked herself away from Duke's arm and skipped over beside me. He flailed for her, too late. I had distracted him just enough for her to pull free.

'I won't forget this,' he growled, pointing at me.

'Don't forget we both know your secret, either,' I yelled back.

He looked around angrily at all of us.

'*Go inside the saloon,*' I ordered. I had been ordered around enough to know how to do it.

He clenched his jaw and stomped back into the saloon.

'Well, well.' Prism Chisholm grinned at me, his multiple eyes shining in the pale light from the saloon. 'So the little guy finally decided to play with the big boys—'

'Shut up,' I said. 'And mount up. I saved you too, you know.'

Prism Chisholm's eyes blinked bright red.

'Aw, forget it. Let's go.' Sniffin' swung up onto his horsite and sniffed again. 'We got a long way to go back to Femur.' He spurred his horsite and rode away.

312

Prism Chisholm eyed me once more in an orange sparkle, but then he mounted up and rode after Sniffin' without another word.

Betsy and I stood watching them go.

When they had cantered off into the darkness, I let out a long, unsteady breath. Tomorrow the drama would continue as the gang chased them, but I was out of it. I was going to stay out of it, too.

Then I glanced at her. She was watching me with the same wide-eyed expression she had been looking at Duke with.

'Come on.' I walked back into the saloon. After a moment of hesitation, I heard her footsteps follow me.

Tether was still swinging back and forth from the chandelier, whooping and hollering. Every so often, he reached down to knock crooked one of the little flowered hats on a young woman dancing. In between those times, he snatched Carver's hat and spun it across the room before someone else picked it up and returned it. When his mug was empty, he dropped down to the bar just long enough for a refill.

Duke was draining a full mug of something light blue at the bar.

Carver was leading the cowboys in the square dance. Sally had been dancing with him, leading the other women, but she took a break and went to sit down by Harris. He had been watching quietly.

Hong and Doc were just spectators too, but they were enjoying the party. Hong's black obsidian foot tapped in time to the music. Doc nodded slightly to the rhythm, himself, as he brushed dust off his silver trouser leg.

The tune was 'Sweet Betsy from Pike', but no one was singing. Under her breath, Betsy made up a new verse.

> *'She rode with the wagons, she rode on a steer.*
> *She reached the last mountains and her father dear.*
> *When she told him off and she cost him his gold*
> *She had a new life now 'cause she was so bold.*
>
> *Singing, too-ra-li, too-ra-li, too-ra-li-ay . . .'*

Betsy glanced up shyly, knowing I had heard her. I smiled weakly and shrugged.

'Well,' I said. 'It's been quite a night. For my part, it's better than dropping an anvil on someone's head, isn't it?'

'Yes. It certainly is.' She giggled, catching my eye.

'Thank you,' I said.

'What for?' she asked carefully, turning sidelong.

'For making Duke return the money. It's honest and got me off the hook with everybody.'

'I didn't do it for *you*. I had my own reasons.'

'I know. Still.'

She shrugged, making her looped braids sway.

I waited awkwardly, not knowing what to say. Then I saw Chuck stick his masked snout through the doors again.

'Say, there's Chuck again.' I moved toward him, talking over my shoulder. 'Did you know I'm going to own the herd? Come say hi. You like Chuck.'

'Own them? You mean you're stealing them?' She followed hesitantly.

'No! Just ask him.'

Chuck worked his way towards us, watching the square dancers with interest. By the time we reached him, near the table where Sally and Harris were sitting, he was swaying his horns back and forth in time to the music.

'Chuck, is it true that Louie is going to own your steerites now?' Betsy asked.

'He sure is,' Chuck said happily. Then he lowered

his head in embarrassment when he looked at me. 'Are you mad at me, boss?'

'Uh – no. Not any more. Now that I'm your owner, your self-preservation is important to me.'

'Whew,' said Chuck. Then he turned to Betsy. 'Say, thank you very much for this mask, but I don't need it any more. Would you take it off, please?'

'Of course.' She bent down to untie the knot, which had grown tighter with the dry air and was caked with dust and sand. Still, she loosened it and slid off the leather mask.

'Thank you,' Chuck said politely. He shook his head a few times and then ambled towards the little makeshift band in the corner.

'Congratulations,' Betsy said to me. 'You have an honest career as a rancher now.'

'It's a start.' I felt someone tug at my shirt.

Harris looked up from his chair. 'Louie, would you like to buy some special parts, cheap?'

'You mean yours?'

'Well, yes. That is, I believe I have had enough of the outlaw life. I should leave it to you experienced fellows.'

'What about getting your name on the cover of a magazine back east?'

He shrugged. The gesture seemed to be contagious tonight.

'Actually, I'm going to start a small ranch.' I thought a moment. 'Say, would you like to work with me? I can't do everything alone.' I waited for him to get all excited.

Instead, he just nodded soberly. 'Perhaps. Let's discuss it in the morning.'

'Come on, Harris.' Sally inched her chair closer to him and leaned her head against his arm. 'You were going to tell me about your adventure tonight.'

315

'Oh, I don't know. You want to dance instead?'

'Dance? Oh ... all right.' She looked disappointed, but followed him to the middle of the floor to join the others, fussing with the feathers behind her head.

'So ... *Betsy?*'

We both turned. I was surprised to see Duke addressing her as he lurched unsteadily forward.

'What?' she demanded suspiciously, backing away.

'I've been thinking,' said Duke. 'Tinny Ginnie's gone south and the loot's gone east. I expect the gang will take off after Mr Chisholm tomorrow, but maybe I'll let them go without me.'

'Why?'

'Maybe I ought to take up something less strenuous.' He shrugged and drank from his mug. 'Anyhow, grudges aren't worth my time. What do you two think?'

'Would you take up something honest?' she challenged.

'Could be. Maybe these new railroads need guards. A guy who knows how outlaws operate.'

'They're all based in San Francisco,' she pointed out.

'And, uh, maybe we could get acquainted. For real, I mean.'

'Maybe.'

He nodded, apparently satisfied.

'Who's in San Francisco?' Smellin' came over to us, drinking out of another full mug. 'Nobody wants to go there.'

'Maybe you do,' said Duke, putting a heavy arm around his shoulders.

'Me? Why?'

'There's a guy there named Snortin' Horton.'

'What?' Smellin' sniffed, then frowned angrily. 'Really? No kidding?'

'No kidding.' Duke led him into a corner, still talking. 'He's got this special nose, you see . . .'

'You know,' said Betsy, as she watched him go, 'ever since I came to Washout and told him off, especially tonight, I don't feel my old grudge, either.'

The current song ended and Grudge and Hackles went to the bar for a break. Chuck stuck his nose over the piano keys, looking around and consulting with Fingers. Many of the dancers moved to the bar or else pulled up chairs and sat down to catch their breath. Alkali was still bouncing for some time after he quit hopping around.

'Would you dance with me?' I asked Betsy. 'When the music starts again.'

'Well, I won't dance with you until it does.' She snickered, but she hadn't told me to shut up.

Fingers began playing the piano by itself, then, in a slow and familiar tune. Chuck stood next to the piano, raised his snout, and sang his song.

'"Oh, roast me not on the lone prairie"—
These words came low and mournfully
From the stainless lips of a young steerite
As he malfunctioned at the fall of night.'

I looked at Betsy and she shrugged. We walked out to the middle of the floor and started dancing together, awkwardly.

'"Oh, roast me not on the lone prairie
'Cause my legs fell off and my eyes rolled free.
On a turning spit, even two or three,
Oh, roast me not on the lone prairie.

Oh, roast me not" – and his voice failed there,
But we paid no heed to his plaintive prayer.

317

*On a turning spit, even two or three,*
*We roasted him there, on the lone prairie.'*

Everyone applauded. Chuck took a bovine bow and opened his mouth to start another song. Before he got started, Hackles and Grudge hastened back to their places and began burning up 'Sweet Betsy from Pike' again, somehow in the proper rhythm. All the dancers rushed back onto the floor. Chuck looked disappointed.

Betsy smiled real big, maybe for the first time since I'd known her. As Grudge called the song, we linked elbows, swung our partners, and danced away.